Tales of the Were

Grizzly Cove
Volumes 1-3

All About the Bear
Mating Dance
Night Shift

BIANCA D'ARC

D1707334

DEDICATION

To the many fans who encouraged me to write this series. Thank you!

And, as always, to my family, without whom none of this would be possible. You are my rock and my anchor in the wide ocean that is life.

CONTENTS

1 All About the Bear   1

2 Mating Dance   68

3 Night Shift   140

Grizzly Cove #1

All About the Bear

BIANCA D'ARC

PROLOGUE

"You want us to what?"

The question came from Brody, one of the highest ranked of John's lieutenants. If he couldn't convince Brody of the genius of his idea, he'd never have a shot at convincing the rest.

"We're going to pretend we're an artists' colony. That's the most sensible way we can fly under the radar around here." He'd researched it, and it was the only plan that made sense for this part of the country.

"But none of us are artists," Brody insisted.

"You can use a chainsaw, can't you?" He pointed at Brody, then went around the circle of his top men who were all gathered to hear the latest mission plan. "We all know Drew whittles in his spare time. And Sven can carve ice. Remember the swan he made when we were undercover as caterers that time?"

"Tell me it's the fucking polar bear that came up with this," Peter the Russian shot a disgusted look at Sven, who flipped him the bird casually as he sat back to listen. Sven could always be counted on to listen first before jumping to conclusions.

As Alpha of this team of misfits, John had his work cut out for him, but he wouldn't have it any other way. All bear

1

shifters, they'd bonded together over years of covert missions and top-secret assignments. And now, when the world had gone to hell and it was time to regroup, John had finally put his long-term plan into motion.

He'd been quietly buying up a huge tract of land near the very tip of Washington State over the past several decades. Every spare dollar he'd ever earned had gone into the project. He considered it an investment, and now that he had finally revealed his master plan to his men, he hoped they would take a more active role in buying up the rest of the land that they needed.

It was wild country with few inhabitants, yet the city wasn't too far away as the crow flies. And there were humans nearby. An Indian reservation and other coastal communities. If John and his team set up house here, they'd have to come up with a plausible cover story as to why there was suddenly a new settlement made up mostly of men in this remote area.

John had a plan to even out the numbers, too, but they'd have to be in residence first before he could put out the call through the shifter community to invite female bears who were looking for a change—and possibly a mate—to join them. There would probably be a few humans passing through on occasion, so they really needed that good cover story for their little community.

John laid out the long-term plan for them all for the first time, and thankfully, they listened. Bears were tricky. Most liked to roam alone, only settling down with a mate and raising their family much later in life—if at all. And they usually didn't live in such close proximity to their Alpha, which was more a ceremonial title than an actual authoritative one.

But John had been commanding officer to every one of the men who gathered around him at one time or another, and the role of leadership fell naturally to him. He might not be the biggest bear in the group, but he was universally believed to be the smartest when it came to strategy. He had hope for his people that they seemed to understand. He wanted to see these men, who had given so much of themselves to help protect the innocent, have fulfilling lives of their own now that they were retiring from the human world and its troubles.

Things had changed drastically in the shifter community. Dark times had accelerated John's plans for his men, but though they remained poised to help, the greater war seemed to be in a lull at the moment. Which left the bears at loose ends. That was why John had brought them all here, to Washington State, to lay the base for what he hoped would be a community that would last for generations.

It was a social experiment the likes of which had never really been attempted in the modern age. At least not on this scale. But if anyone could do it, John knew his men could. Bears were both strong and patient.

It took some doing, but eventually, he talked them all around, and they started planning in earnest for the settlement they were going to build. The community of Grizzly Cove would soon be a reality.

CHAPTER ONE

Brody walked along Main Street, marveling at the way the men had risen to the challenge when John set out the parameters for this new mission. They had drafted in a bit of help from the Clan of shifters that had their own construction company in Nevada, to plan and build the small town square. Other than that, everyone had built their own little den in the woodlands that surrounded the cove.

A few also had houses and cover businesses in town. Brody had chosen to build his home on the outskirts of town, closer than most of the outliers. His job as sheriff of the newly incorporated town of Grizzly Cove, Washington, demanded his full attention. Now that humans were coming into town with more regularity, he needed to stay on his toes so his brothers and their secret would be safe.

The town square had a plethora of art galleries that were filled with all kinds of stuff the bears had thrown together. Most of it was garbage, as far as Brody was concerned, but there were a few standouts. Drew's figurines had always been nice, and they were bringing in big bucks, mostly by accident.

Drew had put the first triple-digit prices on them as a joke, probably also hoping nobody would buy them. Much to his surprise, the rich humans who had bought the carvings on their way through town hadn't even blinked at the high prices.

That set the tone. After seeing the kind of money Drew was bringing into their community, it became a point of pride among the bears to try to do better. Even Brody had gotten caught up in the competition, learning how to use his chainsaw to carve logs into—what else—bears. He liked the irony, and the humans seemed to like the bears. They didn't bring in the same prices as Drew's miniatures, but Brody was working on improving his technique and learning to carve other things besides his self portrait.

When he wasn't busy being sheriff, that is. Not that there was much crime in their small town, but Brody's unofficial job was to keep an eye on the humans. In particular, he was watching over a trio of new arrivals who had gotten permission to open a business. Though humans had passed through, none but this group of three sisters had been brave enough to go before the town council—made up of the Alpha and his top lieutenants—to seek permits to open a business here.

There had been long, high-level discussions about the newcomers' bid to open a bake shop. Over a case or two of beer, the town council had decided to expand their social experiment to include the occasional human female in the town, under strictly controlled conditions.

Those conditions included discreet surveillance by the sheriff and strict limitations on where the females in question could live. In town. That was the only option open to them. Luckily, the sisters didn't seem to mind.

And so, Nell Baker—with the suitably ironic surname— and her two younger sisters, opened the Grizzly Cove Bake Shop and lived in the tiny apartment above the small store. Business was booming, because bears liked sweet things and because Nell and her sisters were easy on the eyes.

Nell, Ashley and Tina were also some of the only females for miles, though they didn't seem aware of it, at first. Only after they had set up shop and fallen into the routine of daily life, a few months after moving in, did they seem to realize there weren't a lot of other women in the area.

Oh, a few female bears had answered the Alpha's open invitation to settle in the cove, but times were tough in the realms of magic and those whose lives were touched by it. Most shifters seemed to want to stay put where they were until things settled down. Apparently, John hadn't really thought about that when he put his plan in motion, but it couldn't be helped now.

The shifter world was still in a holding pattern and would be until the enemy started up their old tricks again. Until that time, the bears were going to live…and live well.

"Afternoon, Nell," Brody said, walking into the bakery and finding the eldest of the Baker sisters manning the shop.

Brody liked to come by a few times a week to check on things and pick up a pie. Nell made the most delicious strawberry rhubarb pies Brody had ever tasted.

"Now how did you know I just finished a batch of pies, Sheriff?" Nell laughed as she teased him.

Brody tapped his nose. "It smelled like lunchtime."

Nell rolled her eyes at him. "Pie isn't lunch, Sheriff." She motioned him to take a seat and brought over a cup of black coffee.

Because there weren't a lot of businesses in town where a person could get a meal, the bake shop had started serving coffee and sandwiches. The sisters baked artisanal breads in addition to the sweet stuff.

There were a few small tables inside, as well as a few wooden patio-style tables with umbrellas out front along the wide sidewalk. A lot of the men who found themselves in town during the day got their lunch from the sisters, and the ladies did a brisk business. The few tourists and hikers who came through loved the bakery too.

In fact, one walked in as Nell set Brody's usual turkey on whole grain sandwich down in front of him. She'd serve him the pie later, but she insisted he eat a proper lunch first, before he devoured the strawberry-honey-rhubarb confection.

Brody watched the tourist covertly as he ate his sandwich. There was something off about the guy, but Brody couldn't catch much of his scent from across the room and with the air conditioning unit blasting in his face. All he caught was the pungent scent of eucalyptus.

Maybe the guy had a sore throat and was sucking on a cough drop. Brody shrugged as he downed his sandwich, continuing to watch the tourist, his instincts telling him there was more wrong with the guy than just a summer cold.

Then the newcomer started speaking in a heavily accented voice, and his words told Brody all he needed to know. The man definitely had a one-way ticket on the bus to Crazytown.

"I heard there's supposed to be a lot of bears around here," the stranger said in a voice that carried to Brody, even as he stood to intervene. "But so far, all I've seen is a whole lot o' nothin'." The man leaned over the counter that separated them and took a very obvious sniff around Nell. Brody felt the growl reverberating in his throat as the man turned. "Finally!" he said, looking with challenge at Brody as he prowled across the floor of the bakery.

"You'd better leave the lady alone, son," Brody growled, moving closer.

"Why? I thought Grizzly Cove was the place where bears could be bears. Or is that just a PR slogan?" The man— scratch that, the *shifter*—was breaking all sorts of rules, including the most important. Don't let the humans find out.

"Let's take this outside, friend." Brody tried to intimidate the man out of the place, but apparently, a dominance contest was about to take place, whether he wanted it or not, and Nell was going to witness it. Goddess help them all.

He tried one more time, pitching his voice so only the newcomer would hear his words. "She's human, man. Don't be a fool."

"A fool! Who's calling Seamus O'Leary a fool?" the stranger demanded, reaching up to unbutton his shirt.

Only then, did Brody catch the underlying scent of alcohol.

"You're drunk," Brody snapped out, hoping Nell would accept that excuse for the man's bizarre behavior.

"I am not," Seamus objected, continuing to unbutton his shirt.

If the moron was going to get naked right here in the bakery and shift, Brody was going to have to do the same and show him who the bigger bear was in the most graphic terms. But Nell didn't know about shifters. And Brody didn't want to be the one to break it to her.

Better to arrest the drunken Aussie and handle all of this down at the station. When the foreign shifter sobered up a bit, then maybe Brody could make some sense out of his bizarre appearance.

Brody put one hand on the foreigner's shoulder. "Don't do this here," Brody coaxed. "Come with me, and we can do it properly."

Seamus shook his head. "Don't want to meet me in public, eh, mate? Why? What are you? A pansy-assed panda?"

Brody personally knew at least one resident of the cove who would take marked exception to that comment, but he was more worried about Nell, at the moment. The Aussie's shirt was off, and he just unbuttoned and unzipped, kicking off his sandals.

And then, he shifted. And got a lot smaller.

He wasn't a big man to begin with. Built more on the wiry side than the massive scale of most of the residents of Grizzly Cove. And he was gray. With tufted ears. And he wasn't chewing cough drops.

He was a fucking koala bear.

CHAPTER TWO

Brody learned, at that point, that koala bears—cute as they seem—have big fucking teeth. The furry little gray monster swiped at him with sharp claws and bared his chompers menacingly. The little bastard wanted to fight?

Brody looked at Nell's pale face. She was in shock, and Brody knew there was no putting this genie back in the bottle. *Shit.*

The crazed koala came after him again, and Brody had had enough. He tugged his embroidered golf shirt over his head and dropped trou, shifting seamlessly into his beast.

As a five-hundred-pound grizzly bear facing a comparatively tiny koala, the match was completely uneven. The koala seemed to realize it about the same time the alcohol he'd consumed when in human form caught up with him. He shuddered once, then collapsed into what Brody belatedly understood was a drunken stupor. The dude just passed out, right there on the bakery floor.

Brody sat back on his haunches, contemplating the hugeness of the mess the Australian had just created. Nell hadn't quite fainted, but she was visibly shaken. Brody didn't know how he was going to fix this.

And then, the Alpha walked in.

Big John took one look at the koala bear passed out on the

linoleum and started to laugh.

Brody snagged his pants in his teeth and ducked behind a display case to shift. He struggled into them while the Alpha chuckled. When he emerged, dressed only in his uniform trousers, he looked at Nell but knew he had to square things with his Alpha first. It would be up to John, what happened next.

Although, if John had any thought about running Nell and her sisters out of town or trying to silence them permanently, he was going to have to go through Brody. He would protect the brown-eyed baker with every fiber of his being.

Whoa. That sounded serious.

Brody realized, in that moment, that all of the lunch hours spent here in the bakery were merely excuses to be close to Nell. He'd made up errands near the bakery, just so he could catch a glimpse of her through the window. And he'd come in more often than he probably should have.

All because of her. Nell. The sweet lady who baked the sweet pies he liked so much.

But he liked her even more.

Probably more than was good for him.

"I'm sorry, John. This guy just came in here and shifted before I could stop him," Brody said to his Alpha, leaving the more troubling thoughts about the pretty baker for later.

"I saw most of it, though I couldn't believe my eyes when he turned into a koala. Never seen a koala shifter in my entire life. Cute little fuckers, aren't they?" John bent down to get a closer look at the snoring marsupial. At that point, he seemed to get a good whiff of the stranger and backed off quick, shielding his nose. "Whew! Eucalyptus and alcohol. Not sure which one is stronger. I'm amazed he was sober enough to walk in here."

"He passed out. I can put him in a cell to sleep it off. Then, he's going to have to answer for his actions." Brody frowned. "And one of us is going to have to deal with the fallout." He glanced significantly at Nell, still standing with her mouth open, behind the counter.

John looked at her too, then frowned. "She saw you shift. You'd better talk her down. I'll take sleeping beauty to the jail." He held out his hand for the keys. "You give me a call if you need help with Nell."

John threw the small bear over one shoulder while Brody bundled the man's clothing into a ball that John tucked under one arm. Without a backward look, the Alpha was out the door and down the street a moment later.

Brody realized he was still shirtless, so he found his golf shirt and spent a few stalling seconds turning it right-side out. He pulled it over his head before turning to Nell, once again. She still hadn't moved.

"Are you okay?" Brody asked quietly, not wanting to startle her.

Nell blinked at him. "Was that..." She paused, then tried again. "Was that real?" She gestured widely to the floor of the bakery and back to Brody. "You were a bear."

Knowing the time for lies was over, he nodded. "Yes, I am."

That got her full attention. She stared hard at him.

"You can turn into a bear?" Shock. She was definitely in some form of shock. "How is that possible?"

Brody shrugged. "I was born this way. It's what I am."

Nell just shook her head, clearly unable to deal with the revelation. Brody sighed.

"Look Nell, I'm the same guy you see every day. Now you just know a little secret about me." He tried to be casual. "And it *is* a secret. You understand? You can't tell anyone about us. The world isn't ready to know about shapeshifters."

"There are more?" She looked slightly appalled by the idea.

Brody wasn't certain if that boded well for getting her cooperation on this matter. And without her cooperation... He feared what the group might decide if Nell couldn't be counted on to keep their secret.

"Honey, this entire town is made up of shapeshifters. That's why it was so difficult for you and your sisters to get permission to open your store here. We weren't sure about letting humans in."

"Humans?" she repeated as if it was just sinking in, despite what she had seen. "You mean everybody is a...a...bear?" She looked outside at the people walking down the street, fear in her eyes. "Don't bears eat people?" she whispered, working up to a full-fledged freak out, if Brody was any judge.

He decided to tease her. Now that she knew the secret, she was fair game. And he'd seen her first.

"Only if they ask very nicely," he said in a husky drawl that made her gaze shoot back to his.

"Are you *flirting* with me? Now?" Outrage wasn't quite what he'd been aiming for, but it was better than panic.

At that moment, the little bell on the door jingled, and two of the town's most recent arrivals entered. Lyn Ling and her daughter, Daisy, had moved in last month. They were Chinese by birth, but the loss of her mate had sent Lyn running from her homeland, looking for a safe place to heal and raise her baby. Daisy was about four years old and cute as a button. She had just about every man in the settlement wrapped around her little finger, Brody included.

Daisy skipped up to the counter, looking with wide eyes into the glass display case as her mother said hello to Brody and Nell. As Nell looked from Brody to Lyn and back again, her eyes widened.

"You said everyone," Nell repeated. "Oh, God. Lyn too? And Daisy? They're...bears?"

Lyn scowled, looking at Brody. "What have you been telling her?"

"I didn't tell her. Some dumb drunk koala came in here and challenged my dominance right here in the middle of the bakery. Nell couldn't help but see. John left me to deal with it."

Lyn huffed at him. "Well, it's clear you're not dealing well." She then lapsed into Chinese muttering, probably saying unkind things about men in general, and Brody in particular, as she lifted her daughter into her arms. Pasting a smile on her face, she turned to Nell. "Yes, we are bears," she said firmly. "No, we do not hurt people. Not unless they hurt us first. We just want to live in peace. In harmony with nature. Free to be who we are. Is that too much to ask?"

Nell was left gaping at the outburst from the normally quiet woman. Slowly, Nell seemed to calm down. Eventually, she nodded.

"No, Lyn. It's not too much to ask. I guess, when you put it that way, it's kind of what everybody wants. Freedom to do what we wanted is why me and my sisters came here too. As long as you guys...bears...are okay with that, I think we can get used to the idea of people turning into grizzly bears."

"Not grizzly," Daisy decided to interject in her high voice. "Panda!"

CHAPTER THREE

"Oh, dear Lord," Nell whispered, completely overwhelmed by the craziness that had invaded her bakery today.

Maybe she was hallucinating. Maybe somebody had spiked the flour with PCP or something. That would explain why she was seeing koalas and grizzly bears in her store, and the cutest little four year old on the planet just claimed she was a panda.

"She better sit down," Lyn said in that no-nonsense way she had of talking.

"Yeah, I think you're right," the sheriff agreed, taking Nell's arm across the counter and guiding her out from behind. He escorted her to the nearest chair, and she let him.

She sat, only then realizing she was trembling from head to toe.

"You gonna faint on me, honey?" Brody asked, squatting down in front of her chair.

He had that boyish smile on his face that usually made her knees weak. But they were already weak. They'd turned to rubber when the men had turned into bears, and only her death grip on the display case had kept her upright.

Nell had had a thing for the sexy sheriff since she first moved into her new shop. He'd come by to welcome her to

14

town and had been by most days since, usually eating lunch here, while she covered the store. Her sister, Ashley, got up with the roosters and stayed until after the breakfast rush. Then, Nell took the afternoons, and little sister Tina covered the evening shift, which wasn't nearly as busy.

Nell was the oldest. She had brought her sisters here. Were they safe? Had she moved them all to an even more dangerous place than the one they'd just left?

Oh, God. Bending over, she wrapped her hands around her middle, feeling ill.

Brody's warm hand settled on her back, rubbing slow, pacifying circles as he moved closer. She felt surrounded by his warmth, but oddly, it made her feel safe.

This was the closest she'd ever been to him. The barrier that had seemed to keep him at a distance was gone. But was her safety gone with it? Nell frowned, worrying.

"It's okay," Brody whispered. "You've had a shock. But you're safe, Nell. Nobody in town would ever hurt you."

A clatter on the table beside her made her look up. Lyn had brought her a strong cup of coffee.

"Drink up," Lyn said. "You need a jolt of caffeine. Only wish I had something stronger to give you." Lyn's smile was friendly, and Nell realized that the woman she'd become friends with over the past weeks was still the same, even if there was some bizarre way she could turn into a enormous bear.

Brody took the mug and handed it to Nell. He was such a gentle giant of a man. She had admired him from afar over the past weeks, glad his habit was to take a late lunch when the shop was quiet, as it was now.

Nell drank a sip of the coffee, and it did make her feel a little better. The heat of the liquid and familiar flavor of the brew grounded her a bit. It wore down the shock that had been riding her for the past fifteen minutes.

"Can you call Tina in to take over a little early?" Brody suggested as she downed the coffee. "Tell her you're not feeling well or something?"

Nell's eyes widened. "Are my sisters safe here?"

Brody nodded solemnly. "Safer in this town than anywhere else," he insisted. "Our residents have all been vetted, and most have known each other for many years. While it's true we recently opened up to new faces, there's a procedure for shifters who want to join the community. That drunken Aussie wasn't supposed to just show up in town and go furry. He's going to face the Alpha when he sobers up, and believe me, that won't be pretty."

"We don't go around advertising what we can do," Lyn said, picking up her daughter once more. "Secrecy is the first rule of our society. You are now one of very few humans who know about us," Lyn went on. "Can you be trusted to keep our secret?"

Nell was surprised by the question. "I won't tell anybody," she promised. "Nobody would believe me anyway. I'd end up in the loony bin." She finished her coffee and put the mug back on the table at her side. Then she realized Lyn had come in to pick up the lunch order she'd called in an hour before. "Oh, you probably need to go. Let me get your bag," Nell said, rising and going behind the counter.

The familiar work helped calm her further, even if her world had been turned upside down in the past half hour. The lunch order was ready and sitting in the cooler. Nell took it out and handed it over the top of the display case to Lyn.

"It's on the house today, Lyn," she said when the other woman reached into her bag. "And there's a treat inside for Daisy."

The little girl's face lit up when she heard that last part. Her mother asked the universal mommy question. "What do we say when someone gives us a treat?"

Daisy responded with a loud, "Thank you!"

Nell couldn't help but smile at the child. "You're very welcome, Miss Daisy."

"I wouldn't leave, but I have a buyer coming to the gallery in twenty minutes. Promise me you'll come by later so we can talk?" Lyn insisted.

"I'll take good care of her," the sheriff insisted. Lyn shot him a doubtful look but left with a nod.

When Lyn had left, Nell found herself staring at Brody. His quirked eyebrow invited her to speak.

"So far today, I've seen a koala, a grizzly and, if Daisy is to be believed, a panda walk into my shop. In human form." As observations went, it was a doozy.

"I told John he should be more specific when he sent out the call for bears." Brody shook his head with a smile. "I was willing to bend the definition for Lyn and Daisy, but that puny Aussie? I don't think so. Besides, he smells like cough drops."

Nell laughed out loud but quickly stopped herself. "Eucalyptus. I think that's what koalas eat." She ran her hand through her hair in frustration. "God. I can't believe I'm even having this conversation."

"Actually, I'm kind of glad we're talking about it," Brody admitted, moving nearer, his arms crossed and his stance contemplative. "I've been wanting to get closer to you for weeks, but until you knew my secret, I had to keep my distance. I don't like lying to people I respect."

That took her by surprise. "You respect me?"

She couldn't imagine why. She was nobody special. She was just another rolling stone who happened to land right side up in the cove, looking for a new start.

"Of course I do," he answered without hesitation. "You care for your sisters. You were strong enough to stand up for yourself, and for them, in front of the town council. You convinced Big John that you could make a go of your business here, and you've done just that. What's not to respect?"

When he put it that way... It was kind of charming of him to have noticed, actually. Nell felt her cheeks heat as she blushed. She'd been covertly watching the big sheriff every day since they'd met. He pushed all her buttons on a physical level, but also on a mental one. Their lunch conversations had ranged from the latest tech innovations in the news to the planning and layout of the town. She'd known he had a hand in it and liked what he had to say about the way he'd designed certain security aspects right into the road system itself.

"I respect you too," she admitted. "I like talking with you when you come in for lunch."

Brody sighed heavily. "But you're not sure what to make of the idea that I can turn into a grizzly at will, huh?" He gazed straight into her eyes.

She shrugged in reply. "I don't know what to think."

Rather than answer her, Brody reached for his cell phone and placed a call. Still feeling a little bewildered, Nell watched him as the call connected.

"Yeah, hi, Tina? This is Sheriff Chambers. I'm over at the bakery. Everything's okay, but I think your sister could use a bit of a break. She just finished dealing with a difficult customer. Is it possible for you to come in a little early?" He paused, listening to her sister's reply. "Excellent. We'll wait for you to get here." Another pause. "Yeah, I'm taking her out to decompress. I think she needs a little TLC after the day she's had. We'll probably just take a quiet walk around the cove." He smiled as her sister said something else. "Thanks. Yeah. We'll see you in a few minutes."

He ended the call with a tap of his finger and put the phone away. That little grin never left his face. He looked a bit smug. Was he feeling satisfied that he'd arranged to take her out? And how did she feel about his highhandedness? She honestly wasn't sure.

"You seem very pleased with yourself," she observed.

"That's because I am." His smile grew wider as he came around the display case, joining her in the work area as if he belonged there.

He took one of the empty boxes off the stack she kept ready and placed a few of the honey buns she knew were his favorites into it. She watched, bemused, as he put the box into a shopping bag and then pulled a few bills out of his pocket and stuck them in the cash register.

"What's that for?" she couldn't help asking.

18

"Our picnic," he answered, still grinning.

"What picnic?"

"The one we're going to take down by the beach while I tell you all about the bears and this town." He took her hand and led her out from behind the display case, even going so far as to remove her apron and fold it neatly before placing it on the counter. "Now that I'm free to speak the truth, there's a lot I want to tell you."

"What about my sisters? Will they be let in on the secret?" she wanted to know.

Brody's smile dimmed as he tilted his head. "I'm not sure. That sort of all depends."

"On what?" She put her hands on her hips as she faced him.

"On a few different things. How you handle what I'm going to tell you. How we proceed from here on out. What the Alpha decides. Any number of things, including your sisters' temperaments." He shrugged. "If it were up to me, I'd probably tell them, but when we agreed to settle here, we also agreed to follow Big John's laws. He's the Alpha. He gets to decide the big questions, like this one. But I wouldn't worry. He was the one who approved of your plans to open this bakery. He checked you all out before he ever agreed to let you into our town."

"He investigated us?" Nell was a bit insulted by the idea, but then again, it looked like these people—if that's what they were—had a lot to lose if they let the wrong sort of person run around loose in their community.

"Don't feel bad. He had us all investigated before he ever made the offer to let us live on his land. You probably don't realize it, but this place was Big John's dream from the get go. He quietly accumulated acres and acres of land around the cove over the past several decades. He plans long-term. And he wasn't about to let just anyone settle here."

"I had no idea. My rent goes to a big corporation, I thought."

"Yeah. A big corporation ultimately owned by John

Marshall. He's got all kinds of paperwork and shell corporations that hide the fact of his ownership pretty well. That's why the lawyer was one of the first shifters he invited to join him here."

"The town lawyer is a...a shifter?" She tried out the unfamiliar term.

"Honey, everybody who lives here, except you and your sisters, are shifters. If you want to stay here, you're going to have to get used to it." He shook his head, his smile still charming, though his words were alarming.

"What if I want to leave? Would you let me go, now that I've seen what I've seen?"

Brody sighed. "That's another thing that would be up to the Alpha, though I would definitely argue in your favor. I don't think you're about to go hunting up the nearest newspaper reporter. And you also had no option when that crazy, drunk Australian forced the issue. It's not like you were deliberately trying to find out about us. You shouldn't have to pay the price for his stupidity."

"What kind of price are we talking about?" She had a bad feeling about this.

Brody started to look uncomfortable. "Well, in the past, some Alphas were known to impose permanent solutions for this kind of thing, but I don't believe Big John would even consider something like that in your case."

"When you say *permanent solutions*, do you mean...?" She couldn't bring herself to say it.

"Death," he said succinctly, nodding as she felt herself go faint. "I won't lie to you, Nell. Not anymore. Not even by omission. That's a promise." He held her gaze, and she felt some of his strength flowing into her, odd as it seemed. "But if it comes to that, I won't let it happen. I'll protect you with my own life, if I have to."

She believed him. She didn't know why, but she did.

"Let's hope it doesn't come to that, but thank you for the sentiment."

Brody moved closer, his hips in line with hers as his hands

went to her waist. "It's not a casual declaration, honey. There's something between us. I've felt it from the first moment I saw you. In a way, I should be thankful to that stupid koala, because now, I'm finally free to talk to you about who, and what, I really am."

CHAPTER FOUR

Tina showed up, and Brody stepped back, but not before her little sister got an eyeful of Brody Chambers standing right up in Nell's personal space. The big wink Tina sent her was almost comical. Nell would have laughed if the situation wasn't so serious.

As it was, she allowed Brody to hustle her out of the bakery in record time, Tina taking over during the slow mid-afternoon period. Nell usually used that time to do paperwork, but not today. Nope. Today, apparently, she was going to learn all about *shifter* bears.

She wasn't sure she wanted to know, but then again, spending time with hunky Brody Chambers was something she'd let herself think about off and on since moving to Grizzly Cove. She didn't think anything would ever come of it, but she'd let herself dream…occasionally.

Now she was getting her wish, but she honestly didn't know if she could handle the *why* of it. Suddenly, Brody was asking her out, but it wasn't for any of the normal reasons she had imagined. No, it was to explain the freakish nature of the town, and only after she knew all about it would the decision be made—by the Alpha, whatever that meant—as to whether or not she would be killed.

Hysteria tried to bubble up, but Brody took her hand and

led her across the street toward the public beach area. It wasn't large, but the town—which was owned and operated by John Marshall, she had just learned—had put a few wooden picnic tables along the side of the road for public use. Beyond the sandy area, down a sloping incline, the waters of the cove lapped at the shore in a hypnotic rhythm.

Nell liked to go down to the water a few times a week to just listen for a bit and commune with nature. The town was out of the way and didn't see many travelers passing through, but that was okay by her. The residents bought enough of her breads and pastries to keep the bakery afloat, and that's all that really mattered. Nell wasn't here to make a killing. She'd come here to start over, with her sisters, and that was just what they'd done.

Now the only question was, would they be allowed to continue?

Brody let Nell sit before he placed the box with the honey buns on the table and sat opposite her. He didn't like the fear and uncertainty in her pretty eyes, but he understood why she was afraid. The unknown was usually frightening.

He hoped he could set her mind at ease, but he'd never done this before. As long as he'd lived, he had never had to explain what he was to anyone. They either had no clue, or they knew all about shifters because they were shifters too. Brody didn't usually hang out with humans.

But he found himself doing all sorts of new things when it came to Nell. From the first, she had stirred something in his blood. She had almost called out to him on some primitive level he didn't quite understand. Following his instincts, he'd spent time near her, having lunch at the bakery as often as possible, trying to figure out her allure.

So far, the only thing that had accomplished was to make her even more intriguing. And after today's debacle, he at least could be completely truthful with her at last. Only time would tell if that was a good thing or a bad thing.

He opened the box he'd packed earlier and bit into a

honey bun before starting the conversation he knew he had to have with her. Honestly, he wasn't really sure how to do it, but he had to try.

"These are truly delicious," he said around a bite of the honey bun.

"Thank you. Ash makes them. I just do the glazing," she admitted.

"That's the best part," he said with a smile, licking his fingers absently. "Look, I'm not really good at this. I've never done it before. I've never had to tell anybody about shifters in my entire life, so I might mess up. Stop me at any time and ask questions, okay? Nothing is out of bounds now that you've seen my bear." He thought about his words. "Well...almost nothing is out of bounds. I'll let you know if we hit on a sensitive topic, okay?"

She smiled faintly and nodded. At least it looked like she was willing to try.

"Good. Now, the first thing you ought to know is that there are all kinds of shifters in the world, not just bears. Though we're among the most powerful, we're also far fewer in number than some of the others. There are tons of wolves, for example. A lot of big cats. Quite a few raptors. Get the picture?"

"You mean there are people that can turn into wolves and tigers and eagles?"

"Yep. But in Grizzly Cove, so far there are only bears. That's the way Big John designed this place. It was to be a haven for bears, specifically."

"Why?" she asked in a quiet but clearly interested tone. "Why only bears?"

"A number of reasons. Each of the original residents worked directly with John over the years. We're all bears, so we understood each other in ways we don't really understand the other shifters. Wolves have their Packs. Cats have their Clans. Bears...well...a lot of us are loners. We tend to stake out large territories and don't often interact with others of our own kind." He shrugged and finished the honey bun he'd been eating. There were still two left in the box.

"That sounds kind of lonely," she observed.

"It can be. But living too close to other bears can also be a problem. That's why most of us own property along either side of the cove. We need our space. The town is great for the times we want to be around other people, but the forest is home to the other half of our souls."

"That's kind of beautiful," Nell said quietly. He liked the soft, open, accepting look on her face. Maybe this was going to turn out okay after all.

* * *

They walked down to the waterline and then began a lazy stroll around the curve of the cove while Nell asked questions and Brody did his best to explain about shifters. He tried to gauge his progress by her mood. She was calmer now, which he took to be a good sign. And when her foot slipped on a wet rock, it was all the excuse he needed to put his arm around her shoulders.

There. That was better. He liked the feel of her petite frame under his arm. She was the perfect height for him. They *fit*, for lack of a better word. Just as he'd always suspected but had never been able to test out before.

It had been hell staying away from her. Not that he'd actually been able to stay *away*. He'd had lunch at her place more days than not, just to be around her. But he hadn't been able to touch her or ask her out. Or even walk on the beach with her.

That had all changed now, and Brody's bear side was pleased. As was his human side. Both wanted to get to know this lady much, much better, and they finally had the chance.

"You know, I'm glad you found out," Brody admitted after he'd explained as best he could and they'd turned their steps back toward the picnic area. They'd walked quite a way down the cove, away from the main street and toward the wilder areas bordered by dense woodlands. "I mean, the way you found out was kind of bad, but the result is something I can endorse, if it means you here with me, walking on the beach. I've wanted to ask you out for a long time, Nell."

"Then why didn't you?" She stopped walking and turned slightly to look at him. She was so close he wanted to bend down and kiss her.

"I couldn't. I didn't want to have to live a lie. I can't be only half what I am. I'm a man, but I'm a bear too. Both parts of me want to be near you." His words were impassioned, and he felt her respond, her small hands coming between them to rest against his chest as she moved even closer.

When her body swayed, he put his hand around her waist, his other arm still at her shoulders. He pulled her against him, and she didn't resist. In fact, she reached upward, standing on tiptoe. The invitation couldn't be any clearer, and he was happy to take it.

Brody lowered his head, and his lips met hers.

Sparks tingled through his body at the first touch of her lips. A sort of magic shimmered around him and through his bloodstream.

Nell didn't quite know how she'd ended up kissing Brody Chambers on a deserted stretch of beach, but she didn't mind at all. Not one bit.

There was something almost magical about his kiss. Something she'd never experienced before in a man's arms.

She felt…safe. Protected. Cared for.

And that was a lot of baggage to tack on to a first kiss, now wasn't it? But even though the undeniable fact that she'd seen him turn into a giant grizzly bear scared her on some level, the feel of his arms around her was something welcoming and warm. Like coming home.

Nell had always been a practical sort of woman. She knew she wasn't the prettiest of her sisters. That honor fell to the middle sister, Ashley. She probably wasn't the smartest either. Tina was the clever puss in her family. But Nell had grit. Determination to see that her sisters had as good a life as she could make for them all.

She'd always thought she had good judgment. But one kiss from Brody and all her best-laid plans of a long spinsterhood and non-involvement with the male of the species went right out the window. In his arms, she found she wanted this—for herself.

She had sacrificed a lot to keep her sisters with her after their parents died, and she'd always put them first. She had let her own desires take a backseat to making sure there was always food on the table and a safe home for her little tribe. But Brody made her want something for herself... Him.

She wanted him, and she couldn't deny the instant attraction she'd felt for him from the get-go. Now that she was finally experiencing his kiss, she could no longer blind herself to the fact that he was just about perfect in every way that mattered.

Oh, there was the bear thing. That had been seriously unexpected. She'd have to find a way to make peace with that in her mind...when Brody wasn't overwhelming her with his delicious kisses that tasted like honey.

CHAPTER FIVE

Brody walked Nell home a little while later, leaving her at the bakery door. She and her sisters lived in the small apartment above the store.

As sheriff of the sleepy town, Brody didn't have much to do normally. Today though, he had a drunk koala shifter in the tiny jail under his deputy's supervision that he had to deal with. Brody smiled as he walked down the main street, which ran along the apex of the cove. He'd finally been able to take Nell Baker in his arms and find out if her kisses were as sweet as the honey buns she baked.

He licked his lips remembering. Her kisses were even better than the buns, and that was saying something. He wanted more.

More importantly, his inner bear wanted more. It was the first time the grizzly inside had sat up and taken notice of a female. Brody knew that meant something special. He had been wondering for weeks if the eldest Baker sister might not just be his mate.

But until the drunk shifter had shown up in her shop today, Brody hadn't been able to cross that final line. He hadn't wanted to get involved with her—with any female—unless she knew about his bear. He hadn't wanted to start something with Nell that could turn out to be serious with a lie of omission between them. Especially not something as big as he was when he shifted into bear form.

Now that it was finally out in the open and she'd seen his alternate shape, the self-imposed restriction was gone. He was free to court her and to talk about his dual nature. Oh, sure, the town council would probably meet and discuss the ramifications of letting the Baker sisters know about shifters, but Brody wasn't too worried about all that. Nell had heart. She would never betray him or any of the bears who called Grizzly Cove home.

Brody was whistling a jaunty tune as he entered his office. He had a koala to corral and a courtship to plan.

* * *

The next day dawned bright and clear. The Alpha stopped by the jail first thing and had strong words with their new guest.

As a result of Seamus's solemn promise to lay off the booze, straighten up and fly right, Big John had agreed to let him out. There was one condition. John demanded that Seamus make his way back to the bakery, with Brody as his police escort, and apologize to Nell for causing trouble.

And so, right before lunchtime, when Brody knew Nell would be manning the bakery by herself, but not too busy yet, he escorted Seamus into the store. Seamus, hung over and looking it, held his hat in his hands, his head down as he shuffled towards the counter.

Brody, by stark contrast, felt lighthearted at the vision of Nell, a little flour dusting the side of her cheek. She looked good enough to eat.

Down, boy.

"Morning, Sheriff," Nell greeted him.

"Miz Baker," he acknowledged with a private smile just for her. When her cheeks flushed rosy under the sprinkling of flour, his smile grew even wider. "Seamus here has something he'd like to say to you. Miss Nell Baker, this is Mister Seamus

O'Leary, originally from Australia."

The shorter man looked up sheepishly. "I'm sorry for the trouble I caused yesterday, ma'am." His voice had a decidedly Aussie twang to it.

Nell had met a few Aussies before and generally liked them. The overall impression she had was that they were hardworking people who knew how to party.

"My only excuse is that I just escaped from the private zoo of some corporate jackass with Gestapo security and cameras on me twenty-four-seven. I couldn't shift until I got free, and it was hard getting out of there as a koala. All they fed me was eucalyptus leaves, which are great normally, but the human side of me likes to have a little protein, now and again. And a few hops, preferably in beer form." He winked as his story lengthened and his manner became easier.

Brody stepped in. "When we founded the town, Big John put out a call for any loners in the various bear shifter populations, hoping to attract females, honestly." Brody chuckled. "A few have applied for residency so far, and all, with the notable exception of Lyn and her child, are brown and black bears. Frankly, I've never seen a koala shifter before yesterday."

"We're rare," Seamus said, puffing out his chest.

Brody rolled his eyes before turning back to Nell.

"It's totally up to you, Ms. Baker, whether or not Seamus here is allowed inside your establishment. You can think over your answer and let me know later today." He didn't want to put her on the spot, and he liked the idea of knowing she would have to talk to him again that day, but she threw a monkey wrench into his master plan.

"No need. I can tell you right now that he's welcome, as long as he behaves. That means no drunkenness and no shifting inside, okay?" She looked straight at Seamus, and the other man had the sense to fidget under her no-nonsense scrutiny.

"I can promise you that, missus. Big John set me straight

about the rules of this town, and I won't go breaking them again. I promise." The golden-skinned Aussie with the seriously Irish name seemed so contrite Brody almost believed him.

But Brody knew trouble when he saw it. And Seamus O'Leary had trouble written all over his furry gray koala ass.

"In that case, are you gentlemen here for lunch?" Nell asked, flashing a smile that hit Brody right between the eyes.

"Yes, ma'am," the koala answered without consulting Brody.

Not that he would argue. Any time spent near Nell was time well spent according to Brody. And if the Aussie was going to stick around in the bakery, better that Brody was here to keep an eye on him.

They placed their orders for sandwiches on the delicious artisanal bread Brody liked and sat at one of the indoor tables. He watched Nell bustle around behind the counter, liking the way her ponytail swayed as she worked.

Seamus nudged Brody's arm with his elbow. "You got something going on with the lady?" the koala shifter asked in a low voice.

Brody nodded once, staking his claim.

"Shame." The other man sat back in his chair. "You're a lucky man."

Brody nodded again, thinking truer words were never spoken.

Maybe Seamus wasn't so bad after all.

Nell came over a moment later with a large tray. It almost overflowed with the two plates holding substantial sandwiches, cutlery, napkins and condiments. Nell laid it all out before them, then pulled a small bottle out of her apron pocket and presented it shyly to Seamus.

"I wasn't sure…"

"Beauty!" Seamus exclaimed, taking the little jar from her. "I haven't had Vegemite in years. Thanks, doll. You're a peach."

Nell smiled, and Brody realized again how thoughtful this

little human woman was. Here she was, facing the idiot who had revealed the existence of shifters to her just yesterday, in the most bizarre way, treating him to something special from his homeland. Brody could see the pleasure she took in providing Seamus with the small treat. It indicated how big her heart really was.

The koala shifter was right. Brody was the lucky one to have found a woman as extraordinary as Nell.

Brody and Seamus spent about an hour in the bakery, eating their sandwiches and finishing off with a slice of pie. Nell was kept busy as most of the people in town came in to pick up lunch. The town wasn't that big, but it seemed everyone who was in the area made it a point to stop by and talk to Nell.

A few of the women—and there weren't that many living here, yet—offered to answer questions Nell might have about their society. More than one gave Seamus the once-over. Apparently, news of the fracas here yesterday had gotten around. Brody was pleased to see the friendly overtures toward Nell. It seemed as if the bear shifter community was welcoming her.

It could easily have gone the other way. But maybe more than a few people had noticed them necking on the beach yesterday afternoon. Brody had been on the receiving end of a couple of envious looks and at least one high five. The latter coming from his deputy, earlier this morning.

Brody felt about ten feet tall, even in his human form. He liked that the others knew he was courting Nell. And he liked the subtle, silent approval from both his male contemporaries and the small, but growing, female population.

Before meeting John, Brody had always roamed alone. Now he was coming to appreciate the feeling of belonging, of being part of the larger bear shifter family.

When there was no longer any excuse to stay in the bakery, Brody parted ways with Seamus and made sure the Aussie shifter left the premises before Brody went up to the counter to speak with Nell. He didn't need an audience—

especially not Seamus—for what he had in mind.

"Are you doing anything tonight?" Brody asked Nell as casually as he could, during a lull in business. The lunch rush was nearing its close, and the few people eating had chosen to sit outside.

"What did you have in mind?" Nell's smile was full of mischief and slightly shy. It was enchanting.

"I thought maybe I could make dinner for you. You've been feeding me for months now. I owe you a steak at the very least. You do eat steak, don't you?" For a moment, he had the horrific thought that she might be a vegetarian.

Nell chuckled. "I like steak. I can bring a salad, if you like. We have some nice ripe lettuce plants on our roof balcony."

"You grow lettuce on your roof?" Brody couldn't picture it.

"There's lots of sun up there, and it's all just wasted space. We put a plastic patio table and chairs up there, and surrounded it with a container vegetable garden. Saves us a lot of money on groceries, and everything is super fresh."

"I had no idea," Brody said, charmed by the thought of a secret garden up on the roof.

"I'll show it to you, but not today. I know for a fact that Tina is sunbathing up there before her shift."

The way she said it made Brody think about Nell lying up there on a patio lounger. Naked.

He almost growled out loud at the image that popped into his mind.

"You should know, there are probably a few raptor shifters in the area. At least one eagle and a couple of owls and hawks. They don't usually have much to do with us, but occasionally, I see one fly over." He could see she wasn't quite making the connection. "If I can see them, they can most definitely see you up there sunbathing on your roof." Nell's mouth dropped open, and Brody had to grin. "It's something to consider." He shrugged. "You're not quite as alone up there as you might think."

Nell nodded. "Good to know." He could see the wheels

turning in her mind.

"So. Dinner? My place?" he reminded her of the most important part of their conversation.

"Oh, yeah. I'd love to. What time?"

"How about I pick you up at seven when I get off shift?" Excitement flowed through his veins as both his human half and his bear half scented victory.

"Sounds perfect," she said, smiling at him with that shy look in her eyes that he found absolutely adorable.

He couldn't resist leaning across the counter and kissing her.

What he meant to be a quick peck turned into something molten as she kissed him back. Brody damned the counter that separated them, but thankfully, it kept him from going too far. The bell above her door jingled as somebody walked in on them, and Brody cursed inwardly.

Nell pulled back, her cheeks flushing a lovely shade of pink while she looked toward the door and the newcomers who had interrupted them. She pasted a bright smile on her face and tried to pretend that they hadn't just been caught red-handed.

Brody whistled as he left, a spring in his step. He had a date, and if he played his cards right, he might just convince her to stay all night.

Or maybe forever.

CHAPTER SIX

Brody picked her up at the agreed time in his Sheriff's Department SUV. It wasn't very subtle, and everyone on Main Street saw him open the passenger door for her and help her in. They also saw the kiss he stole as he was assisting her up into the off-road vehicle, which had massive tires that made it a climb for her to reach the seat.

He chuckled at her momentary struggle, then solved the problem by lifting her around the waist and tucking her into the car. She squeaked, not expecting the move, but in the end, was grateful for the assist.

"I'm going to have to install running boards for you," he murmured. "But I like helping you in, too. Any excuse to touch you is a good thing as far as I'm concerned."

His words, coupled with the audacious wink he gave her as he closed the door, made her blood warm in her veins. He walked around the front of the large vehicle, and she noted he had no problem climbing into his own seat. The car was made for someone his size.

Suddenly, she felt small and feminine, which wasn't a sensation she often experienced. The oldest of the three Baker sisters, Nell hadn't had much time for dating after they lost their parents. She'd been eighteen and just barely able to hold her little family together. With the help of their elderly

35

grandparents in those first few years, she'd been able to provide for the small family. When their grandparents died, too, the girls had been old enough to make their way in the world on their own.

Moving here had been part of the new start all three of them needed. They'd sold the home their grandparents had left them and unanimously decided to strike out on their own. After working for a successful bakery chain for years, all three of them knew the business and were able to take their skills with them.

Finding a place in the country had been ideal because of the lower cost of living. Their rent on the building wasn't much, and they had been able to squirrel away a bit of savings since opening the store, which they hadn't really expected.

Oh, they'd wanted to show a profit, of course, but hadn't projected any until next year at the earliest. But the people in Grizzly Cove had been amazingly receptive to the bakery, and business was booming. Well, as much as business could boom in a tiny town like this.

"How far is it?" she asked, to make conversation as they rolled past the last of the small businesses on Main Street.

"Not far. I live closer to town than most because of my job, but I managed to snag some property up on the hillside, with a lovely view of the cove. I think you'll like it."

Brody suddenly realized this was the first time he'd brought a woman to his new den. It was important to him that she liked the place. More important than it probably should be, but he found himself thinking in terms of forever where Nell was concerned.

If she liked the place, maybe she'd consider moving in with him? Maybe, if he could get even closer to her, he could discover if she was truly meant to be his mate. The bear inside him was still on the fence, but it was leaning more and more toward her each time they were near.

He'd deliberately held the bear back until yesterday because he couldn't have contemplated getting involved with her until she knew about shifters. Now that she knew, he had released his tight hold on his inner bear, and the cranky animal was being stubborn, withholding from the human side just for spite. Otherwise, he'd know already whether or not Nell was meant to be his.

Or so he believed. His parents always said they knew at first sight that they were meant for each other. In fact, Brody had spent an hour on the phone last night with his dad, trying to figure it out, but his dad had seemed to think that it was different for each shifter. Many, like his folks, knew immediately. Others had to be hit over the head with it.

Brody hoped he wasn't one of the latter. He wanted a mate. And a family. And a home that was more than just a house.

"I built into the side of the hill to take advantage of the views but did my best to leave the natural habitat intact," he told her. "Though there's plenty of room for a garden," he said, thinking of her rooftop oasis.

He looked over to find her smiling in a shy way that he found adorable. Pretty much everything about Nell was adorable. If he could pick a mate, he'd want a woman exactly like her. But one thing his dad had impressed on him in their talk last night was that shifters really didn't have much choice. True mates were granted by the Goddess and brought together by fate.

Brody pulled into the drive and drove up to the house, holding his breath to see her reaction.

"Oh, this is lovely," she exclaimed, and he started to breathe again. "I love the way the house blends into the woods. It's like it grew out of the hillside naturally."

Brody felt his cheeks heat as he flushed with pleasure at her compliment.

"It's my attempt at a human grizzly den. All the comforts and safety of being in the ground, and yet, the beautiful views and natural light my human side craves." He had never really put it into words before, but he found himself wanting her to understand.

She turned in her seat to look at him. "You really are two in one, aren't you? I mean, I've been thinking about it pretty much non-stop since yesterday, and I'm so curious about how it all works...being a bear, I mean."

He liked that she was interested. It was a good sign, as far as he was concerned. If she could accept his dual nature, maybe she would be amenable to being his mate. If the Goddess blessed them, of course. For now, the bear was withholding the knowledge from him, the furry bastard.

"Well, the first thing you need to know..." he said, pulling to a stop in front of the house and shutting off the engine, "...is that the bear side of me will never hurt you. I'm still me when I'm in my fur. I still know all my friends, and my protective instincts are in full force. You never need to fear the bear in me, Nell."

When she was silent, he turned to look at her and found her mouth open in shock again. Finally, she seemed to process his words. "I hadn't even thought about that. I mean, you were so great in the bakery yesterday, I guess I just didn't even consider it."

"Great?" She thought he'd been *great* in the bakery? He thought he'd scared her half to death, but apparently, she remembered it differently.

"Yeah, I mean, you could've torn up the place, or roared, or something. You could've wiped out that little koala with one swipe of your claws, but you showed enormous restraint, I thought. You were great," she repeated, nodding.

He was blushing again. He could feel the heat in his cheeks. He hadn't been so emotional since he was a teen, but something about Nell brought out all sorts of strange reactions in him.

"I probably should have sat on him at least," Brody joked, uncomfortable with the praise he didn't quite know how to handle.

Nell chuckled. "Then I would have had squashed koala in the middle of my shop." She giggled some more. "I shouldn't laugh. It's just a funny visual, you know? Like a cartoon or something."

"It would've been a little ridiculous," Brody admitted, smiling with her. "I just couldn't bring myself to hurt the little guy. I mean, he was stupid and drunk. And did I mention stupid? But there's something about a koala. They're not a real bear, you know? But they're kinda cute if you hold your breath."

"Why hold your breath? Oh! You mean the eucalyptus smell?" She chuckled again. "He kind of smelled like a cough drop to me."

"Well, I've heard that smell is intense for humans, but imagine how my nose reacted to that. We smell things, hear things, taste things...a lot more than you do. Our senses are way more acute. His scent is literally an assault on the nostrils."

"I had no idea, but I guess it makes sense. Wow. You continue to amaze me the more I learn about you," she said candidly.

He liked that she wasn't holding things back from him. He'd seen her shock and her fear, though thankfully not too much fear. Her honesty was fresh and welcome.

"Then let me amaze you even more with my grilling skills. I've got everything set. All I have to do is light the fire and get things cooking." He gestured toward the house. "Shall we?"

She smiled at him, and his heart stopped for a moment. "Sure. But I'm going to need some help getting out of your car, or I might fall on my nose."

"Say no more. Your wish is my command."

He got out of the vehicle and walked quickly around to her side, opening the door and lifting her out.

He took his time lowering her to the ground, allowing her body to slide against his all the way down. And even when both of her feet were on the ground, he didn't let her go. He paused, letting her decide if she wanted to step away and break their connection.

When she didn't, he lowered his head and stole the kiss

he'd been wanting since the night before. A kiss with no holds barred. Nobody watching. Nobody gossiping. Just the two of them, in the forest evening.

His arms swept around her when her knees crumpled, and he felt the sharp stab of pride knowing he'd nearly made her swoon with pleasure. Just from a kiss. He wondered what would happen when they finally made love. And then, he almost growled out loud, thinking about how much he wanted that to happen tonight.

He tightened his hold, wanting to feel every one of her luscious curves against his starving body. But then, he made himself release her, one agonizing inch at a time. He couldn't rush this. He had to remember she was human. She probably didn't feel the same raw urgency as shifters did. He had to do this right and give her all the space she needed.

Of course, that didn't mean he wasn't going to do his best to seduce her, but he'd lured her to his den with the promise of dinner. He could at least feed her before he tried to convince her to go farther. Besides, he liked spending time with her. Sex would be great—no, it would be awesome—but he also wanted to just have her in his space for a little while, all to himself, to enjoy talking with her and basking in the sparkle of her eyes.

CHAPTER SEVEN

Nell's head was spinning when Brody let her go. She was dazed and didn't really comprehend at first why he'd stepped back. She had been on the point of climbing his body like a tree and removing his clothing with her teeth. Even now, she had to fight the impulse to step closer and demand he give her more of those addictive kisses.

She wanted to run her fingers over his body, to learn the curves and hardness of his muscles. Brody was, by far, the finest specimen of a man she had ever gotten this close to. She hadn't been in town long before she noticed that he filled out his clothes with amazing detail, his shoulders straining at the seams of his embroidered uniform golf shirts.

She liked the casualness of this town's sheriff's uniform— those nice, stretchy golf shirts that showed off every muscle when he moved a certain way, and cargo pants that showcased a tight ass she had found herself watching every time he walked out of the bakery. Brody Chambers had a great butt.

And he was a truly nice guy too. Not vain, he didn't even seem to be really aware of how good looking he was. As she was getting to know him, she had figured out that he came by his muscles honestly, doing all sorts of physical labor around the town when needed. He wasn't the kind of man to sit on the sidelines when something needed doing, and she really admired that.

As her head began to clear, she realized he was looking into her eyes as if to gauge her reaction. She felt like a fool, caught staring at him, probably with a goofy expression on her face.

The man was lethal. His kisses should come with mandatory warning labels. *May cause dizziness, light-headedness, lack of oxygen to the brain and gooey, lovestruck appearance. Oh, yeah.*

"Ready to eat?" His voice rumbled through her body, warming her in very private, sensitive places.

You bet she was ready. But it didn't sound like he was on the menu at the moment. Nell tucked away her disappointment and tried to sober up. He'd invited her here for dinner. She had to get with the program!

"Where did you put the bag I gave you?" she asked, buying time to settle her nerves.

Brody went to the backseat of the big SUV and removed the big shopping bag she had packed earlier and given him when he'd picked her up. He closed the car door and hefted the bag in one hand as he motioned for her to precede him up to the front door.

He reached around her to open the door and let her walk through first. The house was lovely. Although built into the side of the hill, there were lots of windows at the front and skylights in the front part of the roof that let the twilight of outside into the structure. It almost felt like a continuation of the woodlands she had just stepped out of. The house was rustic and majestic all at the same time.

Rough hewn beams and giant poles that had to have been entire tree trunks dominated the entryway but gave way to more modern materials at the back where the house entered the hillside. There was a techno-forest vibe where the wood blended with poured concrete slabs and brick that had been artfully arranged as walls and supporting structure. The house was definitely built to last.

"You built this yourself?" she asked, not quite believing it.

42

This house should be on the cover of a design magazine.

"Every beam and every brick," Brody said, and she heard the hint of pride in his voice. He should be proud. What she could see of it was amazing.

"Wow." She moved farther into the giant living room, which fronted the house, probably to take advantage of the awesome view.

"So you like it?" He seemed unsure.

"Like it?" She turned to meet his gaze. "Brody, this place is like nothing I could have imagined. It's ingenious. I love it."

Hearing her sincere approval of his efforts did something to Brody. It was like a great weight had been lifted off his shoulders, and a smile started inside his heart, working its way outward. She liked the den he had built for his mate.

Oh, he hadn't been consciously aware of it, at the time, but Brody had always had a little ray of hope, somewhere in the back of his mind, that he might find a mate to settle with after he put down roots in Grizzly Cove. He'd designed the house on a much larger scale than he'd need just for himself. He'd also put in every modern convenience a woman—or a growing family—could need. And safety had never been far from his mind. The entire back half of the house could be sealed off like a fortress if attack came from the open front half, and there was even a secret tunnel escape route if they got trapped in the underground section.

He'd tried to think of everything. He had put a lot of effort into both the design and the construction. This was his home, and he would hate to have to leave it, but he would, if his mate didn't approve.

Whoa. There was that word again. *Mate.*

Why was it that he kept thinking about a permanent arrangement when it came to Nell? She was human, which would make life difficult, but she was also so…incredibly perfect. Maybe the shifter mate he'd always envisioned in his life wasn't meant to be. Maybe he was meant to have a human mate. Oddly, the thought didn't bother him as much as he thought it would. Not when the human woman in question was Nell.

For her, he'd do just about anything. She was delicate, so he'd have to temper his more animalistic tendencies, but his bear was starting to think of her in *mate* terms too, so it wanted to protect her. If the bear decided she was it, then the human half of his nature wouldn't argue. His human side had been attracted to her from the very beginning. It was the bear that had reserved judgment.

And now, the bear was puffing out Brody's chest, proud that the small woman liked the den he had built.

"Come on back to the kitchen. We'll just get the grill started, and I'll put the steaks on," he said, focusing on the task at hand.

He'd invited her over for dinner. He would make sure he actually served the food before he lost complete control and pounced on her. It was the least he could do.

The kitchen was in the front part of the house that stuck out from the hillside. It was off to the left side and had a door that led to an outdoor deck that was secluded by pine trees and the surrounding forest. There was a wooden table and chairs out there Brody had carved from tree trunks and stained to match the environment. He'd spent many evenings out on this deck, from which he could see the front of his property through the screen of branches but remain hidden from view.

"It's like a hidden grotto out here," Nell observed as he led her outside.

He'd left her shopping bag on the kitchen island before heading out to light the grill. If he didn't get the fire going, it would be a long wait for those steaks he'd promised her.

"I eat out here most of the time," Brody admitted, rolling back the wooden cover he'd made to camouflage the giant grill that was his pride and joy.

"Wow," Nell said, peering at the propane-powered giant that filled the back of the deck. "That's some grill."

Brody beamed. "One of my little indulgences," he admitted. "Bears like meat, and my human side likes it cooked to perfection. This grill is the compromise, so I went all out to get the best one I could afford when I built this place. I cook out here almost every night."

"What about when it rains?" This part of the country received a lot of rain, but he'd come up with a way around that too.

"Behold," he said, like a showman, as he pressed a button and the canopy he had painstakingly designed deployed to cover the deck.

"That is so cool," Nell whispered as she looked up to admire the dark green canopy he had rigged so that any rain would slide off to either side, away from the house. It kept the deck and grill area dry while not cutting them off from the night air or the view. She turned back to look at him. "You've really thought of everything. I'm impressed."

Brody couldn't resist. He leaned down to steal a kiss.

The taste of her mouth was like ambrosia to a starving man. Honey and light. Sweetness and life.

Brody lifted her in his arms and seated her on the wooden table, moving between her thighs. The feel of her soft body flowing around him made him tremble. How much better would it be when they were skin to skin and he could sink inside her tight warmth, learning the feel of her body taking him...accepting him?

He wanted that with every fiber of his being. He wanted to belong to her and have her belong to him. The human side was totally on board with that concept, but the bear was still reserving judgment, though he was starting to see the merits of having a soft human woman share his den. She would bring laughter and wonder...and cubs.

Even if she could never run with him in the woods and hunt by his side in bear form, he would have cubs to teach and play with. Young to raise and love. His mate would love them, and he would love her. They would make a family. The bear approved of that idea wholeheartedly.

"Brody." His name was a whispered plea on her lips, driving his passions higher.

He lowered his lips to her throat, nipping a little, enjoying her flutters and the little squeak when he pushed a little too hard. He drew back, meeting her gaze.

"I'm sorry. We should eat first." He stepped away, though it was one of the hardest things he had ever had to do.

"First?"

He had turned away but looked back at her to gauge her reaction. Her tone had been flirty. The look on her face was...daring. She was smiling, and one eyebrow was raised in question.

"Uh..." He cleared his throat. "I mean..."

Nell hopped off the table and walked slowly over to him, placing her right hand over his racing heart. She was still smiling, and he wasn't entirely sure he knew what to make of her expression. She looked...confident, as if she knew something he didn't. Hell, she probably did. Women were mysterious creatures, and Nell was a prime example of her species.

"It's okay, Sheriff, I know what you mean." She tapped her fingers over his heart playfully, and his breathing hitched. "As it happens, I think we're thinking along the same lines." She stepped back when he would have given in to his instincts and reached for her. "I'd like my steak medium well," she said brightly, and it was some time before he could make his brain work again, and figure out that she had just placed her dinner order, as it were.

So much for thinking along the same lines, he thought sadly. But he had promised her dinner, and it looked like she was hungry, so he would feed her. And bask in her presence.

He liked having her in his home. She added a liveliness to the place that didn't normally exist.

"I'll just go get the steaks," he said, heading back into the kitchen after lighting the grill.

She followed on his heels, going straight for her shopping bag. The bag was full of plastic food boxes, which she unpacked neatly, and he realized as they worked in the kitchen together that she'd brought way more than just a fresh salad.

"What is all that?" he asked, unable to contain his curiosity.

"Just a few other things you can put on that massive grill to go with the steaks. It all came from our garden."

"Seriously?" His jaw practically dropped when she opened and unwrapped savory green and red peppers, sweet potatoes, zucchini, and what looked like a small gourd or squash of some kind. "That can all go on the grill?"

She smiled up at him. "Give me a little corner of that rack, and I'll show you what can be done with roasted veggies." The largest plastic bowl did, indeed, contain the promised salad. She'd also brought a bottle of homemade dressing. "I hope you like raspberry vinaigrette."

"Bears love berries," he answered, his stomach rumbling a bit in anticipation. Usually the bear inside him was placated by meat, but it craved sweet things too, which is why he often stopped in at the bakery for a slice of pie or a honey bun. "In fact, there's a wild patch a short way up the hill. I go there sometimes, when the berries are ripe," he found himself admitting.

He had never told anyone about his private berry patch and felt a little foolish for doing so. Rolling around in a berry patch in his fur was one of his sweetest memories of childhood. His mother would take him out in the forest behind their home and forage with him. Those were some of the best days he could remember as a child.

"You know, you could probably cultivate more berries up here." She looked around as they stepped back onto the deck. "Berries love this volcanic soil and climate. I bet I could get blueberries, blackberries, even raspberries to grow here."

He liked the sound of that. More than the berries, he liked the idea that she would even consider nurturing the land around his home and making things grow. She had a giving nature and both his human and bear side liked it. A lot.

They worked side by side at the grill for a while. She grilled her vegetables, teaching him a thing or two, while he took care of the steaks. Before long, they had full plates and, not long after that, full bellies. They'd eaten her salad, then followed that with the steaks and veggies. All in all, it was one of the most memorable meals Brody ever had in this house.

"How long have you lived here?" Nell asked as they lingered over the dessert she had also brought in her shopping bag of tricks.

"Not too long, really. About two and a half years," Brody admitted. "The town sort of sprang up overnight once Big John told us his plans. We all pitched in, and we got some help with the legal side from the shifter leaders. We call them the Lords. They have connections in every state and in the federal government."

"Bears in the government?" she asked with a teasing smile.

"Actually, they're werewolves, but it's the same concept."

"Werewolves?" she repeated the word incredulously. "Like in the old movies?"

"Not really. They turn into wolves, just like I turn into a bear. Technically, you could call me a werebear, or weregrizzly, but I like just plain ol' *shifter* better." He thought about the old movie creatures and tried to give her a more complete answer. "There is a battle form though, which is probably where those old movies got their start. It's the halfway point between human and wolf—or human and bear—that is a bit of both, and it's pretty effective for fighting, if you can hold it. Only the strongest of us can hold the shift in the middle for any length of time. As youngsters, we practice it, and it helps us figure out the hierarchy of strength and dominance."

"The whole concept is kind of fascinating," she said, making him glad he had tried to explain things for her. "And I'll admit, it's a little scary too."

He didn't like that.

"You don't ever have to be afraid of me, Nell. I would never hurt you, no matter what form I'm in. Even if my instincts are sharper as the bear, I'm still me. I still think and feel and know what I'm doing."

She paused, and he held his breath, but then, she met his eyes. "I'm not too worried about you, per se, Brody. It's the others. I don't know all of them, and I worry for my sisters. What if they say or do the wrong thing? A regular guy who wasn't very nice might get abusive, but what would happen if a guy who had the strength of a bear got angry?"

"I won't lie. We're stronger and more dangerous than the average human man. For one thing, we can sprout claws and sharp teeth, and we don't shy away from using them. But we're also somewhat better at curbing our baser instincts. Shifters have been living in secret among humans for centuries. Millennia, even. And for the most part, we've been able to fly under the radar. We couldn't have done that if we had poor impulse control." He wanted her to be sure about him and about the other bears in town. He didn't want her to be afraid. "And even before you moved in, Big John read everyone the riot act about how you and your sisters were to be treated. Bear society might not be as hierarchical as say, the wolves, but the Alpha's word is still a law. Until that silly koala rolled into town yesterday, you and your sisters were not to be told—or shown—the truth about us."

"But how could we have lived here for any length of time without the truth coming out?" Nell wanted to know.

Brody sighed. "John had you vetted carefully. He seemed to think that, if you did find out, you weren't the kind of people who would go running to the tabloids. But the whole thing was supposed to be a test run, to see if we could let more humans into the neighborhood and live among them without anybody being the wiser."

Nell sat back in her chair, thinking. "Well, until yesterday, it was working. I had no idea."

"Yeah, I know." He had to smile. "It was killing me, you know? I wanted to be able to talk to you. To ask you out. But I didn't want to start anything unless you knew the full story about me. Yesterday sort of untied my hands, and in a way, I should be thankful to that damn troublesome Aussie."

Nell looked kind of...angelic, in that moment. The lighting on the deck was dim and yellow, to keep down the bugs. They were sitting on the same side of the table, closest to the grill. It didn't take much to lean forward in his chair and kiss her.

She didn't resist. In fact, she leaned closer to meet him. And then, the fire truly started. He lifted her out of the chair and positioned her on the clear end of the large wooden table, taking his place between her thighs as he had before.

He kissed her deeply, enjoying the taste of her, the feel of her soft curves against him. He liked the way her hands moved over his body, almost petting, clenching when he did something she liked, the little rounded, human nails digging into his skin through the fabric of his shirt.

And then, her fingers were undoing the buttons of that shirt, and his breath caught. She seemed so eager. Was she ready for what he had in mind? Did she want him like he wanted her? Would she let him go all the way? Was she ready for the consequences?

What if she really was his mate?

CHAPTER EIGHT

The thought stilled him. Brody lifted his lips from hers and moved back a tiny bit so he could meet her eyes.

"I want you to know…" He paused to catch his breath. "There's a very real possibility that if we do this, I'll want to keep you."

The way her eyes lit up made his heart clench.

"What if I want to keep you too?" Nell countered after a moment's pause.

"Honey, if you're my mate, you won't be able to get rid of me." He needed to make her understand. "And that's the truth. Mating is for life among shifters. So if you're not sure about this…"

Goddess, he was going to kill himself later for being so noble. But if she really wasn't sure and wanted out… He had no choice. He had to let her go if she asked. His honor demanded no less.

"How will you know if I'm your mate?" she asked, her fingers running up and down his arms in a playful way that made him want to growl.

"Once we make love, my inner bear will either want to claim you or be indifferent. If the bear is indifferent, there's not much the human side can do about it." He had to be brutally honest with her. She deserved the truth.

"So it's all or nothing?" He didn't like the way her eyes shifted to the side. That she wouldn't meet his gaze told him something.

"It would never be nothing. Not between us." He stroked a strand of her hair back to tuck behind her ear. "I admire you. I think you're amazing in almost every way, Nell. I just want to be honest with you. I value the truth, and you deserve it. I wanted you to know that if, and when, the bear gets a taste of you and decides he likes it, there's no turning back. If the bear recognizes you as his mate, it's for life, so I wanted you to be forewarned."

"How likely is it?" she whispered shyly.

Brody stifled a growl at her unconsciously sexy tone. "I think it's very likely."

"So mates means…what? Is that like, you'd want to marry me?" She sounded so hopefully unsure it was kind of a turn on.

"Mating is more than marriage. It's forever. It means everything a human marriage does and more. Like building a family together, if that's what fate has in store."

"Children?" She seemed happily surprised. "Would they be like you? Little bears?"

"Probably," he admitted. "Either way, they'd be loved." He sensed her approval of his words. "The thing is, mating is not something you can end with a legal document. When I say it's forever, I mean *forever*. I could never let you go, Nell." He cupped her cheek in his palm. "You would be mine, and I would be yours. For the rest of our lives."

"So…um…how does the bear know?" she asked, moving closer to him, almost breathing her words against his lips. "I mean, you'll be human when we…um…"

He thought he knew what she was driving at, so he helped the conversation along. "I will only make love to you in my human form, since you are human. Frankly, doing it as a bear has its limitations, so I won't miss it. Though it might be fun to play chase with you occasionally. The bear likes to hunt."

Her eyes widened, but he didn't let her talk anymore. The

important things had been said, and she hadn't run from him. No, she had stuck by him through the awkward revelations. She had seemed more intrigued and hopeful than fearful. There was nothing more to say. Now was the time for action.

His words gave Nell pause, but not enough to want to stop. She'd never responded so completely to a man, never wanted a man so much. She felt in her heart that Brody was someone special to her, even if he was a being totally outside her previous experience.

The whole concept of shapeshifters still kind of blew her mind, but she'd known Brody for a while now, and in all that time, he'd always been a man she could admire, respect, and definitely want to get to know better. Now was her chance, and she was going to reach out and take it with both hands.

She was going to reach out and take him with everything she had. The need building inside her would not be denied. And, somehow, she trusted that the future would take care of itself. If they were supposed to be together forever, it would happen.

She liked the idea a lot. Brody was the kind of man a woman could build a life with. He had all the qualities she admired in a man—and then some. The whole bear thing... Well...even though it was still a little scary, it was also kind of a turn on. All that leashed power was very attractive in an uncivilized, throwback sort of way. Nell hadn't realized she was so old fashioned, but something about Brody holding all that magic and strength inside him was incredibly attractive.

He wasn't hard on the eyes either. Muscles on muscles, Brody had the kind of physique women drooled over. In fact, she and her sisters had noticed how well most of the men in the area were built. It had been the topic of conversation between them, for weeks now. They'd put it up to the rustic setting, and the fact that most of these men worked hard at physical jobs and tasks around town and on their properties. Now Nell knew another facet—they were all shapeshifters who could turn into bears.

Her sisters would never believe her if she tried to tell them. Smiling inwardly at that thought, she didn't resist when Brody moved closer. And then, she didn't have any truly cohesive thoughts for a very long time as he showed her how a shapeshifting man could worship a female body.

More than that though, she felt like, of the few men she'd been with, Brody was the first one to think more of her comfort than his own. He undressed her as if she was made of some priceless, fragile substance. And when she pushed at his shoulders and fisted her hand in the fabric that still covered him, he took the hint and quickly removed the offending material.

His skin was hot and only slightly rough against her palms. For a guy who turned into a bear on a regular basis, he wasn't all that hairy. She loved the feel of his muscles moving under taut skin, and his big hands were as patient with her as she could have dreamed. He was a considerate lover, which was something she'd always looked for in a man. A gentle giant.

Exactly like Brody.

She gasped as he cupped her bare breasts, his fingers rubbing her nipples. He teased her skin with deliberate touches that drove her passions higher. Each little lick of his tongue over hers, and his fingers over her breasts, made her want more.

His mouth moved downward, over her jaw, into the sensitive hollow of her neck and then, lower. His palms positioned her breasts for him to lick and suck. Little noises of pleasure issued from her throat without her conscious volition.

He lay her back on the table, coming down over her, blanketing her with his warmth. Her remaining clothes disappeared as if they had melted away, and her mind spun as he kissed a trail down over her abdomen and into the warm crevice between her thighs.

Never in her life had she felt such sensations. Brody played her body like a master, and she suddenly realized that any other sexual experiences she'd ever had could never compare to this moment...to this man. Brody was unique.

"Mmmm," he rumbled against her most sensitive spot, making her quiver. He paused and looked up at her, meeting her gaze from between her thighs. "Know something bears really like?" he asked rhetorically, pausing a beat as their gazes held. Then he smiled. "Honey."

Leading with his tongue, he renewed his gentle assault, driving her higher until she shattered. She came, and he rode her through it, gentling her and drawing out the climax.

When her body started warming up again—much to her surprise—he stood and removed his pants, the final barrier between them. The shape and size of him was impressive. She almost laughed, thinking of the way she and her sisters had been speculating about all the hunky guys in town. Based on what she was seeing here, her sisters would have to revise their estimates...up. Way up.

Brody was hung like a bear. The thought crossed her mind, and then she nearly dissolved in giggles. The only thing that saved her was that, at that very moment, Brody stepped closer once more, tugging her downward on the huge table until her splayed thighs were in the perfect position to receive him.

And then, all thoughts fled her mind once more as he joined them. Skin to skin. She would think about that later too, once her mind was out of the clouds and back on Earth. For now, though, everything was perfect. Brody was perfect. Big but perfect for her.

He touched places inside her body—and in her heart, as well—that no man had ever touched before. He filled her, claimed her, and made her his own.

Even if his bear didn't think she was his mate, Brody the man was going to have a hard time getting rid of Nell after this. Just let him try. She could be every bit as possessive as a grizzly bear.

Then he began to move.

Sweet mother in heaven, Nell wasn't sure she was going to survive. The pleasure built in slow waves as he began an advance and retreat, like water lapping at the shore. The gentle lapping turned into an ocean current as his motion increased and then into a torrent as they were both swept up in something beyond control.

The tempest was upon them, pushing her to the height of pleasure, demanding and giving all at the same time. She clung to Brody's shoulders. He was her one solid presence inside the raging storm. He was her anchor and her rock. He was the one who would protect her and push her beyond all boundaries. He was her lover and, if she had anything to say about it at all, her mate.

She screamed his name as the crashing wave broke, casting her higher than she had ever gone before. His muscles tightened as her body clenched around him, and together, they rode the gentler waves of completion, held secure in each other's arms.

CHAPTER NINE

Without saying a word, Brody carried her into the house and back to his bedroom. Something profound had just happened, but he'd be damned if he was going to tell her she was his mate while they were still wrapped up in a quickie on the picnic table. Even if it had been the most earth-shattering quickie of his life.

He lay her down in his bed, marveling for a moment at how good she looked there. Her body was luscious, curved in all the right places and a perfect fit for him in every way. Much as her personality and sharp mind seemed to mesh with his. She challenged him and fascinated him. Theirs would be a really good match, he'd thought from the first.

Now he knew his inner bear was on board. All he had to do was tell her...and hope she felt the same.

It was a tricky business, mating with a human. They didn't have the same instincts as a shifter. There was no inner furball telling her what must be.

Brody was taking a big chance here. He was fully committed—but could she be, without the inner beast driving her? He didn't know, but he'd sure like to spend the rest of his life finding out.

He settled in the bed next to her, his arm lying over her waist, his legs tangled with hers. He needed the skin contact even as their breathing started to return to normal.

He felt her move. He looked over to find her leaning up on one elbow, smiling at him.

"So, what's the verdict?"

Brody wanted to laugh. He should have known his Nell would take life by the balls and face whatever would come of their joining head on. He loved the way she didn't back down.

He levered himself over her, kissing her and aligning their bodies, reveling in the feel of her softness beneath him. If all went well, he'd feel these sensations for the rest of his life.

But he had to tell her and see what she'd say. He couldn't put it off any longer, even if he was just a tiny bit afraid of rejection. He had to be a man and face her. If she didn't want to be his mate, he'd just have to spend the rest of his life finding ways to convince her. He could do that, couldn't he?

Brody lifted his head, ending the kiss, and met her gaze.

"You're mine, Nell. My mate. Now and forevermore."

She gasped but didn't say anything while his heart climbed quietly into his throat. Why didn't she say something?

Finally, she took pity on him. Her smile gave him hope as she leaned closer to whisper against his lips.

"I like the sound of that. Because you know what? You're mine too. And I'm not ever letting you go."

She sealed her words with a kiss, nearly tackling him with her enthusiasm. She ended up on top this time, and he didn't mind a bit. She sank down onto his hardness and began a slow, perfect ride that sent his senses soaring.

He let her do with him what she willed. He was her slave. Her partner. And her protector. Now and forever.

As that crossed his mind, another thought occurred, and he broke their kiss, taking her by the shoulders to still her movements.

"Does this mean you'll marry me?" He had to know she was willing to be his in the eyes of the human world, as well as by shifter standards.

"You're asking me this now?"

She was laughing, her face aglow with the dew of her exertions. He wanted to lick her all over. Her breath came in labored pants as she tried to squirm on him. She had been nearing a peak, and he'd stopped her as his thoughts overcame his instincts.

"I need to know," he said softly, hoping she would understand.

But she was his mate. Of course she understood. He saw the softening of her expression as she looked deep into his eyes. He had the sensation that she could see down all the way into his soul.

"Yes, Brody. I will marry you. It would be my honor to spend the rest of my life with you and make this house a home."

That's all he needed to hear. He kissed her, rolling with her so he was on top. He took over the work of grinding into her, driving her pleasure as high as he possibly could before he took his own. She came at least three times before he lost count and joined her in bliss.

He'd found his mate, and she was going to marry him. More than that, she liked his den enough to want to share it with him. Life couldn't get much better than that.

It was after they had both come back from the biggest climax yet and were laying side by side in the bed when she spoke again.

"We're going to have to tell my sisters, you know." She sounded both worried and amused.

He liked the little designs she was tracing over his arm with her finger, absenting petting him in a way he knew he would love getting used to over the next several decades. He looked over at her to find her staring at the art he'd painted on his bedroom wall last winter. It was a mural of a grizzly being followed by two cubs. It had been a hopeful bit of whimsy on his part, a dream of what he hoped someday might be in his future. And now, with Nell in his life, he finally had a chance at a family, if the Goddess so blessed them.

"I'm trying to think how to tell them without scaring them," Nell went on, oblivious to his deeper thoughts. That was okay. There was plenty of time to discuss both of their hopes and dreams for the future.

"I'll have to clear it with the Alpha first," Brody said, drawing her attention. "I'll talk to Big John first thing tomorrow."

"Do you think he'll object?" Nell bit her lip, looking adorably worried. Brody leaned over to kiss her, then relented once he felt her tension dissolve.

"I'll convince him," he promised her as he drew back to look at her. "You've been here long enough for him to get to know you and your family. I know you can all be trusted, and my counsel counts for a lot with the Alpha. I'm one of his top lieutenants. Which means you'll have a pretty high rank just by virtue of being my mate. Plus, everybody already knows you're a total badass, which means you've already earned some clout of your own." He winked at her, and she frowned.

"Where in the world did you get that idea? I'm no *badass*."

"Are you kidding? That was a direct quote from Lyn after you threw Sig out of your store for coming in stinking of fish guts. You put the fear of Nell into him, and I can tell you Sig doesn't scare easy." Brody was laughing as he remembered the incident. "Sig's a Kodiak when he shifts, which means he's one big-assed bear. Nobody throws him out of anywhere if he doesn't agree. Frankly, we were all pretty glad you told him off because most of us wouldn't have dared tell him to take a shower before he walks around town after one of his week-long fishing trips."

She chuckled, and he laughed with her. It was so easy to be with her. They just...fit.

The Goddess really knew what she was doing when She sent Brody his perfect mate. He had never expected his mate to be human, but he couldn't argue with the Mother of All's wisdom. Nell was perfect for him, and he would do all in his power to be the perfect mate for her.

CHAPTER TEN

Brody talked to John the next morning, and as he'd thought, John had only slight reservations about letting the other Baker girls in on their secret. The Alpha was more than pleased by the news that Brody had taken a mate. A big celebration was being planned to commemorate the mating, which John said he hoped was the first of many in their new community.

But first, Brody had agreed to invite Nell's sisters to dinner at his home, to break the news of their engagement and talk to them privately about his ability to shapeshift. Brody figured a demonstration would be necessary, but he didn't mind putting on a little show for his sisters-in-law, if it would help them accept the truth. He was a little nervous about how they would react, frankly, and he knew Nell was even more worried.

He'd given her a key to his home and knew she was spending her afternoon, after her shift at the bakery ended, up at their house. She was getting things ready for their family dinner that night, and Brody loved the way she was making herself at home in the den he had built with his future mate in mind. That she liked the place made something inside him stretch with pride. He'd built a house, and now, the Goddess had blessed him with a mate to make it a home.

Everything was going along great until that stupid koala got drunk and started waving a gun around the local pub. Brody had to wade in and break up the standoff, taking a shot in the shoulder before he could wrestle the peashooter away from the drunkard. It wasn't a serious wound, but dragging the koala's drunk ass down to the station and locking him up ate up precious time.

Brody was going to be late to the very important dinner he was supposed to be hosting at his den. Nell wouldn't be happy, and being late wasn't a good way to impress the in-laws either.

There was only one way he'd get there on time. Straight through the forest.

Brody shrugged out of his bloody uniform and left it on the chair in the back of the jail. Shifting to his bear form, he used one paw to open the back door of the jail and made a beeline through the forest at the back of the building, running on all fours toward his den. He could cover a lot more ground a lot quicker in his fur than if he'd had to drive around the long way on the winding road.

And shifting shape had mostly healed the bullet graze across his arm. He couldn't do much about the blood until he got a chance to clean up, but at least bleeding had stopped with his shift. The only blood left in his fur now was what had been on his body before he'd changed into his grizzly form.

He had left his watch and phone behind at the station, but he thought he might just make it before the sisters arrived. He saw his house and made for the side of it, hoping to sneak in from the deck, shapeshift, and clean up a bit before the girls arrived.

"Brody!" Nell met him in the woods a few yards from the deck, running to him and dropping to her knees to look at his shoulder. "John called and said you'd been shot in the arm. Are you okay?"

She was touching his furry front arm, her hands coming away bloody. There were tears in her eyes, and he knew he had scared her. Dammit. He hadn't meant to worry her.

Brody shifted shape right then and there.

"I'm fine, Nell. It was only a graze, and it healed when I shifted."

"But the blood..." She gestured with her faintly red hands.

"It stopped. Look." He twisted to present his shoulder to her and waited while she touched him gently, probing the area around the wound, wiping away the residual blood with her fingers.

They were both still kneeling on the ground, and he urged her to her feet, taking her into his arms.

"I'm sorry you were scared. John shouldn't have worried you like that." He frowned. The Alpha was going to hear about making Brody's mate cry. The tears in Nell's eyes bothered Brody. A lot.

He rocked her gently in his arms. He was stark naked, but as a werebear, he was used to that after a shift.

"He said you were on your way, but that you'd been shot," she said, tucking her cheek against his chest. She was trembling, so he held her closer. "I didn't listen after that. All I could think of was that you were hurt. Thank God you're okay." She squeezed him tight, making his heart do a little flip at the undeniable evidence of how much she cared. She loosened her hold and moved back a little, meeting his gaze with teary eyes. "You are okay, right? You didn't lose too much blood, did you? And the bullet didn't go in, it just grazed your arm?" She looked at the wound again, as if making sure.

"Yes, I'm fine," he assured her, smiling. "I didn't lose much blood. It was just a scratch, and all evidence of it will be gone by morning. I promise." He moved his hands to her shoulders. "I'm sorry you were worried. And I'm sorry I was almost late for the big dinner." He lifted her off her feet and onto the deck, following close behind. "I need to get cleaned up before your sisters arrive."

"Too late." It was Ashley's voice, coming to him from the

far end of the deck.

Looking up quickly, he saw both Ashley and Tina seated at the table with half-full glasses of wine in front of them. They'd been there for some time already.

Dammit. He really was late, after all.

And naked.

Though that didn't bother him as much as it seemed to bother Nell. She'd placed herself strategically in front of him, blocking the sisters' view of his privates, for the most part.

Surprisingly, the sisters didn't look all that alarmed. They had to have seen him shift. He hadn't been all that far away from the deck when he'd changed.

Leaning down beside Nell's ear as she stood with her back to his front, Brody asked, "Do they already know?"

"Oh, you're going to love this," Nell said, turning to face him. The expression on her face was a strange one. She looked sort of angry, but not at him, thank the Goddess. "Apparently, I'm the last one in the family to figure out the big secret of Grizzly Cove. They've known for weeks!" she said in an accusatory tone.

"How?" Brody frowned. Everyone in the cove knew to keep things quiet. If someone had been blabbing, he'd have to have words with them.

"Oh, come on," Tina said, lifting her glass and taking a swallow of the wine. "You guys are terrible at keeping secrets. I saw your brother strip and shift the second day I was in town."

"He shifted in front of you?" Brody was shocked.

"Hello? Roof garden," she sing-songed, rolling her eyes. "We have a hell of a vantage point from up there. I was up there putting the planters together when I saw him getting naked in the woods behind our building. He's kinda hot, so of course I watched. And then, he turned into a freaking bear." Tina downed the rest of the wine and reached for the bottle to refill her glass.

"And he's not the only one we saw from up there," Ashley chimed in. "Nell, did you know that Dr. Olafsson can become a polar bear? He likes to skinny dip, then come up as a bear. And hubba hubba. Doc is built."

"I had no idea you two were such voyeurs," Nell said over her shoulder. She seemed more hurt than mad. Brody put his hands on her shoulders, stroking gently, hoping to soothe his mate. He didn't like seeing her upset.

"See?" Tina said in an accusing tone. "That's exactly why we didn't tell you." Tina drank more wine. "You would have totally spoiled our fun."

"Can you believe them?" Nell said, moving more into Brody's arms. "And here I was all worried about how we were going to tell them. I agonized over this big revelation, and it turns out I'm the only one who was in the dark."

Brody tried to think of the best response. "Well, at least now you know they're not going to run screaming into the night at the idea there are shapeshifters in the world."

He tried giving her a lopsided smile, and she responded with a faint one of her own. He felt relief flow through him. She was recovering from both the shock of hearing he'd been shot and from learning that her sisters had known about the town's secret all along and neglected to tell her.

"Ashley, Tina, we wanted to tell you that we're getting married." He let that announcement fall without waiting for a response. There would be time for congratulations later. First, he had to get some pants on and comfort his mate—not necessarily in that order. "Now, if you'll please excuse us for a few minutes, we'll be right back," he said firmly, as he walked slowly backwards into the house, Nell still in his arms. The sisters watched but didn't move from their seats on the deck.

Once inside, he couldn't wait. He had to take her into his arms. He had to comfort her and hold her. The bear inside him demanded he make her happy again, and Brody could do no less than agree.

He dipped his head and claimed her lips in a gentle kiss that quickly turned into something much hotter.

"Way to go, sis," Ashley called from the other side of the screen door while Tina let out a wolf whistle. Brody paid them no heed. He was way too busy kissing his mate.

# # #

Grizzly Cove #2

Mating Dance

BIANCA D'ARC

CHAPTER ONE

Tom Masdan was the one and only lawyer in Grizzly Cove, Washington, and he liked it that way. Tom figured if there was more than one lawyer in a town, they'd be obligated to fight things out in court, which was one aspect of his profession that he loathed. The conflict of the adversarial process annoyed his inner bear and made him want to scratch, claw and just beat his opponent into submission rather than wait to hear what some old guy wearing a dress and sitting on a podium had to say.

Tom thought, not for the first time, that maybe studying law hadn't been the brightest idea he'd ever had. Then again, shifters needed legal representation every once in awhile, just like everybody else. That's where he came in.

He enjoyed helping people like himself—people who lived under the radar of the human population. Shapeshifters had to learn to adapt to the modern, human world. That included following the laws of the countries in which they lived.

Tom had been born and raised in the United States. He'd gone to an Ivy League law school back east. Since then, he had offered his services solely to the *were* of North America, or any *were* that needed legal representation in the States. He filed claims, did a lot of paperwork, and helped shapeshifters of all kinds create the paper trail that humans found so necessary to their existence.

He had traveled all over, but he had never found the one woman who could complete him. He'd never found his mate.

So when his long-time friend, John Marshall—known simply as Big John to most folks—proposed the idea of forming their own little enclave on the Washington coast and putting out an open call for any bear shifters who wanted to move there, Tom was cautiously optimistic. The idea of gathering a relatively large group of usually solitary bears in one town was both novel and intriguing. It could also be dangerous as hell, but Tom trusted Big John's ultra-Alpha tendencies to keep everybody in line.

John had asked Tom to begin the process of turning the large, adjoining parcels of real estate John had bought over the past several years into a new town. There were lots of forms to file with the state of Washington, and quite a few building contracts to oversee. He'd also overseen the real estate deals of neighboring properties for each of the core group of bear shifters that had joined John on this quest. It had taken a good portion of the last several years of Tom's life, but the town of Grizzly Cove had finally become a reality.

It was a really good reality too. The town was small by human standards, but already a few dozen bear shifters had answered John's call for settlers. There were still more males than females, but with the recent decision to allow a few select human-owned businesses to open up on Main Street, things were beginning to change.

Just last week, the sheriff had found his mate in the human woman who, along with her two sisters, owned the new bake shop. It was a true mating, and Tom was happy for them.

But, it had become clear that the so-called secret of Grizzly Cove hadn't really been that much of the secret to the other two sisters. They'd taken the news about shapeshifters in stride. It seemed they'd already figured it out.

Which meant that the shifter residents weren't being

careful enough. And that the two remaining sisters needed to agree not to spill the beans.

A job for Tom, the Alpha had said. Tom wasn't so sure. He might be a lawyer, but he wasn't necessarily a smooth talker. He did his best work on a computer, in an office. He wasn't the kind of attorney who schmoozed clients over three-martini lunches.

But Big John had asked him to try, so there Tom was, approaching the bakery he had never stepped foot in before. It wasn't that he was shy. It was more that he hadn't really wanted to interact with the new humans in town until the experiment had been proven a success. The bakery was the first of many applications Tom had received from business people who wanted to open stores in their town.

The decision had been made to allow the bakery—and the three sisters—as a trial run. Their food was excellent, from all accounts, and most of the shifters in town liked the women and were glad one of their comrades had found a mate.

Humans made decent mates, and bears couldn't be picky. There weren't a lot of bears in the first place, and it wasn't uncommon for them to find mates outside their species. A lot of bear shifters took human mates. It didn't diminish the magic. Bears had more than most shifters, and Tom often thought, that's why they were kind of rare. But what did he know? Only the Mother of All—the Goddess who watched over all shifters—knew for certain.

The bell over the door tinkled as Tom pushed into the bakery. Immediately, he was surrounded by the most scrumptious scents of baking bread, honey and some kind of cheese. He took stock of the place and realized he was the only customer this early in the day. Only one of the sisters was there, working in the back.

That would be the middle sister, he'd been told. She worked the morning shift, and her name was Ashley Baker. The irony of the Baker sisters owning a bakery had struck Tom as suspicious when he'd first seen their application, but he'd done thorough background checks on all three women, and they really were named Baker and had been since their birth.

The blonde woman came out from behind one of the ovens, wiping her hands on her apron as she greeted him. She took up her position behind the counter with a brisk sort of efficiency, and Tom was struck momentarily dumb when she smiled.

"Good morning," she said brightly. "What can I get for you?"

Sonuva... Tom's bear sat up and wanted to roar. It liked the woman.

Hell, it more than *liked* her. It was thinking *mate*.

No way.

Tom cleared his throat, realizing the woman was looking at him strangely. She'd asked him something...

Oh, yeah. She wanted to know why he was there. He stuck his hand out over the counter with a jerky movement.

"Hi, I'm Tom. Tom Masdan."

Smooth, buddy. Real smooth. Tom grimaced inwardly at his own awkwardness.

She wiped her hand once more and took his for a brisk shake. She was eyeing him with a sort of amused wariness as she looked more closely at him.

"You're the town lawyer. I recognize your name from the contracts we signed when we moved in."

His turn to talk. Dammit. He wasn't ready for this. He'd been caught completely flat-footed by the woman. His discomfort turned to anger as he shook her hand. Anger at himself, for being such a dork.

Then he got lost in the feel of her soft skin against his palm. She was delicate and womanly, and her hand held a faint grit of powder. Probably flour, he reasoned with the small part of his brain that was still functioning.

She was looking at him strangely again. Oh, yeah. He was supposed to say something.

"Yeah, uh..." He cleared his throat as she withdrew her hand, and he had to let her go. He didn't want to let her go, but he couldn't very well drag her over the top of the counter by her fingertips, now, could he? "Yes. I'm the lawyer."

Also, apparently, he was an idiot. Stating the obvious. He mentally kicked himself and cleared his throat again, looking around the bakery, searching for something to say that wouldn't make him appear even stupider. Breathing in the delicious aromas, he was struck with inspiration.

"So, uh, what are you baking back there? It smells really good."

She smiled again. He'd said the right thing.

"I've got one oven full of artisanal breads, a tray of honey buns, and I'm just putting the finishing touches on some cheese danish. Any of that strike your fancy? The danish are delish." Was she teasing him or was this her normal manner? He couldn't be sure, having stayed far away from the Baker sisters since they'd moved in.

"I'll have a danish if they're ready," he replied, needing time to think.

He asked her for a cup of coffee too and decided to stay for a bit, using one of the tables scattered around the front of the shop to eat and spend time getting his sanity back.

She moved away from the counter as he scrambled for equilibrium. She bustled around in the back for a bit, but it wasn't long before she returned with a cheesy confection on a plate that smelled really good. Tom's stomach grumbled as she placed the steaming cup of coffee next to the plate on a small tray. He paid her for the snack and took his tray to the closest table without another word.

CHAPTER TWO

Ashley Baker was intrigued by the tall man. He'd seemed gruff and a little odd, but maybe he was just having a bad morning or something. It was early, even for the early risers of Grizzly Cove. The sun was just barely breaking over the mountain to the east, painting the dark waters of the cove in cheery golden ripples. It was her favorite time of day, and she seldom shared it with anyone, for the simple reason that nobody ever really came into the bakery this early.

Normally, she would take a break as dawn arrived, sipping her coffee while staring out at the waters of the cove, the sun rising from behind her, giving her a stunning view of the cove and the wildlife that inhabited it. She saw all kinds of birds, even a few seals occasionally. And she had a pet seagull she threw crumbs to every morning when he came up to the door of the bakery.

Sure enough, there he was now. Ashley grabbed the little dish of bread crumbs she saved for the old bird and headed for the door.

"If you feed that thing, you'll have the whole flock here in no time," the man said as she approached the door.

Ashley laughed. "Gus and I have an understanding. You'll see."

"Gus?" Tom got to his feet.

He walked closer while Ashley opened the door of the bakery and stepped out. She wasn't surprised when Tom followed, though she noticed he kept his distance when she went right up to Gus and held out the dish of crumbs.

Gus the seagull came right over, used to their routine by now. After a few vigorous pecks, Ashley placed the dish on the ground and stepped back, watching Gus demolish the bits of bread she'd saved for him. Tom came up beside her, and she felt oddly comfortable with him, though they'd only just met.

She'd wondered what the town lawyer might be like when she'd helped her older sister settle the paperwork for their new business. Ashley was the one with the business background, and she did most of the bookkeeping for their little business. She'd liked the orderliness of the lawyer's correspondence and the clarity of his instructions. He'd laid out everything in a sensible way, which was something she'd come to learn wasn't always the case with lawyers.

She had looked forward to meeting him when they moved in, but he hadn't come by the bakery. Until now. She wondered why he'd waited so long, and why he'd chosen this odd hour and this particular day to drop by.

He seemed nervous, so she didn't press him. She had sympathy for socially shy people, since she'd been one in her younger days. It was only after she'd gotten involved in the speech and debate club in high school and developed those skills in moot court competitions in law school that she had really blossomed. She'd lost her fear of talking in front of people and was better able to handle social situations as she gained confidence.

But then all hell had broken loose soon after she took her first job, and she'd come running back home to her sisters. She was better off with them, doing something she enjoyed even more than her former profession. Law was work, but baking... That was fun.

Baking had always been her outlet, even before she had gotten serious about her education. Baking for her was creating, and she came up with a lot of the unique recipes they used in their shop. She liked spending the quiet hours before dawn beating bread dough into submission and experimenting with new flavors and textures.

She liked being in the shop alone from about four in the morning until her older sister came in to help with the breakfast rush, such as it was in this small town. Ashley left the store in Nell's capable hands after the breakfast crowd dwindled, and she had the rest of the day to herself.

"You named a seagull Gus?" Tom said quietly, picking up the question she hadn't answered on her way out of the store.

She shrugged. "Gus the gull. It seemed appropriate."

"I can't believe the rest of his flock hasn't show up to fight him for those crumbs."

"I don't think Gus really has a flock. He's kind of a loner. And he's been living rough. See his wing?" Ashley pointed to the way some of Gus's feathers didn't quite sit right. "I've tried to get close enough to examine why it's like that, but he won't let me. I'm hoping someday we'll build enough trust up that he'll let me help him out, but for now, feeding him in the morning is all we've managed to agree upon." She sighed as she looked as closely as she could at the seagull's injuries. He'd been through the wars and had a few scars on his legs to prove it in addition the wing issue.

They watched in companionable silence while Gus finished his breakfast, then flew away.

"It doesn't seem to affect his ability to fly," Tom observed as the seagull flew off toward the water.

Ashley watched the bird go and sighed once more. "No, he can fly well enough, but something's not right there, and I'd love to see if I could help him be more comfortable."

Tom turned and she looked at him, meeting his sharp brown gaze. "You have a good heart, Ashley Baker. Not many people would care so much about a dumb animal."

"Gus isn't dumb. He's smart enough to con me out of breakfast every day." She smiled and opened the bakery door.

"Point taken," Tom said, following behind her as she went

back indoors.

She didn't seek the imaginary safety of the counter. Instead, she leaned against one of the tables and turned to confront her guest.

"So, what brings you to my door this early in the morning, counselor?" She folded her arms and watched him squirm a bit before he came up with a reply.

She wasn't sure why, but it seemed she made him nervous. Imagine that.

"What makes you think I didn't just come for breakfast?" he countered, leaning on the table opposite her.

She should have expected the counter-argument. He was a lawyer, after all.

"Well, let's see. In the months since we've been open, just about every resident of the cove has been in here at least once—if only to check us out and grumble." There were a few notable curmudgeons in the area who would gladly buy their baked goods but weren't exactly friendly about it. "You, however, have never been in. Not once. I noticed."

"Why would you notice something like that, especially?" His tone challenged her. The single arched eyebrow dared her to tell him the truth. Ashley squirmed.

"If you must know, I've wanted to put a face to your name ever since we started the application process to move here. I liked your style, counselor. Your papers were precise and orderly. That's not something I've seen all that often, and I admit, I admired your work. Can you blame me for wanting to meet you?"

Tom shrugged those massive, muscled shoulders. Ashley had noticed how fit he was. Then again, most of the residents of this town were fit and what she'd call *buff*. They were shapeshifters, after all. She and her younger sister, Tina, had seen a few of them shifting into bears from their rooftop garden within the first few weeks of living there.

At first, Ashley hadn't been sure of what they were seeing, but as time went on and more men got naked in the woods behind their building, and then bears stood in their places,

Ash and Tina had put two and two together, as it were. Incredible as it had seemed, they were living in a town full of bear shifters.

And then their oldest sister had gone and gotten engaged to one of them. The sheriff, a hunky guy named Brody Chambers, was a hottie, no doubt about it, and he'd be their brother-in-law in the not-too-distant future. They had been planning the wedding for the past week, ever since the happy couple had made the announcement at a dinner party at Brody's home in the woods.

Brody and Nell were supposed to break the big news about him being a shapeshifter at that dinner, but Ashley and Tina had already known. It was Nell who had been out of the loop on that big secret. The younger sisters had opted not to tell Nell until they were all well-settled into town because they didn't want their overprotective sister uprooting them. They were done moving around. The sisters liked this cove full of extraordinary beings, and they wanted to stay.

The lawyer was just as hunky as Brody. No, he was even more handsome to Ashley's mind, because not only did he have those broad shoulders, narrow hips, and muscles that showed through his clothes, he also had a demonstrated ability to use his brain. Ash had always found a man's mind as attractive as the outer packaging.

And Tom definitely had superior outer packaging to go with his orderly mind. She'd liked his style even before she'd seen him, and now that she'd finally met him, she found him very, very attractive.

"I guess your sisters let you handle the paperwork, considering your background." Tom's eyes dared her to confirm his suspicions, and they held far too much knowledge.

"You know?" She sucked in a breath, truly surprised, though she probably shouldn't have been.

"Honey," his tone dropped, turning the word into a soft endearment, "I did background checks on all of you. Big John trusts me to vet whoever we allow into our community."

She grabbed the back of a nearby chair and sat, her knees almost giving out on her because of his stunning news.

"Does everybody know?" she asked in a broken whisper.

Tom crouched before her, taking her shaking hands in his. "No. Only me. I just told John that you were okay, and he took me at my word."

CHAPTER THREE

"I was cleared. Cleared of all charges, I mean." Her voice was weaker than she liked when she finally looked up to meet his warm brown gaze.

"I know. I looked into it. The New York press treated you badly. You did all you could for those kids. It wasn't your fault."

His strong, solemn tone touched her, even as the horror of the past that had sent her running from her big corporate job in New York with her tail between her legs came back, hitting her once more. It had been a long time since she'd been confronted by such an out-of-the-blue reminder of everything that had happened. She'd run home to her sisters, and they'd taken her in and let her join them on their next adventure.

"Then you know it all," she said, knowing her tone was as bleak as the desolate place inside her that had been utterly destroyed by the events that had run her out of New York on a rail.

"Most of it." He stood and pulled a chair over, close to her, sitting opposite her.

He was easy to be around. He didn't rush her to speak or bombard her with questions. She liked that. But even so, she knew he expected her to say something.

"Nell and Tina already had a successful bistro in Portland. They had a regular customer who had retired to the west coast, and he got me the interview with his old firm in New York after I graduated law school. If I'd known what I was in for though, I don't think I would've done it. Hindsight is twenty-twenty, isn't it?" She had to laugh, or else she'd cry. And she didn't want to cry about this anymore. Especially not in front of this man. "So there I was, fresh out of school, full of myself and not knowing that I was as green as grass and ripe for a fall. They put me on the Hilliand case, and I did my best to follow orders and file all the motions for custody. Well, you probably saw what happened as it played out in the media. I became the public face of the law firm for software billionaire Bob Hilliand. And I got the blame when his ex-wife won custody of their three little ones and whisked them off to Slovenia. When they were killed in the plane crash..." Her voice trailed off.

"The press hounded you, blaming you for their deaths. If you hadn't screwed up the paperwork, they would never have been allowed to leave the States. Isn't that how it went?" Tom's voice was neither accusatory nor sympathetic.

"Something like that. But...I didn't," she whispered. "I didn't screw up. What I filed should have worked. When the papers were released... That wasn't my work. Only, no one would believe me."

"Whose was it? Do you know?" His question was gentle but firm.

She met his gaze. "I know who it was, but there's no way to prove it. She set me up for the fall in order to climb right over my back into a better position in the firm. She didn't care about the client, at all. In fact, she probably counted it lucky that the mother and children died. It made me look even worse than losing the custody battle. I left the firm in disgrace, and her way was clear to advance."

"People like that are the reason I hate our profession," Tom said, sitting back in his chair and blowing out a gusty sigh.

"You believe me?" Ashley searched his gaze, surprised by his open attitude after the horrible reputation she'd earned in the press.

"No reason why I shouldn't." He spread his hands on his jeans-clad thighs, and she followed the movement with her gaze. He had big hands. Rough and calloused. Not like most lawyers' hands she'd ever seen. This was a man who worked with his hands as well as his mind.

He also had a mishmash of faded paint stains on his fingers. She knew he was a painter of some renown. All the residents of Grizzly Cove did some kind of art. The place had been founded as an artists' colony, though Ash and Tina had figured out soon after moving here that a lot of the residents were also shapeshifters.

First off, most of the men didn't act like artists. They weren't flamboyant. Just tall, muscular and hunky. The place was populated mostly by men, which the sisters had discussed at length. It was a less civilized stretch of the coast, to be sure, but they were slowly bringing the comforts of small-town living to the area. The three sisters were the first outsiders they'd let in to their growing community, and there were very few females besides the three human Baker sisters.

In fact, she could count the other women in the area on one hand. There was Lyn Ling and her adorable four-year-old daughter, Daisy. Lyn made art out of bamboo, and it was said she kept a grove of the stuff growing out by her home in the woods. She was Chinese by origin, but had lost her husband and come to this town for a fresh start.

Maya Marshall was Big John's sister. She had a lovely little workshop just down the street from the bakery, where she sold the most amazing pieces of one-of-a-kind handmade jewelry. Jayne Sherman was Maya's best friend, off-and-on partner in the jewelry business and the town's only registered nurse.

The final female of note was a reclusive watercolorist named Mary MacDonnell, who came in to the bakery twice a week or so to stock up on breads and buy a few pastries. All of the ladies were likely shapeshifters of some kind, though Ash had thought it rude to ask.

Tom was probably one of the grizzly bears she and Tina had seen roaming the woods behind the bakery. He was certainly large enough. And muscular enough. She liked the look of his broad shoulders and bulging biceps.

Was it getting hot in here? She thought momentarily about the ovens in back, but the timers would beep when the bread was done. There was no beeping, just the pounding of her heart as she talked to this gorgeous hunk of man who—*saints preserve us*—seemed to be keeping an open mind where her colorful past was concerned. He was getting even more attractive, by the moment.

"Besides," he went on, blissfully unaware of her perusal, "I know when people are lying to me. I'm also a really good judge of character. So is just about everyone here. Especially our mayor. You and your sisters are okay with Big John, so that means you're okay. End of story."

"But that isn't really the end of the story, is it?" she countered, still uncomfortable that he knew her deep, dark secret. "My sisters moved here, in part, to help me start over. The press hounded me. You have no idea…" She ran a hand over her hair, feeling the sorrow and frustration of those days all over again. "It was awful."

"I won't tell anyone." His voice was reassuringly strong, though the deep tone created a sort of intimacy that warmed her.

She looked up, meeting his gaze. "How can I be sure, though? It would kill me to have to move again. I'd have to leave my sisters behind now that Nell is marrying Brody, and Tina's so infatuated with all of you people and your abilities…"

Tom actually chuckled, and Ash couldn't figure out why. She scowled at him until he held up one hand, palm outward.

"Honey, that's the reason I'm here. Big John asked me to come talk to you and your sister, to make sure you wouldn't go telling the rest of the world about *us*."

"Huh." She sat back in her chair, nonplussed. "So we both know something about the other we don't want getting out." A dark thought occurred to her. "Were you going to threaten me with exposure if I didn't keep your secret? Because if that's your game—"

"Peace, Ashley," Tom interrupted her, this time raising both hands in a gesture of surrender. "That wasn't my angle. I was simply going to ask, but I couldn't quite figure out how to do it. I wanted to get to know you a little first, and see what you were like. I should've come in when you first moved to town, like everybody else did, to check you and your sisters out, but…well…I didn't. I'm sorry for that now." He smiled at her, and she was glad she was sitting down. His smile packed a wallop. "Truce?"

How could she say no when the handsomest man she'd ever met looked at her with those puppy-dog eyes and asked so nicely? She couldn't help herself. She caved.

"Okay. Truce." She reached out to shake the hand he offered. "I won't tell if you won't."

Something almost electric passed between them as she touched his hand. He held hers for longer than strictly necessary, and her breath hitched. Time seemed to spin out, stretching as she looked deep into those stunning brown eyes of his…

And then he let go. At least she had the satisfaction of realizing that he seemed as shaken as she was by the strange moment. His eyes gave him away. They held a trace of the same confusion she was feeling, along with a sort of wonder that made her breath catch again.

This man had the most amazing effect on her.

Beep. Beep. Beep.

"I think your oven is calling." Tom grinned at her.

"What?" She shook her head to break the daze she seemed to have fallen into. "Oh!" Ashley ran around the counter and saved the bread, moving pans around while keeping one eye on Tom, to make sure he wasn't going to just leave without saying goodbye.

She put the bread onto the cooling racks and loaded the next batch, which she'd already prepared before he came in. Task done, she wiped her hands as she went back up front. He was still there. Just on the other side of the counter.

"That bread smells really amazing," he offered, looking over her head at the cooling racks that were just visible behind her.

"Thanks. Want some?" She motioned with her chin back toward the bread.

"Yeah, I could take some to go, I guess."

Oh. He had to leave. Why did her heart sink at the thought?

"There's just one more thing." He looked kind of hesitant to speak, and that intrigued her.

Ashley's heart went pitter-pat wondering what the one-more-thing could be? Would it be something personal? Would he ask her out? She felt...sort of...giddy. Yeah, that's what it was. Giddiness.

When was the last time Ashley Baker, disgraced lawyer and therapeutic baker, had felt giddy? She couldn't even remember, and that struck her as kind of sad. Yet, here was a man who made her feel things she hadn't felt in a very long time. Things were looking up—as long as he stuck around.

"What is it?" she asked, unwilling to wait for him to get around to speaking again.

"It's your sister."

Hmm. Her heart sank a little.

"Which one?"

His answer to that question was key. If he was asking about Nell, no problem. Nell was happily engaged. But if he was asking after pretty, younger, gets-all-the-boys Tina...

"Tina."

There it went. Her hopeful, foolish heart hit the dirt.

"What about her?" Ashley stood strong, not letting her disappointment show. She hoped.

"Well, I don't know her. How can I be sure she won't go blogging about *Grizzly Cove, Home of the Rare Bear Shapeshifters* or something?" Tom diffused his tough words with a

84

charming grin that Ashley fought against. She refused to be charmed by another guy who might just be using her to get to her sister. "Can she be trusted?"

Wait. Was he asking Ashley's opinion? Did he not want an introduction to Tina to find out for himself?

"Tina's always been trustworthy. She doesn't tell tales, and she doesn't have a blog." Ashley chuckled at the thought. "My sisters have sort of rallied around me since I came home with my tail tucked between my legs. They mostly stay off social media and try to run under the radar for my sake. It's old news now, but every once in a while, when we were still in Portland, some enterprising reporter would jump out at me from the bushes, or try to get to me through my sisters on the internet. Since then, they've pretty much closed ranks to protect me. I don't think Tina would seek attention from anyone in the media, lest it somehow bounce back on me again. She wouldn't do that to me. We moved this far to get away from my past. Tina wouldn't ruin that. She likes it here."

Ashley wouldn't tell him how much Tina enjoyed spying on the hunky guys who dropped trou in the woods and turned into bears. It had become a bit of a sport for her to sit up on the roof and try to spot them. That was about as exciting as things got around here, after all.

Moving up here had been hardest on Tina, but she never complained. She'd had an active social life back in Portland, though no serious boyfriends. Not any that lasted longer than a few months, at any rate.

"I trust your judgment, but I'd still like to talk with her," Tom said, depressing Ashley further.

Maybe he *was* interested in her younger sister. Ashley wouldn't be surprised. It had happened before. Quite a few times, in fact.

"She works the night shift," Ashley replied in as bland a tone as she could manage.

"Yeah, I know, but..." He trailed off, and she became intrigued despite her better judgment. "Will you be here tonight too?"

Ashley dusted off the non-dusty counter with her towel. "There's no reason to fear Tina. She's harmless. You're a big boy. You can introduce yourself."

"Oh. Well, yeah," he agreed quickly, seeming somewhat surprised by her brusque answer. "But I was hoping to see *you* again. I mean, I'd like to talk to Tina, just to be sure, but I was wondering if maybe you'd like to have dinner with me."

CHAPTER FOUR

For a lawyer, he wasn't all that eloquent.

And there went her heart again, going pitter-pat. Had he really just asked her out?

"Since this is the only place to eat in town, at the moment, I thought maybe I could meet you here, then talk to your sister before we grab a bite and then maybe take a walk on the beach after?" He seemed nervous, talking quickly when she didn't answer right away.

Damn. He really did just ask her out. Her. Not Tina. Inside, Ashley raised a mental fist in victory.

"How about we meet here and you can talk to Tina, but then, maybe instead of eating in here, could I offer you the setting of our rooftop garden? It's really pretty up there. We strung white twinkle lights among the flower pots, and we sit up there at night sometimes, and stargaze."

Was she talking too much? It felt like maybe she was. Ashley stuttered to a halt and waited to see what he'd say.

He gave her one of those electrifying grins that made her knees wobble. "I'd like that very much. What time is good for you?"

She wanted to say right now, but it wasn't even eight o'clock in the morning. She'd have all day to prep and worry and try to get ready.

"Is seven too late?" She picked a time she knew Tina would be the least busy.

If needs be, Ash could take over for a few minutes while Tom talked to Tina. Seven was right in between the dinner crowd and the folks who strolled in for latte and dessert.

Tom's smile widened. "Seven is perfect. I'll look forward to seeing you then."

"Me too." Not a witty answer, but it was the best she could do under the circumstances. Tom's smiles made her feel all warm inside, and they sort of melted a part of her brain—the thinking part, no doubt.

She jumped, realizing he was probably waiting for her to get the bread they'd talked about a minute ago. She went back and quickly selected one of the best loaves, packaging it in the special bags they'd had printed, that were both long and wide enough for the special shapes Ashley liked to make. She handed him the still-warm bread across the counter.

"This one's on the house. Hope you like it. It's honey walnut." She felt a little shy all of a sudden. Should she have given him one of the plainer selections?

"Sounds delicious. You know, we bears love honey. And I am particularly fond of walnuts." He brushed her hand with his as he took the loaf from her, and she swore she could feel little sparks against her skin, like little zaps of static electricity. "Thank you, Ashley."

His warm, deep voice made a meal of her name. She liked the way he said it.

He stood there for a moment, gazing at her from across the counter, and then, he sort of shook himself and headed for the door. It looked to her like maybe he was reluctant to leave, which made her feel all tingly. Maybe he was as attracted to her as she was to him? Could she be so lucky? Well, he had just asked her out—sort of.

There wasn't much night life in the cove, so his suggestion about sharing a meal—even if it was in her family's establishment—pretty much made it a date. Ashley felt that giddiness again. She hadn't been on a date since all the trouble started back in New York.

She watched him walk away, noticing again what a fine backside he had. These shifters were built to last, every single one of them, but Tom seemed to have that little extra sex appeal that made her want to jump his bones. Not that good girl Ashley had ever really gotten wild enough with a man to jump him. Still, Tom made her think about it. Very seriously.

The bell above the door tinkled as he left, and Ashley sighed, watching him walk down the street. The town lawyer really had a great ass.

* * *

Tom was prompt, which was a good thing for Ashley's nerves. She'd frittered around the apartment upstairs all day, cleaning, setting up the table in the rooftop garden, and figuring out what to wear. As a result, her entire wardrobe was now scattered all over her room, but the little garden had been weeded and pruned until every leaf shone.

She'd been hanging around downstairs in the bakery for the past half hour, chatting idly with Tina and helping out here and there. The dinner rush—which only consisted of about a half dozen people that night—had come and mostly gone. And then, there he was. The man himself walked in the door.

He seemed only to glance at Tina before his gaze met Ashley's.

Tom saw Ashley standing there, and every other thought went straight out of his head. His inner bear liked what it saw, which was a first. Never before had his other half weighed in this strongly about a female.

He walked straight up to her, but social convention barred him from doing what he really wanted to do, so he settled for smiling at her and saying hello. If they hadn't been in public, he might've given into his baser instincts and pulled her into his arms, greeting her with a kiss…or more. Whatever she'd let him get away with. As it was, he had to be polite and make conversation, which wasn't exactly his strong suit.

"You look great," he said, knowing it wasn't polished, but at least it was true.

"Thanks." Her smile lit his world, and he was glad he'd opted to speak the first thoughts that jumped into his head. "You too." A throat cleared nearby, and Ashley jumped. "Sorry. Tom, this is my sister, Tina. Tina, this is Tom."

The younger sister stuck her hand over the counter and gave Tom a speculative smile as she looked from him to Ashley and back again. He shook Tina's hand, but there was no spark. Not like when he touched Ashley.

So it wasn't a Baker sister thing. It was just an Ashley thing. Good to know.

"You're the town's lawyer, right?" Tina asked, letting go of his hand.

"Yeah, that's me," he agreed.

"Ash said you wanted to talk to me?" Tina went on. "Don't worry, your secret's safe with me. Nell read me the riot act already, but it wasn't necessary. I get that you guys have a good thing going here, and I won't ruin it for you—or for my sisters. Are we cool?"

Tom's head was spinning a bit by the speed of Tina's words, but his inner bear scented the absolute truth in her words. There wasn't much guile in this young woman. Tom's built-in lie detector knew she was on the level, even if she left his human side in a whirl.

"Yeah," he said, his human thought processes catching up with his bear's instincts. "I think we're cool. I can tell you don't intend to make trouble for us, and most especially for your family." Tom decided to take it a step further. "You know, now that Nell is part of the Clan by mating with Brody, you two are under our protection too. If you ever have any trouble, you just come to me, or better yet, go to John. He looks out for all of us. He's the man in charge. Our Alpha. Did Brody explain about that?"

"You mean he's leader of the pack, right?" Tina said

offhandedly.

"Packs are for wolves. We're bears. We call our groupings Clans," Tom told her.

"Wolves?" Ashley piped up, sounding surprised. "You mean there are people who turn into wolves too?"

"Duh," Tina intoned before Tom could say anything. "Where do you think the legends about werewolves come from, Ash? Seriously." Tina shook her head as she wiped the counter with a dish towel.

Ashley blushed rather becomingly, Tom thought. He decided to tell her a bit more about the world the sisters now found themselves in.

"Wolves, big cats, raptors. There are all sorts of shapeshifters, each with their own hierarchy. But we all answer to the Lords."

"Like nobility?" Ash asked him, then turned to her sister. "There's shapeshifter nobility?"

"Sort of, but it's not a hereditary title. The Lords are always twin Alphas, and the duty usually falls to a different group in each generation. The current Lords of North America are wolves, but we've heard rumors that the next generation will be from a bear Clan." Tom felt a swell of pride knowing that the next Lords would be bears.

"How do they decide which group gets the leadership? Is there a vote or something?" Tina asked.

Tom shook his head. "No. No voting. Identical twins are rare among shifters. When a set is born, we know the Mother of All has chosen them to be the next Lords." That's just the way it was. The way it had always been.

"Mother of All? Is that like Mother Nature or something?" Tina asked.

"The Goddess has many names and many guises. I know most of your human religions feature a male deity, but shifters have served the Goddess for as long as there have been shifters."

"Wow," Tina commented. "Progressive."

The bell above the door jingled and Tina went over to

assist the newcomers. It was Lyn and her daughter, Daisy. Though most four-year-olds would be going to sleep soon, shifter kids had a bit more energy than their human counterparts, so it looked like mother and daughter had come in for dessert.

CHAPTER FIVE

"Shall we go upstairs?" Ashley asked after greetings had been exchanged.

"Lead the way," Tom answered, knowing he was smiling and unable to stop himself.

He hadn't been on a date in way too long, and he'd never really experimented with human women. There was something so incredibly alluring about Ashley though...something primal that demanded he get closer to her.

Tom followed Ashley through a door marked *private*, up a flight of stairs and into a cozy apartment that took up the entire top floor of the building. Everything up here was feminine, with soft edges and colors. It was nice, Tom thought, though his own taste ran more toward hunter green and navy blue.

She kept going, leading him to another set of stairs that took them onto the roof. Tom followed, bemused by what he found up there. The sisters had turned a plain, flat roof into an oasis in the middle of the village. There were planters of every size and shape—most made of wood that the ladies must have built themselves—all over the roof. In the center was a patio table that had been set with silverware and china. In the center of the table, a thermal bag held something warm that Tom could scent was some kind of beef.

A green salad with tomatoes sat under a net cover, and a small rack of condiments lay nearby. Ashley had gone all out, and Tom was duly impressed, though he also felt a little guilty.

"I didn't mean to make you go through all this trouble, but it looks great, and the food smells great." He looked at the views in the early evening light. "This is really nice up here."

"It's our little getaway. We spend a lot of time up here, tending the plants and just enjoying the sunny days." She led him toward the table in the center of their magical garden. Fairy lights were woven throughout the planters, lighting the path with a soft illumination.

The salad, Tom learned, had come fresh from the garden, as had most of the vegetables and herbs. Tom admired the sisters' ingenuity in growing their own fresh produce in a town that didn't really have much in the way of groceries. Some of the shops stocked various meats, and there was a fresh fish market, but getting fresh lettuce, for one example, wasn't a high priority for most in the town.

Ashley had made a roast that was cooked to perfection. Some kind of herbed potato dish went with it, along with the salad and a green bean dish that was absolutely delicious. Tom complimented her cooking many times throughout the meal.

"I didn't mean for you to go to all this trouble, but it was fantastic," Tom said, as they finished the meal. "Thank you. Next time, I'm going to cook for you." He gathered his courage, knowing his inner bear wouldn't allow him to wait. This woman was too special. "In fact, how about tomorrow? I can pick you up and bring you out to my place. I've got a huge grill, and I've even been known to marinate a steak or two in my time."

"Really? Do tell." Her answer was flirty. Tom took it as a good sign.

"I even have the beginnings of a small wine cellar," he told her with a knowing nod as he raised his glass to her. She'd paired the roast with a very nice red wine that he truly appreciated. Wine was one of his little hobbies.

"I'm impressed. Are you going to offer to show me your etchings next?" She was still flirting with him. A tiny bubble of joy rose up from the center of his being. He couldn't remember having this much fun with anyone in a good, long time.

"No etchings, but I do have a studio overlooking the cove. In fact..." he said, getting excited as he looked at the view from the rooftop, "I'd love to paint the cove from up here sometime. It's a unique perspective, and the light is phenomenal."

They'd moved to sit on a bench the sisters had placed at the front of the roof where they could look out over the cove. The dusk had given way to dark, and the only illumination was the soft twinkle of the fairy lights in the garden behind them, the dusting of stars and quarter moon overhead, and the occasional flutter of the lights from a ship out at sea.

The cove itself wasn't large or deep enough for any serious docks. There were a few small boats, at least one of which was used exclusively for fishing by the same shifter who owned the fish market. He supplied everyone who didn't want to do their own fishing. The other boats belonged to various residents who enjoyed occasional sport fishing or just sailing along the coast.

"You could," Ashley said softly. "I mean, I don't think my sisters would mind if you wanted to use our garden as your studio for a little while. I've seen some of your work in the gallery next door, and it's very powerful."

She'd seen his art? And liked it? That touched him more than he thought it would.

"I never really painted much before coming here," he admitted. "But I've discovered a passion for it." He had to laugh. "I thought John's idea of disguising ourselves as artists was a little nuts at first, but the man has vision. A lot of us have discovered hidden talents and a real joy in creating things. It's somewhat therapeutic, and while my inner bear doesn't truly understand the point of it all, it does appreciate beauty. Painting calms the beast a bit, which is a nice added benefit. Having so many of us living in such close proximity could have been disastrous otherwise. Usually, we don't group together like a lot of other shifters do. Mostly we just have our small family units as part of a larger Clan that we see every once in a while, but we don't all live together in the same place."

"So this place is a sort of social experiment," Ashley mused.

"In more than one way," Tom agreed. "John's also managed to turn us all into artists. That was a pretty massive undertaking in itself. I honestly thought—if anything—we'd have an entire community of chainsaw carvers."

Ashley laughed, and the sound warmed Tom's soul. There was something so enchanting about this woman, and he wanted to get closer to her.

Trying out one of his rusty moves, he put his arm along the back of the bench, behind her. When she didn't object, he relaxed, enjoying her nearness.

"Brody carves with a chainsaw," she said quietly, her tone amused as she moved closer and practically snuggled into his side.

"Don't get me wrong; I like your sister's mate. Brody and I go way back. But applying the term *art* to those tree stumps he attacks with a chainsaw isn't something I care to do. Besides, all he does are self-portraits." Tom liked being close to Ashley. She smelled divine, and his inner bear grumbled happily in the back of his mind.

"He does seem to carve a lot of bears," she allowed.

"Look closer. They're all the *same* bear."

She chuckled, and he felt a small sense of triumph that he'd been able to make her laugh. Brody's ongoing series of self-portraits had become something of a running joke within the Clan.

"Just think of all those poor, ignorant tourists, totally

unaware that they're stuck with a self-portrait of your brother-in-law on their front lawn."

This time, she laughed outright. Tom liked making her laugh. He enjoyed the cheerful tones of her amusement and the way her eyes lit up.

Unable to let the moment pass, Tom followed his instincts and leaned over to cover her smiling lips with his. Their first kiss, and it was one of joy.

It quickly turned into something much sultrier as she turned into his arms, and he drew her against his body. She tasted of the peppery wine they'd had with dinner and her own unique essence. He couldn't get enough.

Tom's inner bear wanted to lick her all over and learn her different tastes, but it was too soon for that. He counseled the grizzly to patience while his human form got to know her responses, cataloging each one and learning what made her tremble.

Her passion was as quick to ignite as his, which was good. It meant they were a good match, and that she was as attracted to him as he was to her. So far, so good.

Tom lifted her legs so they stretched across his lap. She let him move her around to suit his mood, her cooperation making him want to growl in victory. She was with him. She was part of this seduction, this initiation, this getting to know each other.

Her tiny hands roamed over his back and then his shoulders and arms, learning him, testing the feel of his muscles against her fingers. He damned the cloth that separated his skin from her touch, but he had to be patient. She was human. He had to let things progress at a slower pace. He didn't want to scare her off.

She was quickly becoming much too important to him for him to mess this up. He told himself again, to be patient. And when she pushed eagerly at his clothing, he wanted to go with her instincts and get them both naked on the roof, under the stars.

But he heard noises in the apartment below. It was late.

Tina had closed the bakery and was making a lot of noise—probably to give them fair warning that she was in the apartment.

It was time to end their first date, even though he didn't want to go. Not now. But he had to.

Reluctantly, he caught her fingers and stilled her movements, ending their kisses.

"I've got to go," he said, hating every word, but knowing it was the right thing. For now. "But I want to see you again. Are we still on for tomorrow? My place? I'll pick you up."

He held her hands gently between his own, raising them to place little kisses on her fingertips. He couldn't help himself. If she was near, he wanted to touch her. To kiss her.

A bang came from downstairs, loud enough for Ashley to hear.

"Damn, it must be later than I realized," she said, blushing prettily now that the dazed confusion was slowly leaving her gaze. He liked that he'd put that dreamy expression on her face. "Tina's downstairs."

"I know." He kissed her knuckles gently. "That's why I stopped us from going any further."

She blushed even more. Tom could see it in the faint light. His night vision was pretty good. And her response made him want to cuddle her.

"I'm glad one of us kept a level head," she muttered as she allowed him to hug her against his chest. Her head fit nicely into the crook of his neck, as if made to belong there. To belong to him, and him alone.

"I will always protect you, Ashley. In every situation. It's part of my instincts. Hard-wired, if you will." He rubbed his hand down her arm from shoulder to wrist and back again in soothing motions. He loved touching her.

"You know, that could sound stalker-ish, but I find it comforting. I feel like I've known you a lot longer than just a day." Her words slipped quietly into the evening breeze, and straight into his heart.

"I feel the same way, honey. Sometimes it happens like

that for my kind. Courtships can be a bit...accelerated. But I give you my word, I will try my best not rush you."

She eased from his arms and sat on the bench next to him, then she met his gaze. "Is that what we're doing? Beginning a courtship?"

Tom took a deep breath, gathering his courage before answering. "I'd like to think so. If you're okay with that. We call it the mating dance."

She looked out over the cove, then up at the stars before answering. "Yeah, I think I'm okay with it. I like you, Tom. That's a good first step."

She stood and walked to the table, gathering the plates and putting them in a plastic caddy she'd had stowed to one side. He helped her clean up, prolonging the moments he had with her, but it didn't take long to put the roof garden back to rights.

Together, they went back down into the apartment after shutting off the little lights on the roof. Tina was nowhere in evidence, but they both knew she was somewhere in the apartment. They dropped the dishes off near the sink, and Ashley motioned for him to follow her down the stairs that led into the bakery.

He kissed her again—a long, lingering but all-too-chaste kiss—in the door of the closed bakery, and then, he left, heading for home. They'd made a start. And for that, Tom sent a little prayer of thanks heavenward to the Mother of All.

He wasn't one hundred percent sure yet, but he had a good feeling that Ashley Baker might just be his mate.

CHAPTER SIX

Tom couldn't stay away. After a mostly sleepless night, he found himself at the bakery bright and early, when only Ashley was there. She welcomed him with a smile, and they shared a quiet breakfast while her bread baked.

They even went outside to watch the sunrise and to feed Gus, the seagull. Little things that were becoming rituals after only two days with her. Tom wanted to spend every moment with Ashley, but he couldn't. For one thing, he had promised John he would work on some permits from the state today. For another, he had to prepare for their date. He'd promised to cook for her, and he had to get some supplies and clean his house a bit.

He left her as the morning customers started coming in and her sister joined her behind the counter. He didn't try to kiss her. Not in public. Not with their relationship so new. He didn't want to make her feel uncomfortable, but he was definitely making plans for kissing her—and whatever else she would allow him to do—at his place tonight.

He couldn't wait.

By the time dinner rolled around, Asheley was a nervous wreck. She'd showered and primped, shaving and putting lotion on every part of her skin she could reasonably reach.

She'd given herself a mani/pedi and spent almost an hour on her hair.

The entire contents of her wardrobe was strewn all over her room again, but that seemed to be the norm now for preparing for a date with Tom. He'd left her at the bakery this morning, and she'd practically waltzed through the rest of her shift, her feet barely touching the ground.

It had been a long time since the mere prospect of a date with a man had made her that happy, and she intended to savor it. Almost as much as she intended to jump his bones tonight if the opportunity arose.

Tom drove up to the bakery and parked in front. He was driving a Jeep with the top down and looked absolutely scrumptious. Ashley stood in front of the display case, fighting the urge to step up to the door. It wouldn't do to let him see how eager she was, would it?

Tina came up beside her, folding her arms as she leaned against the case beside Ashley. The bakery was quiet for the moment, though a few of the locals were sitting outside at one of the tables they'd been able to set up on the sidewalk in front of the shop. They all seemed to stop and look when Tom pulled up.

Ashley noticed the way the men greeted Tom with nods of respect, but Tom didn't stop to chat. He had a rather intense look on his face that matched the way Ashley was feeling.

"He looks good enough to eat," Tina commented as they both watched Tom walk toward the door.

"Hush," Ashley chastised her sister.

"Well, he does," Tina protested. "I'm just sayin'…"

Thankfully, Tina didn't say anything more as Tom opened the door and the bell over it jangled. He strode in, and Ashley's mouth went dry. He really was the most handsome man she'd ever seen in person. Certainly the nicest—both in looks and personality—she'd ever been on a date with.

Tom walked right up to her, a smile stretching his face. "Hi," he said, meeting and holding her gaze.

"Hi," Ashley replied in a breathy tone.

"Well," Tina's loud voice intruded on the moment. "It's good to see you again, counselor."

"Good to see you too, Tina." Tom seemed to have trouble tearing his gaze away from Ash to acknowledge Tina's greeting.

Tina chuckled and flounced away, clearly amused at them, but Ashley was just glad to see her go.

"Are you ready to go?" Tom asked.

"Yeah, just let me grab one thing," Ashley turned around to find Tina standing behind her, holding up the box of pastries she'd put together earlier.

She and Tom walked out together, Tina snickering behind them, but Ashley didn't care. She felt like Cinderella being picked up by Prince Charming, in the pumpkin coach, heading for the ball.

The locals at the table outside gave them speculative looks as they passed but didn't say anything. Ashley wasn't sure what they thought about another of their kind dating a human, but so far, the response to Brody and Nell's relationship had been mostly positive.

Tom helped her hop into the vehicle then jogged around to the driver's side and got in. Within moments, they had left the small Main Street behind and were out on the back roads that led around the side of the cove.

Tom's home was set a short distance from the shore, on a high point in the terrain that would afford some protection if the tide rose during a storm or something. It was a beautiful structure, with numerous tall windows that probably let in lots of light during the day. As it was, in the early evening twilight, Ashley got to see the beautiful views Tom had of the cove as the sun set in the west, turning the waters all sorts of vibrant colors.

"This place is just lovely," Ashley complimented his home as they walked in, and she got a good look at the floor-to-ceiling windows that showcased the natural beauty of the cove.

"Thanks. I designed it around the views, and my studio is

all about the light." He led the way around, showing her each of the rooms on the main floor. The house had a mostly open floor plan, so the tour didn't take very long.

She was impressed by everything she saw, but when he led the way into his studio, her breath caught.

On an easel in the center of the room was a massive canvas that looked nearly finished. It was a view of the cove at sunset with the vibrant colors of the dying sun reflected off tempestuous waves. The piece spoke of the power of nature and the majesty of their surroundings. Its subject matter was rugged, and yet, the painting was refined in its technique. It was a masterpiece.

"Oh, wow. Tom, this is brilliant." She moved into the room, drawn by the beauty of the image.

"John asked me to do something for the new town hall he's building. This will hang across from the front entrance, so you see it when you walk in."

"It's magnificent." She stood, just admiring the big canvas for a while. "It looks alive. I can almost feel the motion of the waves." She looked at Tom. "You're really talented."

He seemed almost uncomfortable with her praise but gave her a gruff thank you before bringing her attention to the skylights he'd installed. He also pointed out the array of windows that he claimed brought in all kinds of light during different parts of the day. Light, apparently, was very significant to painters, which Ashley had known in a sort of abstract way but was becoming much more educated about as he expounded on the virtues and drawbacks of the light at different times of the day.

She saw a few more of his canvases, propped up around the room. Several were drying, he said, in preparation for being moved to the gallery in town. And a few more were being held aside for a showing at one of the exclusive little galleries in Portland.

"We had the gallery owner come through town on his way back from a fishing trip, and he asked several of us to exhibit," Tom told her, downplaying his part in the event.

"I heard about it from Lyn. And Nell sent the guy off with a box full of pastries. He talked to her the whole time he was in the bakery about the art in the town. He was really enthusiastic, she said." Ashley remembered the incident, which had happened just after the bakery was finally up and running smoothly, about a month after they'd moved to town.

They talked about the upcoming show and their reluctance to draw too much attention to the town. John had finally agreed to the showing as long as the gallery owner kept silent about where the artists lived. John was willing to entertain the occasional tourist in their new community, but they didn't want to attract people who might want to take up permanent residence—or worse, reporters wanting to do a story about where the artists lived.

Tom and several of the others were going to drive down to Portland for the opening, and they would make sure nobody asked too many questions about where they came from. The gallery owner would rake in his commissions, as long as he kept mum about where he'd found the art. At least until the town was better established and they'd gained experience dealing with humans and hiding in plain sight as a group.

"Are we ready for dinner?" Tom asked as his short tour came to an end.

He'd led her onto the patio, off to one side of the house. It was screened by the forest in back, the house on the right, but most of the left side, and the entire front, faced the water. Again, the view was breathtaking.

"How far are you from town? Less than a mile or so, right?" Ashley asked, to make conversation as he busied himself starting the enormous grill.

"Just under a mile. I wanted this view in particular, so when we were figuring out who would live where, the guys let me have it. Most of them wanted to be farther into the forest, anyway, but a few of us like the water more than others." He looked up and pointed to the left, farther up the cove toward the ocean. "Drew lives next door that way. You can usually see his boat at the little dock he built, but I guess he's out late tonight. Sometimes, he stays out on the water fishing for days when the weather is nice. On the other side, back toward town, is Sven's place. His home is practically right on the beach but well hidden. He's a polar bear, so he loves the water, but John wanted him closer to the center of town because he's our only doctor. The beach house was the compromise."

"You sound like you've all known each other a long time," Ashley observed.

"Yeah, we have. Most of us congregated around John when we served in the military. John's always been more Alpha than any of us, and he was a great squad leader. The man has a strategic mind, and he thinks so far outside the box, you can't even see the box from where he is. This whole artists' colony concept was his idea. You should've heard the grumbling when he first proposed it, but he sold us on it, and here we are. It's working. And I really think it will work for years to come. We can finally settle down, stop fighting our way across the globe, and start living."

"I had no idea you had served." Ashley was impressed. She had a great respect for any person who gave of themselves to help protect others.

"We don't talk about it much. We're retired. We've put all that behind us now. The squad was sick of combat by the end. We'd put in too many years fighting human wars in faraway lands. Plus, we had about reached our limit for fooling folks. See, shifters don't age the same way you humans do. We live a lot longer."

"How much longer?" she asked quickly. "What about Nell and Brody? Is he going to stay young while she ages?"

The stricken look on her face made him answer quickly. "No, honey. Don't worry about your sister. She is Brody's true mate. The magic that makes us able to shift will also make it so that they grow old together—and Brody's rate of aging. So your sister has a very long, happy life ahead of her."

She still seemed skeptical. "As for how long that could be, well, Brody's about my age now, so maybe another century or two. That's about all we'll get. We're not immortal, like the fey or the bloodletters."

"Fey?" she repeated, looking stunned. "Bloodletters?"

"Fey are about what you'd expect. Beings from another realm where magic is a way of life, not just an exception to the rule, like it is here. And bloodletters are what vampires like to be called. They usually don't like the word undead, so I'd avoid that if you ever run into one."

"Vampires are real?" Ashley looked shocked. Adorably so. Then she shook her head. "What am I saying? I'm talking to a guy who can turn into a bear, for crying out loud."

CHAPTER SEVEN

Tom thought, all in all, Ashley was taking everything rather well, but he definitely didn't want to overwhelm her with new information about the world she was just coming to understand. There would be time for her to come to terms with it all. At least he hoped she would stay with him long enough for her to get comfortable with the truth about this brave new world she had stumbled into.

Deciding a change of topic was in order, he led the way back into the house. The grill was warming up. It was time to bring out the meat.

Ashley helped him retrieve the platters he'd stashed in the fridge the night before. He had marinated some steaks overnight, as well as a platter of chicken.

"I wasn't sure what you liked best, so I figured I couldn't go wrong with a little variety," he explained.

"This is great. It all looks delicious." She helped him carry things back outside, and they worked together as if they'd done so a million times before.

Ashley was comfortable to be with, yet her mere presence stimulated his senses in ways that made him think of long-term togetherness and commitment. He'd never thought of such things before with any other female, which argued for the fact that she might just be his mate.

He figured he'd know for sure after they made love. If his bear was still on board the Ashley forever train after that, then there was no doubt about it. They were meant to be.

There was a large round wooden table at the center of the patio, with a few cushioned chairs around it. Ashley set the table and arranged the condiments they'd brought out. She also poured the wine and brought him a glass as he stood over the grill.

"To a lovely evening," she said, raising her glass to chime with his.

"To a lovely companion," he echoed, holding her gaze as they sipped the wine. He'd pulled out one of the special bottles for this evening.

Ashley's eyes widened when she tasted the vintage. "Oh," she exclaimed softly. "This is delicious."

"Remember those vampires I was telling you about?" Tom put his glass down so he could attend to the chicken, flipping it expertly with his tongs. "The only thing they can actually ingest is wine. It has healing properties for them, so they say. As a result, some of the best vintners in the world have been perfecting their craft for a few centuries, if you know what I mean." He gave her an exaggerated wink that made her smile.

He flicked on a small radio, and soft music spilled out. Setting her wine glass down, he took her into his arms and began dancing around the patio in a slow, swaying rhythm.

"You like wine?" Ashley asked in a tone that was casual, but the question seemed important to her.

"I do. You saw the wine fridge in the kitchen, right? I have a little bit of a wine cellar under construction right now. Every season, my colleague at the Maxwell winery sends me a few cases of their best."

"A colleague?" Ashley seemed intrigued. Tom liked that she was interested in his life.

"Their lawyer is some kind of big cat shifter. I helped her out a few times after she graduated from law school, since there are only a few of us who are both shifters and attorneys. We all know each other, and help out where we can. This girl, though, she was practically raised by vampires. She doesn't know much about shifters, but we worked together via email a time or two, and for that, her boss put me on the VIP list when he found out I truly appreciated his work. Maxwell's is one of the finest wineries in the States, and Maxwell has been at his craft for a very long time."

"Seems so odd to be talking about vampires working in actual businesses. In fiction, they're all mega-rich and don't ever have to work."

"Oh, Maxwell is mega-rich too. He's had centuries to amass his fortune, but the money has to come from somewhere and has to go somewhere too. If he just rested on his laurels, with the rate of inflation, he'd be broke in no time flat. Like anybody else, he has to make his money work for him. In his case, he puts it to work doing something he enjoys and can actually benefit from himself. It's a good situation for him."

"You sound like you admire the man," Ashley observed.

"I do," Tom admitted. "I only met him once, but he's a very charismatic fellow. Personable. Even friendly, after a fashion. We talked wines after the business part of our meeting was over, and I hear he's experimenting with bringing shifters in to work in his vineyard. He's not a snob. He treats people fairly and seems willing to try new things."

"A paragon," Ashley agreed wryly. "For someone who drinks blood."

Tom laughed outright at that. Ashley had a dry sense of humor he was only just beginning to discover. He liked it. Just as he liked pretty much everything about her.

He spun her around, back toward the grill. He dipped her, stealing a quick kiss before letting her go. It was time to tend the meat on the grill, or else they'd be eating charcoal.

She retrieved her wine glass and sat at the table, watching him cook. Everything was nearly done, so it wouldn't be long now.

They shared a companionable dinner, discussing topics ranging from wine to art to politics and religion. Tom liked the way Ashley asked what she wanted to know directly. She'd learned from her sister's mating with Brody that shifters worshiped and served the Goddess, and he was gratified by the open mind she kept when he explained a bit more about his beliefs. She wasn't rejecting anything right off the bat, which boded well for the future.

When time came for dessert, Ashley unpacked the bakery box she'd brought with her. Honey buns and other delicacies the bakery had become known for came out of the box, and Tom wasn't above devouring two of the pastries in short order. Ashley laughed at him as he licked sticky honey off his fingers, but he didn't mind.

"I guess it's true about bears and honey," she observed, watching him with a little flare of heat in her gaze that made him sit up and take notice. His inner bear was ready to get on with the rest of the evening—especially if it included shared pleasure with the enticing female sitting across from him.

"Oh, it is most definitely true. Just about everyone in town loves honey—except maybe Sven. Polar bears are weird." She laughed as he finished licking his fingers. "One of the main factors in favor of your business was the box of samples you brought when you made your presentation to the town council. The fact that you used natural ingredients—including a lot more honey than most commercial bakeries—is what sold everyone who tasted those first samples."

"So, honey was our ticket into town, eh? Tina will get a kick out of that. She's the one who first started tweaking our recipes and led us down the back-to-nature path. She'd have us go totally organic, if we let her, but the costs are just too high right now to make it worthwhile." Ashley began gathering the used plates together, naturally organizing things to take back inside. "Tina's the one who came up with the idea for our roof garden too. We all helped build it, but it was her idea. It's been great for us. Saves us money on produce, and considering how far off the beaten path this town is, it's allowed us to have fresh greens whenever we want them rather than whenever the delivery truck shows up."

"Yeah, not many of us are salad lovers," Tom admitted. "So, we didn't place that high a priority on that sort of thing. We all can hunt our own game, though we can also have beef and chicken delivered. Just like my wine. We pool orders and have a truck drop off a whole load every couple of months. Everybody's got a big freezer to stash their supply."

"I heard someone was starting up a ranch up the mountain that is supposed to be able to supply the town with chicken, turkey, pork, beef and even bison, eventually," she said as they worked together to clear the table, moving in and out of the patio doors, brushing each other from time to time as they carried things.

Tom's mind wasn't really on the conversation. He was thinking more about what would come next. Was she cleaning up in preparation for leaving? Or was she cleaning up because she was just a neat person who wanted to have everything in order before they sat and drank more wine…and maybe did other things? Tom was eager to find out.

"Yeah, that's the plan, but it'll be a while down the road yet. Livestock tends to be nervous around us, so we're looking into outsourcing the labor, but every applicant has to be vetted. As we learned from you and your sisters, we're not very good at keeping our secret yet. We have to be careful who we allow access to our town."

"I'm surprised you have such control. I mean, I thought people could come and go wherever they wanted in the U.S."

"Technically, we're only partly in the U.S.," Tom explained. "Much of our land is on the outskirts of the reservation. We have a good relationship with the elders, and they know we are excellent stewards of the land. Native Americans are some of the only humans who are raised to believe in us. The local shaman knows what we are, and he trusts us to do right by the land, and by their people. In fact, that ranch will probably employ a large number of the tribe's younger folk, when it finally gets up and running. We have a few other irons in the fire to create employment opportunities, and the tribe gets a percentage of our art sales. It's our way of giving back to their community, since they welcomed us so warmly. We're even looking at constructing a new building on Main Street for the tribe's artists to run, where they can sell their own work."

"That's really impressive. I didn't realize the reservation boundaries were so close. I mean, I knew they were nearby, but I didn't realize…" Her words trailed off as she went back into the house for a moment to drop off the last of the dishes.

When she returned, Tom watched her to see what she would do. Much to his relief, she poured more wine for them both and moved over to the padded bench that faced the water at the far end of the patio. Tom joined her there, sitting next to her as they sipped their wine and watched the dark waves rippling in the moonlight. The dim light from the patio behind them didn't interfere with the stillness of the night all around them.

Tom reached over and put his arm around her, gratified when she moved closer, snuggling into his side. They sat there for a while, watching the stars twinkle and the water wash against the sandy shore. It was a peaceful night, the sound of the water soothing, even while the feel of Ashley against him heated his blood.

CHAPTER EIGHT

Ashley was about to scream in frustration. If Tom didn't make a move in the next five seconds, she was going to jump him.

Oh, to hell with five seconds!

Ashley got up and rearranged herself so that she straddled Tom's thighs, her hands sliding around his neck as she lowered her mouth to his. And then, she was kissing him. Thank God.

She couldn't have taken one more quiet moment without jumping his delectably handsome bones. Tom's only fault—if it really could be called a fault—was that he was too polite. Any other guy would have been all over her by now, but something was holding Tom back. He seemed a little nervous, maybe even a little shy, but Ashley didn't mind showing him that she was ready. More than ready. She had been going a little nuts just sitting there, next to him, feeling his warmth, and breathing in his enticing scent.

Things were better now. She could taste him and feel him under her. She liked the way his cock stood to attention as she introduced her thighs to his, rubbing all over as she squirmed on his lap. Tom's arms went around her waist, supporting her, then subtly moving her in the direction he wanted her to go...right against his hard cock.

She could feel him through the layers of clothing, and he was…impressive. Oh, yeah. Impressive was definitely the word for him.

Her head swam when he whirled with her in his arms, changing positions as he put her beneath him on the wide, padded bench. He was so damn strong. It was a total turn on. He lifted her as if she weighed nothing at all. She felt petite next to him, which wasn't something she normally felt with guys. She was the tallest of her sisters, and though none of them were waif-thin, she was built a little more…uh…substantially than her sisters.

Her height and curves had made her feel self-conscious with a lot of guys, but it seemed none of those old insecurities plagued her when she was with Tom. He was a big man. Taller than she was, his body was coated in hard, rippling muscles. He treated her like she was a goddess, and with him, she felt it. Just a little.

Make that a lot.

He undressed her, moving faster now that he knew she was eager for more. She urged him on, helping by tugging at his clothes, undoing the small buttons on his shirt and his dress pants. He dressed very urbanely for a bear, she thought, smiling.

And she'd give anything, right about now, to see him in nothing at all.

Apparently, that's what he wanted too because he didn't stop stripping her, even while he was kissing the breath from her body. He let her up for air, only to begin a new assault as his mouth trailed hot, wet kisses down over her skin, pausing at all the interesting places.

He laved her nipples with his tongue, making her moan. He nibbled his way down her ribcage and over her tummy. And then, he was there, between her splayed thighs, his mouth giving her the most intimate kiss imaginable while his hands roamed over her thighs, caressing and squeezing, holding them far apart for his pleasure.

She felt mastered and cherished, all at the same time.

Never before had she felt this way with a man. Tom knew what he wanted, and he made it exactly what she wanted too. Anything. She'd give him anything by the time she came apart under the powerful influence of his tongue on her clit and up her channel. He knew just how to play her to make her scream.

And scream she did. His name echoed through the trees around the patio a split second before he rose up and slid into her quaking body. He held her thighs high and wide while he took possession of her spasming channel, his gaze holding hers while her orgasm went on and on...to heights she'd never visited before.

He began to move, and she kept climaxing in the most intense experience of her life.

Multiple orgasms. She thought maybe that's what they called this. Wasn't it supposed to be some kind of unattainable phenomena?

If so, nobody had told Tom. He rode her hard and kept the sensations running hot as he escalated quickly into his own raging climax. When he stiffened above her and she felt him come, tears leaked out of her eyes at the beauty of the moment...and the man.

He'd given her something she had never had before. He'd made her feel...almost...loved.

Tom wanted roar as he came inside her, but he did his best to leash the bear's howl of triumph. Everything inside him shouted *mate*, but though he inwardly crowed, he knew he'd have to take it slowly with Ashley. The last thing he wanted to do was scare her off.

He wouldn't talk about mating until she had seen Brody and Nell's relationship at work for a while, he decided. She needed to understand that mating was for life, and that he'd never treat her badly. He would live only for her, but he had to finesse her agreement. He had to show her that he was serious, and that the mating impulse, though quick to make itself known, wasn't capricious in any way.

Tom rolled to his back on the wide base of the padded bench and draped Ashley over him as they both came down from a glorious climax. She fit him perfectly, as he had hoped she would. She was his match in every way, and he would spend the rest of his life proving himself worthy of her.

If she let him.

When the night air started to cool, Tom knew it was time to go indoors. Would she stay? There was only one way to find out.

"Shall we move this party to where it's warmer?" he asked, hoping with every fiber of his being that she'd say yes.

Ashley leaned up, her hair tumbling around them, creating an intimate space in which their gazes met and held. She smiled, rubbing one finger along his collarbone.

"I thought you'd never ask."

She made a move to get up, but he stopped her, taking her easily into his arms and rising from the bench. Kicking the wad of clothes toward the patio door, he set her down right in front so he could open the door without fear of dropping her.

Ashley scooped up the pile of their discarded clothing, though he would've left it, and scampered into the house before he could stop her. He followed her in, finding her sorting and folding their clothes on the kitchen counter. She was a neat little thing, which amused him.

But there would be time for clothes folding later. Much later.

Tom scooped her into his arms and carried her straight down the long hall to his bedroom.

* * *

Sometime well before dawn, Tom came awake. Ashley was moving quietly around the bedroom.

"What's up?" he asked, yawning as he scratched his chest.

"Me, unfortunately," came Ashley's swift reply. "Sorry to wake you, but I really have to go."

"Go?" Maybe he hadn't heard her correctly.

"Yeah. I've got to open the bakery. Actually, I'm already late." She ducked into the bathroom while he got out of bed.

Dammit. He had heard her correctly. After the most glorious night of his life, his new lover had to leave.

But he understood. Her family was depending on her to take the first shift, as she always did. They hadn't made any prior arrangements that would allow someone to cover for her. Events had just unfolded the night before. There hadn't been a whole lot of planning or premeditation.

Frankly, Tom hadn't expected anything beyond dinner when he issued his invitation. He'd hoped. But hope wasn't the same thing as certainty. The fact that Ashley had spent the night in his arms was something he would never regret. It was a special gift. A blessing.

And he would do everything in his power to keep her. Forever.

Part of that kind of relationship, he knew, involved allowing the other person room to grow, and be who they were without interference. It was accepting them as they were, and not trying to change them to suit his needs.

Ashley was a baker. She was a vital part of her family's business. She worked while most other people slept. It was her routine.

Tom wasn't going to interfere with that. Not on what was, essentially, their second date. It would be up to Ashley, if she wanted to change her schedule, now that they were a couple.

She probably didn't realize it yet, but in Tom's mind, being a couple was a foregone conclusion. He just had to ease her into the idea. Eventually, though, she would see them as he did—two halves of a whole.

Ashley came out of the bathroom, a towel wrapped around her and a fragrant cloud of steam following on her heels. She'd used his soap and shampoo. His bear scented the familiar fragrances, plus the essence of Ashley that made those plain scents much more alluring. Tom liked that she would wear his scents—his soaps and his touch—all day.

"I hope you don't mind. I won't have time to clean up when I get back to the bakery. The bread has to go in the oven as soon as I can prepare it, or I'll have a few angry patrons in a couple of hours."

"No problem," Tom said, gently reassuring her. He wanted to be supportive, even if he would rather have slept until morning, with her in his arms. "I'll drive you back."

Tom ducked into the bathroom, pausing only to place a smacking kiss on her lips as he passed her. He saw her head out of the bedroom and figured she was going after her clothes.

He grabbed some clean clothes out of his wardrobe a few minutes later, dressing quickly. Venturing out in search of Ashley, he found her in his kitchen, fully dressed, if a little rumpled. She looked nervous, and he hated the uncertainty that marred her pretty face.

"I'm sorry," she said, as he came into the room. "I know this is a strange way to end the evening."

"Don't worry." Tom walked up to her and took her into his arms, rocking her gently. "I didn't exactly plan last night either, but I'm really glad it happened. I want to spend more time with you, Ashley. And I don't mind if I have to do a little readjusting of my schedule to make it work. I'm mostly an artist, these days. I don't have to be anywhere at a particular time, most days. And my legal work is mostly paperwork, which can be done in the middle of the night, if need be. I've got more flexibility in my hours than you do. We'll figure something out." He kissed her, then moved back to meet her gaze. "That is…if you want to continue exploring this thing between us. I know I do." He smiled at her, hoping she'd give him the answer he really wanted. "How about it, Ash? What do you say?"

"I say…yes." She reached up to kiss him quickly, smiling brightly. "I want to see where this leads, but right now, it better lead me to the bakery pretty soon, or the morning's bread will never get made." She stepped out of his arms, and he felt momentarily bereft. He craved the feel of her in his embrace already.

But she hadn't told him to get lost. That was a plus. He could work with it. He just had to be cautious and not rush her.

CHAPTER NINE

Ashley had expected Tom to just drop her off. Instead, he'd come into the bakery with her, keeping her company as she rushed through making the day's bread. He was a good companion. He didn't get in the way, and his conversation was both interesting and subdued, befitting the early hour.

When she had the first batch in the oven, they took a break together. He'd made the coffee and poured her a cup when she came out from behind the oven door, ushering her to one of the tables, where they could look out at the view. They sipped the hot liquid in companionable silence for a few minutes as the sun's first faint rays began to make an appearance.

"If I didn't say so before, I had a lovely time last night," Ashley finally opened the topic she'd been avoiding for the past hour. When it came down to it, she was actually somewhat shy, even if she had jumped Tom's bones a few hours ago.

"So did I," he agreed amiably. "Want to do it again tonight? I can get some fresh fish from Sig, if you like grilled salmon."

She felt a smile bloom inside her soul. "I'd like that."

"I'll come by and pick you up again?" he asked, though it wasn't really a question.

"Sounds good." She grinned. Just like that, she had another date with him. Another chance to prove to him that they were good together. No. Not just *good*. Spectacular.

Tom stayed for breakfast, sharing what was fast becoming a ritual with them, of feeding Gus the seagull and sitting outside for a bit, watching the sun rise. When the first customers started trickling in, Tom sat quietly at one of the out-of-the-way tables, reading email on his cell phone while he ate a Danish and drank coffee.

Everyone greeted him in some way, either nodding or going over to shake hands, and she got the idea that a great deal of speculation was flying as they looked from him to her and back again. Ashley didn't know what to make of it. For her part, she didn't mind anybody knowing that she was dating Tom, but she didn't really know how he felt about their possible notoriety. It was a very small town, after all.

She watched him carefully as each new person said hello, but he didn't seem to care that the other townsfolk were putting two and two together and coming up with four. Maybe he didn't mind that they knew. Or maybe—and this sort of speculation could get her in trouble—just maybe, he *wanted* them to know that he and Ash were an item.

Maybe his very obvious presence in the bakery this morning was meant to stake some sort of claim, or warn other men off. A little thrill of excitement sizzled down her spine at the thought, but she had to be careful. She could be totally misreading the situation. Maybe he just wanted to hang out, drink coffee, and eat pastries. It wasn't all that uncommon.

Although…up 'til a couple of days ago, Tom hadn't even set foot in the store before. And now, it seemed he couldn't get enough of the place. At least in the morning, when she was there.

Nell showed up mid-morning. Brody dropped her off and stopped by the table Tom had claimed to chat. Tom wasn't sure he wanted to talk about anything serious just yet, but if anyone would understand how he felt about Ashley, Brody would be the man.

"How's it going?" Brody asked casually, taking one of the empty seats at the small table. He placed his cup of coffee on the table and bit into a honey bun he held in his other hand.

"It's going really well, I think," Tom said, his gaze following Ashley as she moved behind the counter.

"You got it bad, bro," Brody commented after a short interlude where he devoured the rest of the pastry while Tom sipped coffee and watched Ashley.

Tom put down the coffee cup and looked at his friend. "Yeah, I do," he admitted. "You got any advice for me?"

"Don't fuck it up," Brody answered immediately, capping off his words of wisdom with a shit-eating grin.

"Perhaps I should have said, do you have any advice besides the obvious?" Tom clarified. They'd been friends for a long time, and he was used to the kind of banter Brody enjoyed.

"Treat her right," Brody added, pausing to think. "Don't rush her." He sipped his coffee. "And make her happy." He placed the empty coffee cup on the table. "Do those three little things, and you should be okay."

"What's it like, mating a human?" Tom felt the need to ask. He knew it was more common for bears to mate with humans than most other shifters, but none of their immediate friends had mated until Brody found Nell.

"She's more fragile than a shifter woman," Brody answered honestly. "But my Nell has a core of steel. She's stronger than she looks—both emotionally and physically. I'm afraid sometimes, that my strength and size is too much for her, but she promised to let me know when I go too far. As of this morning, she's only had to do that once."

Tom frowned. What had Brody done that his mate objected to?

"She doesn't like the teeth every time," Brody explained without Tom needing to ask. He pointed to his own neck. "She said she's proud to wear my marks, but not every single day. And she did have a good point about not knowing who might wander into the bakery. She can't pass in the human world with bite marks on her neck very well, and this town is open for visitors, even if we still control who stays."

"Wise decision," Tom agreed, seeing the logic of Nell not wanting to wear visible bite marks that would raise questions if humans saw them.

Brody stood, collecting his trash. "Are you going to John's for the planning meeting?"

"Yeah, I was just about to head over there." Tom stood also, noting the way the business in the bakery had picked up in the past few minutes. "I'll go with you," he told Brody, since they were headed in the same direction.

Not wanting to interrupt Ashley's work, he waved to her as he walked toward the door with Brody. Ashley smiled and waved back, even as she waited on a customer. Tom went out the door with a feeling of joy in his heart. She had put it there. Ashley. His mate.

CHAPTER TEN

The planning meeting was something they held every week. It usually started just before noon and went on most of the afternoon. Tom's date with Ashley wasn't until later. He calculated he'd have just enough time to drop by the fish market and pick up the salmon from Sig before picking her up.

They discussed the applications for business permits that had come in over the past few weeks and the plans for further construction John had initiated. They were going to do most of the building themselves, but for the new town hall, John had sought proposals from two different construction companies, both shifter-owned.

They discussed the two approaches, and Tom wasn't surprised when the better design proved to have come from Redstone Construction. Those werecougars had a top-notch operation and a well-earned reputation. If it was solely up to Tom, he'd give them the contract and be done with it, but John liked to think his little town was something of a democracy with a benevolent Alpha running the whole thing. He was putting it up for a vote next week after the two plans had been discussed and dissected to his satisfaction.

They were winding down the meeting when Brody's radio squawked.

"Sheriff, there's a situation at the bakery," came Zak Flambeau's disembodied voice over the walkie-talkie.

Tom stiffened. Ashley was probably off-shift at this time of day, but it was still her family's business, and her sisters were there. If there was a problem, Tom needed to know what it was, so he could help.

Brody looked upset as he keyed the mic on the radio. "Sitrep," he ordered, falling back on their military training.

"A reporter was just in, asking a whole lot of questions. Nell called the station, looking for you, but when I told her you were in a meeting, she hung up. I ran over to the bakery to find out what was going on, and now, I'm calling you."

Tom knew that when Zak said he'd *run* over, he meant it literally. The sheriff's office was only a few doors down from the bakery on Main Street.

"Good man," Brody commented. "Stay there and keep watch. I'm coming."

Tom stood as Brody nodded at John. "I'm going too," he said to the room at large, nodding as well to the Alpha.

"Is there something I should know?" John asked, some of the Alpha tone of command entering his voice.

"Yes," Tom answered without hesitation. "But it's complicated. And it's not really my secret to tell, though I don't think the ladies will mind now that they know about us. But I will tell you this—Ashley Baker doesn't know it yet, but she's my mate."

Tom saw the varied reactions of his closest friends. To a man, they all looked happy for him, and several undoubtedly would have jumped up to congratulate him if he wasn't on his way out the door. As it was, they were all smiling and most nodded to him, acknowledging the claim.

That was significant. He'd let them know that Ashley was his. By acknowledging his claim, they were saying that they wouldn't interfere. In fact, these men—the closest he had to brothers in the world—would probably do all they could to help him along in his pursuit of the lady.

"Understood," John said, nodding. "And congratulations."

He didn't smile. The Alpha was probably more concerned about what the women—and Tom—could have been hiding. "I'll be right behind you. Expect me in a few minutes. I'll want an explanation as to why you didn't give me the full briefing before we invited them into our midst," John said with a bit of menace in his tone as Brody and Tom headed for the door.

Tom didn't regret exercising his judgment on what to tell John and everyone else when he'd been tasked to investigate the Baker sisters' backgrounds. But he knew he would have to do some fast talking when John arrived. Tom wasn't worried about it, but he knew John could growl with the best of them, and he wouldn't let John's intimidation tactics frighten the ladies.

Brody and Tom stormed the bakery a few minutes later, much as they had once stormed enemy strongholds together in far off lands. Only this was friendly territory, and nothing more sinister than a few loaves of bread awaited them inside.

Brody's deputy, Zak, was waiting for them in the seating area. He came forward to meet them at the door when Brody and Tom walked in. Tom kept going, leaving Zak to give Brody the sitrep, while he went to check on the women. At this hour of the day, it was the overlap period between the end of Nell's shift and the beginning of Tina's.

Nell was up front with Brody, having gone straight to him as soon as he walked in. That left the youngest sister, Tina, in back behind the counter.

"Are you okay?" Tom asked, coming right around the counter and checking things over to satisfy himself that everything was secure in the back. "Where's Ashley?"

"I'm spitting mad, but okay. Ash is upstairs, hiding," she answered succinctly.

Seeing that Tina was all right, Tom had to get to Ashley. He pushed through to the stairs that led up to the sisters' apartment and took them two at a time. Ashley pulled open the door at the top as he neared it, and when he cleared the threshold, she launched herself into his arms.

He held her, feeling her body tremble with fear. He didn't like the sensation, and he vowed again to protect her from anything that could possibly harm her.

"Ssh, honey. It'll be all right." He tried to soothe her, but she was going from scared to angry and back again. He could feel the fluctuations in her temper as he held her securely in his arms.

"How can you say that?" she demanded angrily. "A *reporter* found me! The bastard was bothering my sisters, asking about me, asking when I'd be working the counter. Threatening that he'd stake out the place until he found me and got his scoop." She was crying nervous tears by the end of her angry speech, but Tom held her, rocking her back and forth.

"We can handle one little reporter, sweetheart. The entire Clan is behind you. They won't let anything happen here. More than that, *I* won't let anything happen. I'll tear the reporter apart with my bare hands before I let him reveal your location to anyone."

But she wasn't really listening. "I'll have to move again," she whispered brokenly.

Tom set her away from him and made her meet his gaze. "Stop right there, Ashley. You're not going anywhere. You're happy here in Grizzly Cove, aren't you?"

She seemed to come to her senses. "Happier than I've been in a long time," she admitted, her gaze still holding echoes of defeat.

"That's good to hear because you've made me happier than I've been in a long time too. I'm not willing to give that up so easily. Are you?" he challenged.

She shook her head, but her expression looked agonized. "I just don't see how this can possibly work out. I've been found. He'll tell others, and then, we'll have no peace here whatsoever. For your people's protection, I'll have to leave and take my troubles with me."

"Honey, you're one of us now. You're part of our community. We're not going to let anything bad happen."

"You keep saying that, but I just don't see how." She

shook her head, her expression pitiful.

"For starters, we're circling the wagons. Brody and Zak are downstairs, and Big John is on his way here. We're going to have to tell him about you, so he understands what he's up against. He's not going to be happy, and he'll probably growl a bit, but don't worry. He's a good guy under the Alpha bluster. He'll do the right thing."

She cringed, but she was listening. "And then what?"

"Then I believe I'm going to have a little chat with the reporter." Tom was looking forward to it. He'd kill the man if he refused to leave. Nothing was off limits when it came to protecting his mate.

"No, Tom! You can't. It'll only be worse if you try to scare him off. He'll know for sure then that I'm here. Right now, he's still wondering. He doesn't know for sure. We need to keep it that way as long as we can."

Tom considered her point. "Okay. So maybe *chat* was the wrong word. What if our reporter friend found himself confronted by a bear? Or two? Or maybe a whole bunch of us?" Tom started to grin, imagining the fun of running the reporter out of town on a rail without ever speaking a word.

"That actually sounds like a really good idea," came John's voice from behind Tom's back.

Tom had heard the Alpha's deliberately heavy tread on the stairs and wasn't surprised by his presence. Nell and Brody were right behind him, and they all trooped past Ashely and Tom into the apartment, moving into the living room.

Ashley stepped back from Tom, leaving his embrace and wiping at her eyes. She seemed to be in a state of mild shock, her gaze following the small crowd that had just invaded her home. She walked toward the living room, but Tom caught her hand.

"We do this together, Ash," he whispered. "Remember, John's growl is worse than his bite."

"I heard that," John groused from the living room.

"Damn shifter hearing," Tom joked for Ashley's sake.

Together, they walked into the living room, hand in hand.

CHAPTER ELEVEN

Tom wasn't exactly happy to have to explain about Ashley's problem to John, but though the Alpha growled a bit—as predicted—it wasn't really that bad. In fact, as soon as John became aware of the full extent of the situation, he was as supportive of Ashley as Tom could have hoped.

"So what can we do to deter this reporter from asking any more questions?" Brody asked once the facts had been fully explained. "If it was the old west, we could run him out of town on a rail, tarred and feathered, but somehow, I don't think that would go over too well in this day and age."

"I liked Tom's idea," John said. "We could go bear on his ass and scare him off. Where's the guy staying?"

"Zak discovered he was camping on National Park land, not too far away," Brody supplied as John grinned.

"That's just about perfect," John said, looking a lot like the cat who swallowed the canary, no matter that he was a big assed grizzly shifter.

* * *

Ashley sat with her sisters, waiting for word of the men. Brody, Tom, Big John and a few of the others had gone off in search of the reporter's campsite a few hours ago. The bakery was long since closed, but the girls couldn't rest until the guys were back safe and they knew what had happened up in the woods.

"Do you think they'll be okay?" Nell asked for the twentieth time, pacing and hugging herself as she worried.

Nobody answered. Nobody *had* an answer. The sisters were handling their worry in different ways. Nell was pacing. Ash was curled up on the couch, hugging a pillow. Tina was by the window, looking out on the quiet street.

Nothing much happened in town at this late hour. The occasional bear might stroll through the woods or down by the water, but they mostly kept well out of sight. Tonight, though, there was a more visible presence as Zak sat in the deputy's SUV, just down the street, on a stakeout. He'd been stationed there, Brody had told Nell, to make sure the town stayed as quiet as it should be while the other guys held their surprise party in the woods.

They'd been gone for a few hours when Tina finally broke her silent vigil. "I see Brody's truck coming down the street," she said, her voice full of intensity.

Ashley jumped off the couch and threw the pillow aside. She stopped before she hit the window, not wanting to be visible just in case the reporter or any of his friends were watching from below. Nell had no such compunction and went right up to the window and looked out on the street.

"What's going on?" Ashley asked from behind her sisters.

"The truck is stopping," Nell reported. "Brody's getting out," she said, then turned quickly. "I'm going down to let them in."

But Ashley was already on her way to the stairs, heading down into the bakery at a fast clip. She halted at the bottom, allowing Nell and Tina to go ahead of her, for the same reasons she'd stayed away from the window. Until she heard how the guys' little raid had gone, she wouldn't take anything for granted.

Nell raced ahead to open the door for Brody. He hugged her as he walked in the door, sweeping her in with him as he stood aside to let the other guys enter. Much to Ashley's relief, Tom was right behind him, laughing at something John said as he brought up the rear.

The men were grinning from ear to ear, laughing like schoolboys, at times, and Ashley felt relief in her heart to see them all safe—especially Tom. She walked forward to meet him and was thrilled when he reached out and swept her into his arms, twirling her around the room for a breathless moment.

When he put her down, he gave her smacking kiss as his enthusiasm spilled over, making her laugh. Whatever had happened, it had left the men in an ebullient mood.

"Ash, you should've been there," Tom enthused. "We had that city slicker crapping his pants and crying for his mama before we let him escape." He made little quotation marks in the air as he said that final word. "He jumped in his car so fast he left behind most of his gear."

"We now know his home address, his name and social security number," John confirmed, flipping through a brown leather wallet that had to be the reporter's. "With that, we can wreak havoc on him, the likes of which he can't even imagine." John's laugh was slightly evil, but in a loveable sort of way.

"You wouldn't do that, would you?" Ashley had to ask.

John seemed to consider. "If he comes back, we can take this one step at a time, but if he insists on screwing with us, I won't hesitate to do all in my power to fuck him up in every way possible." John's tone of voice was as serious as Ashley had ever heard it.

"And when Big John says the reporter is screwing with *us*, he means all of us, honey. You, me, your sisters. We're all family. Clan. We protect each other." Tom's arms came around her from behind, hugging her. "Believe me now?" he asked in a rumble right next to her ear.

She turned around in his embrace, pulling him close. She couldn't speak for a moment, overcome by emotion. When she had a bit of control again, she turned to face the others.

"I can't thank you enough for this," she said finally.

"No problem, sweetheart," John answered, his smile returning. "I haven't had this much fun in a long time. You should've seen that guy run." John and the others dissolved into guffaws and laughing comments about the way the reporter had screamed and scampered away when confronted by a half dozen big, angry bears.

"I don't know what he made of the polar bear," Brody mumbled, setting the men off laughing again. "I didn't expect Sven to come on the raid, but it was good to have him along. Confused the hell out of that reporter."

"Maybe he thought he was seeing a ghost. All that white fur in the pitch black forest," John added, chuckling.

As the laughter died down again, Ashley turned to hug Tom. "I was so worried the guy might've had a gun. I know you're fierce and all, but what if he'd shot you?"

"Oh, honey," Tom crooned to her, stroking her hair. "It takes more than one or two conventional bullets to stop one of us. And we're all ex-military. We've faced guns before. Many times. We know what we're doing. Even if he had been armed, he wouldn't have been given a chance to get even one shot off at any of us."

"As it is, we confiscated his weapons as well as his personal belongings," Brody put in.

Ashley whirled to face the deputy who was now part of the family. "He *was* armed?"

"*Was* being the operational word there, Ash," Brody reminded her. "When he saw us bearing down on him, he ran. The little arsenal he had in his tent was useless to him, but it'll provide further ammunition—if you'll pardon the pun—against him. Most of those firearms aren't quite legal for him to be carrying here. I've got them locked up in the back of my truck, and he's not getting them back."

Ashley couldn't believe how casually they were all taking this news, but then again, they were vets. Maybe weapons weren't that big a deal to them, like they were to civilians.

"Regardless, I'm glad you guys are whole, and I'm really

incredibly touched that you'd help me this way. Thank you from the bottom of my heart." Words were inadequate to express the wealth of feeling, but they would have to suffice for now. She'd find a way to thank everyone for standing by her. Somehow. Someday. She'd return the favor, with interest.

"Think nothing of it, Ashley. Welcome to the community and just know that you are under the protection of our Clan, such as it is. You may not be a bear, but you have the heart of one," John said, looking from Ash to Tom and back again. "I'm out of here. Gotta get some sleep to be properly mayoral tomorrow. I'm hoping the reporter will call." He grinned as he walked out, leaving the two couples and Tina.

Tina was the next to leave. "I'm going upstairs. I'm glad everybody is okay." She yawned as she headed for the stairs, leaving the two couples behind.

"We're outta here too," Brody said next, ushering Nell toward the door. His truck was still parked at the curb. "See you guys tomorrow."

"Thanks, Brody," Ashley called after them. "See ya tomorrow, sis."

"At last, we're alone," Tom mused as the door shut behind the other couple.

Ashley laughed, despite the worry that had come before. "I'm so glad you're okay," she said, running her fingers through his hair. "I was so worried."

CHAPTER TWELVE

"Wanna go to my place?" Tom asked, but Ashley shook her head.

"I don't want to leave Tina here alone, just in case that reporter comes back." Tom looked resigned, but he nodded. He seemed about to pull away from her when she placed one hand on his shoulder. "But my room has a queen size bed, and the walls are pretty thick. Why don't you come upstairs?"

Tom grinned, and it was as if the sun had come out in her soul. "I thought you'd never ask."

Ashley paused to lock up, Tom at her side. When all was secure, they went up the stairs together, eager steps taking them quickly through the apartment to her room, which was at the front of the building. She had one of the two bedrooms that had the great view of the cove.

Nell had claimed the other front room but had been spending most of her nights at Brody's since they'd gotten engaged. Poor Tina had been stuck with the bedroom at the back of the building, but that worked in Ashley's favor now, since it was doubtful Tina would hear anything, even if Tom made Ashley scream with pleasure. Which, after last night, she realized, was a very real possibility.

But Tom didn't pounce on her the moment the door was

shut. Instead, he sat with her on the edge of the bed, taking her hands in his. The moment felt serious, and Ashley frowned, feeling doubt creep in. Was he going to ask to slow things down? Was he going to dump her?

"Ashley," Tom began, his tone so serious she began to fret. "There are a few things I want to discuss with you."

He seemed to be waiting for her to respond. "Yes?" She was proud that her voice sounded much steadier than her nerves.

"I hope you know by now that I will protect you to my dying breath."

Whoa. Heavy. But was there a silent *but* on the end of that amazing sentence? When he didn't continue right away, she felt the need to make another response. Was he waiting for her to acknowledge every sentence, or maybe... Was he nervous too? Her fears started to recede a little.

"I hope it never comes to that," she said with a nervous laugh. "But I'm grateful that you feel so protective of me. I can use all the help I can get with my past coming back to haunt me like this."

"Honey, you'll never have to worry about that again, as far as I'm concerned. In fact..." He paused, turning a little more toward her, rubbing his thumbs over her knuckles as he held her hands in his. "I don't want to rush this, but, Ash, you should know that when a shifter meets his mate, he often knows almost right away. Like how quickly Brody and your sister got together. That was pretty quick, right?"

"Yeah, sort of a whirlwind romance, you might say," she agreed, wondering where he was going with this. Could he possibly mean...?

"Well, that's normal for us. Some species know on first scenting their mate. Some—the big cats—know they've met their mate when they purr in human form, which is something only their true mate can bring about. We believe that the Mother of All has a hand in helping us find that one special person meant just for us. Ashley..." he moved closer to her, his voice very serious, "...I knew last night, when we

BIANCA D'ARC

made love, that you are my mate. I want to be with you for the rest of our lives, and your happiness and safety is at the center of my world."

Ashley was speechless for a moment as an incredulous sort of joy filled her being.

"Really?" She could hardly believe what he was saying. This wasn't a whirlwind romance. This was a tornado. A benevolent but still shocking tornado. "You know that fast?"

"I do," he answered solemnly. "But the question is, can you return my feelings? Will you be my mate? My wife, in human terms, though you should know, mating is forever. There will never be another woman for me. Just you, Ashley Baker, 'til the day I leave this world. And even then, I'll await you on the other side, until we can be together again. I love you. And I will always love you."

Ashley felt tears gathering behind her eyes. They spilled down her cheeks at his profession of love. It was the most beautiful thing any man had ever said to her, made all the more poignant because it was Tom who was saying such wonderful things.

She launched herself into his arms, talking next to his ear, though her words were garbled with happy tears.

"I love you too, Tom. So much. I can't imagine how this happened so fast, but I can't imagine my life without you in it." She kissed him, little kisses wherever she could reach—the side of his face, his ear, his neck. "Yes," she whispered, her heart in her throat. "Yes, I'll be your mate. I don't want anyone else. After you, I could never be with anybody else. You're it for me, mister."

He moved her head so he could claim her lips, cradling her face in his warm, strong palms.

They wound up on the bed long minutes later, having undressed each other with careless abandon. Ashley had taken charge, coming down over Tom while he smiled up at her, his hands on her hips, guiding her motion as she rode him. She liked the feeling of power, the hard ridges of his muscles under her thighs and against her palms.

Tom liked it too. She could see the indulgent smile and lazy enjoyment in his half-lidded eyes. He was such a handsome man, in every way. When he'd been tough, ready to take on the world earlier this evening before he went out with the other guys, she had seen the warrior side of his personality. Now she was seeing the lover, once again. She liked everything she'd seen of him and still couldn't quite believe she'd get to watch him grow old with her for the rest of their lives. She would enjoy learning everything about him—especially how best to please him.

She tried different rhythms, different motions, until she found one that he seemed to particularly enjoy. She rode him hard and kept increasing the pace until, at the last, he had to guide her hips as she lost control. She spasmed around him, and he came soon after, jerking his body upward, sealing them together for long moments as he came deep within her.

They lazed in the aftermath, before round two, side by side in her bed. It was just barely big enough for both of them, but neither one was complaining. Ashley drew little patterns on his chest with one finger as she lay on her side, his arm tucked around her.

"You know, after you marry me, you could practice law again, if you want. I could use some help. I get a little too adversarial, sometimes, when a tenacious human lawyer gets combative. You could run interference so I don't accidentally, on purpose, rip some jerk's head off." He chuckled as she stilled. "Plus, you're a great lawyer. Nothing that happened to you was your fault. And when you marry me, you can take my last name and begin again with a new identity. Nobody needs to know about your past. You'd be a great help to the town as it grows, and to the Clan. It'd be a shame to let all your education and hard work go to waste. That is, if you want to. No pressure. You can do whatever you like. I'm just offering up the possibility."

"I hadn't even considered every practicing again, but you're right. I went to law school because I really wanted to help people. I've enjoyed the bakery, but that was my sisters' dream. Not mine. Not really. I've liked helping them, but I would like to at least look into the idea of reclaiming my profession, if you really think it's possible." She reached up to kiss him. "You're amazing for even thinking of it. I love you, Tom. You're a heck of a great guy."

He grinned at her. "I love you too, my mate. I never thought I'd find you, and you've been here for months. I should've come into the bakery a lot sooner. I'm sorry it took me so long to get here."

"All that matters is that you're here now, and I'm not ever letting you go."

"Amen to that."

# # #

Grizzly Cove #3

Night Shift

BIANCA D'ARC

CHAPTER ONE

Zak really liked the new duty Sheriff Brody Chambers had him working. Every night since a reporter had come to town to try to make trouble for Ashley, the middle of the three Baker sisters, the sheriff, who was now mated to the eldest sister, Nell, had sent Zak to watch over the youngest sister, Tina. Tina worked the night shift at the bakery the three sisters owned, and since it was the only place that served food in their new town so far, a lot of people frequented it.

The baked goods were downright delicious. The sisters used natural ingredients, including a lot of honey, which was a favorite of Zak's and most of the town, for that matter. It was true that bears really did like the sweet stuff.

Zak had been admiring Tina from afar since she'd moved to town, but hadn't really had much chance to get close to her since they both worked the night shift. He hadn't had much reason to stop in at the bakery while on duty until now, and he was taking full advantage of the sheriff's request that he keep an eye on the one remaining unmated sister.

Brody had claimed the eldest sister, and about two weeks later, Tom Masdan, the town lawyer had announced his relationship with the middle sister, Ashley. Turned out they were both lawyers, though Ashley had given up a high-powered career when a rat in her New York firm had made her look bad and inadvertently caused grief for her client. Unfortunately, the client had been very high profile, and tragedy had resulted from the poorly handled court case. Ashley had needed to go into hiding from the press, which she had, right here in Grizzly Cove, working at her sisters' bakery.

In this tiny town, there were only two lawmen, at the moment. Brody worked days, and Zak overlapped in the afternoon, then worked the evenings alone, unless there was trouble. Both of them were always on call, but then again, since all of the men who formed the nucleus of the new community had served together in the military, just about everyone in town could act as backup, if needed. It was just that Brody and Zak had been handed the roles of sheriff and deputy when the Alpha, Big John, had been assigning tasks according to each man's abilities and desires.

They'd all retired from the military now, though none of them were old by human standards. They were all bear shifters of one kind or another. The majority, including the Alpha, were grizzlies, but there was at least one polar bear, a couple of Kodiaks, a big-assed Russian bear and a few black bears. Zak Flambeau was one of the latter. Smaller than his grizzly friends, Zak was no less deadly. And though he'd taken his share of guff from his buddies over the years, he knew they respected his skills as a marksman and as a shifter. He was smaller, but that also meant he was a lot quicker and more agile than some of his larger comrades. He'd used that to his advantage many times in the field. But now, all that was over. He was retired from that life. It was a bit of an adjustment.

Big John had come up with the insane idea to build their own town from scratch. He'd been quietly buying up land over the years, and when the time came, he'd laid out his idea for the rest of his men. They'd balked a bit, at first. After all, Big John wanted them masquerade as an artists' colony, for cripes sake. They weren't artists. Although, most of the guys had given it the old college try and had come up with some passable *objet d'art*, Zak had to admit.

He couldn't draw his way out of a paper bag. He couldn't even do self-portraits of his bear half, using a chainsaw and a stump of wood. He left that to Brody. Zak didn't have a talent like that. Nothing in the visual arts, anyway. If he had any talent at all, he'd have said it was for cooking, but he couldn't see a way to turn his Cajun heritage of spicy, down home dishes into an art form that could contribute to the town's artists' colony status.

So he contented himself with being the deputy. Good ol' Barney Fife to Brody's Andy Taylor. That he could handle. Blindfolded. And with one hand tied behind his back.

Running security was second nature to him. Zak had left home at eighteen, leaving the bayou and his bastard father behind, striking out to join the Army. He'd never looked back. Not even once.

When his mate had died of illness, Zak's father had turned mean. Or maybe he'd always been mean, and losing his mate just made him worse. Zak didn't know for sure. His mother had died when he was still a boy. He missed her to this very day, but he felt like maybe, sometimes, she was watching over him from above—or wherever spirits went when they left this realm.

"You know, deputy, I'm going to have to start charging you rent if you keep coming in here every night." Tina brought over the carafe of coffee, pouring him a fresh cup without even asking. She knew by now that he would never say no to good coffee.

"Just following orders, ma'am. Though to be honest, I'm enjoying these orders way more than any other I've been given to date in this town. It's nice to have an excuse to sit here, drink coffee and eat your marvelous pastries." He popped a slice of the danish he'd been eating into his mouth to emphasize his point.

"But you ran the reporter off. Nobody's seen him since. I don't think he's coming back, and even if he did, I could handle him. I'd tell him to go straight to hell, like I did the first time he came sniffing around."

Tina was a little more outspoken than her older sisters, and Zak liked that about her. She had spirit. But that sort of spirit could sometimes get a person into trouble.

"I won't argue the point, but Brody asked me to keep an eye on the place, and I'm just as happy to do so. Come on, *ma chere*, don't tell me you don't enjoy my company, at least a little."

The little bell above the door tinkled out its merry tune as the door opened, and every hackle on Zak's body rose in alarm. He spun to face the newcomer, taking in the dark, wet clothing, the blood-red eyes and the hesitant gait.

"Holy shit." Zak grabbed for his radio as the newcomer eyed him.

"Call your Alpha, little cub. I am hanging on here by a thread."

Zak's sensitive nose smelled the blood—new and old—on the creature in the doorway. That he was probably outgunned and outclassed entered his mind briefly, but he dismissed the idea. All that mattered was protecting Tina. And hopefully, getting them both out of this confrontation alive.

"I beg your pardon, miss, but do you happen to have any wine on the menu? I am greatly in need," the newcomer asked politely, though Zak could see that every word cost him.

Then he remembered what he'd heard about vampires and wine. The creature was seeking something that would help him, not attacking. That was a good sign. Zak keyed the mic, calling for Brody in low, urgent tones. Then he palmed his cell phone, hitting the speed dial that would bring the Alpha on the run.

"I'm sorry, sir, we don't serve alcohol. Our liquor license hasn't come through yet," Tina answered politely, though Zak could hear the confusion in her tone. Bless her little human heart, she didn't recognize the danger standing in her doorway.

Zak didn't take his eyes off the vampire. "Tina, don't you

have some wine upstairs? Go get it, honey. Bring as many bottles as you can down here on the double. Leave them at the bottom of the stairs and then go back and get more. Everything you have. And then stay the hell upstairs for me, will you?"

She opened her mouth to argue. He could just feel it. But the vampire stepped forward and left a trail of blood across her doorstep. She gasped as the man's fangs showed.

"Get the fuck upstairs now, honey. And whatever you do, do *not* invite this guy up there. Vampires are big on invitations. Do *not* issue one, okay?"

"I won't. But, Zak…" She sounded worried now.

Zak couldn't tell if she was concerned about him or the bleeding bloodletter. Either way, she was a sweetheart for her concern, but right about now, with a vamp on the edge like this one clearly was, such weakness could easily get her killed.

"Take your bear's advice, little one. I am not to be trusted, at the moment. I have lost too much blood. The wine might help," the bloodletter said as he all but collapsed into one of the chairs at the front of the bakery. He leaned back, blood and seawater pooling beneath him as he sat.

Zak didn't take his eyes off the man, but—thank the Goddess—he heard Tina leave. Her scent went upstairs, and she closed the door behind herself. Zak almost sighed in relief, but he was too keyed up to relax even that much. Everything in him recognized the threat that now sat in front of him.

"I'm Zak Flambeau, the town deputy," Zak introduced himself to the bloodletter, hoping the man could keep his wits a little longer.

Zak knew that bloodletters could go mad when starved of blood, either by being unable to feed or bleeding from serious wounds, like this one. The red eyes gave it away. They were just on the good side of sanity, right now, but that could change in an instant.

"I am Hiram Abernathy, master of this region. I am headquartered in Seattle but was enjoying a few nights on the ocean when my yacht was attacked and destroyed by...something." The red eyes looked confused and sort of haunted. "I seek your aid and will apply to your Alpha for safe harbor, though as you seem to understand, I am *in extremis*. I need blood, or I will run mad. I am trying my best to stay sane, at the moment."

"If I give you my blood, will you leave the girl alone?" Zak asked. He'd do anything to keep Tina safe.

The vampire licked his lips in an unconscious gesture. "Shifter blood..." His flaming eyes seemed to glaze over a bit. "It would heal me much faster than mortal blood. I wouldn't need as much, and it would safeguard your human playmate. But I will warn you, feeding from you will create a link between us. That could be both good and bad. It will also give me some of your strengths for a short period, making me even more powerful than I already am. Bears are very magical, I hear. Still, I have lived many centuries," the vampire said, seeming to consider the situation, laying it all out for Zak. "Even with your inherent magic, I do not believe anyone in this town is my equal, so giving me your blood will probably not matter in the long run. My powers are already superior to everyone here."

Zak had to chuckle as he moved closer to the vampire. "I'd like to hear you say that to Big John."

"Is that your Alpha?" the vampire asked. "John Marshall, right?"

"How'd you know?" Zak asked, eying the man once more with suspicion.

The vamp smiled tiredly. "Why do you think I was sailing around the entrance to your cove for the past few days? Recon, my friend. I like to know who is setting up house in my territory, even if you don't come under my dominion."

"I can understand that, I guess," Zak allowed. He knew Brody and John were on their way.

They'd be here any minute, but every second the vampire had to wait for blood was a second Tina was in danger. He had to stave off the vampire's need for as long as he could, until help could arrive. If this guy was as old as he claimed, Zak knew he would be no match for the bloodletter in a fight, even with his native bear magic. Plus, if Hiram was going to feed from any of the shifters in town, it might as well be him. His bear was small by comparison to the others, and less magical. He was the logical choice, so there was no sense in delaying.

"How does this work? I've never entertained one of your kind before," Zak said with a deceptive grin. Inside, he was nervous, but he refused to show it on the outside.

"Just give me your wrist, and don't fight. I will do my best to control myself, but regardless, if you pass out, I will stop feeding. I won't kill you."

"Good to know," Zak nodded, swallowing hard. The vampire smiled, showing his pearly white fangs.

"You are giving me a great deal of trust, young one. I will not forget this. And I do realize it is to protect your people and your lady. All worthy goals. You have earned my respect, Zak Flambeau." The vampire nodded to him in a very old-world sort of way.

Zak bet the bloodletter didn't say those words to too many people. Oddly, he was flattered, which somehow made it easier to take that final step toward the vampire. He held out his arm, and faster than thought, the vampire had grabbed his hand and elbow, positioning his wrist upward for the fangs that descended with lightning speed.

Zak was unprepared for the wave of energy that washed over him. He felt his magic battling with the vampire's for a moment before some sort of accord was reached and the blood began to flow.

CHAPTER TWO

The door opened with a tinkling chime of the bell.

"What the fuck?" Brody stopped short as he came upon the scene of the vampire sucking blood from Zak's wrist.

"It's okay, Brody. Hiram needs this, and I'm the logical choice of all of us. Where's John?" Was it Zak's imagination or was his voice sounding a little weak?

"I'm right here," John said from behind the bakery counter. He must've come in the back way. The stealthy way. Good ol' John. Once a commando, always a commando. "And I'll thank you, sir," he was speaking pointedly to the vampire now, "to let go of my friend, Zak, there."

The vampire took one last long swallow, then licked his tongue across Zak's wrist in a move that could've been weird but felt healing, instead. He let go of Zak's arm, and when Zak looked, there were no marks left to show that the veins in his wrist had just been opened and resealed. That was some funky vampire mojo Hiram had going on there.

"A moment, if you please, Alpha." Hiram held up his hands, as if in surrender.

He closed his scary blood-red eyes and seemed to meditate for a few seconds. As Zak watched, he seemed to internalize the blood and energy he'd just taken in, his skin taking on a healthier cast as his own bleeding appeared to stop, judging by the lack of droplets adding to the puddle beneath his chair.

When he opened his eyes again, they were a sort of topaz brown. No longer red. No longer too close to the edge of sanity. The vampire still looked quite weak, but he was definitely better.

"Forgive me for this abrupt arrival in your town, Mayor Marshall. It was not my intent to arrive here in this fashion, but the creatures of the deep apparently had other ideas."

"Really?" John seemed unimpressed by the fellow's pretty speech. "Are you trying to tell me a sea monster ate your boat and spit you out in my cove? Pull the other one."

Hiram stood and tugged off what was left of his tattered shirt.

"Son of a bitch," Zak muttered, seeing the evidence of the wounds Hiram had suffered.

It looked almost as if he'd been bitten by a shark, but if so, it was a freaking *huge* shark, with massive *rows* of teeth. At least *five rows* of teeth, if Zak was counting right. And stinging suckers, but again, much larger than any octopus, squid or jelly Zak had ever seen.

John came closer, moving in front of Zak to inspect the wounds. They were healing even as Zak watched. He knew the power of his blood gave the vampire the ability to heal his wounds, but if they still looked this bad now, what must they have been like when they were made?

"I stand corrected. And I'm willing to admit when I'm wrong," John said magnanimously. "What the fuck happened to you?"

"A sea monster ate my boat and spit me out in your cove." Hiram repeated John's earlier words, earning a grin from the big Alpha that turned into an outright laugh.

"Guess I deserved that. I'm John, as you already know. You're Master Abernathy, right? From Seattle?" John held out his hand for a shake.

Zak held his breath. He didn't think the vampire would try anything, but now was a moment of truth, of sorts. Would the bloodletter turn on them now that he'd been fed?

Hiram took John's hand and shook it. Zak breathed again. One hurdle overcome.

"Please call me Hiram," the master replied. "I regret coming to you in such strange circumstances. I was trying to be stealthy, observing your settlement from the water for a bit before I made overtures."

"I know. My bears saw your yacht out there, and I traced the registry to you. I figured you'd come in when you were ready."

John wasn't Alpha for nothing. Zak hadn't known about the vampire's surveillance, but John had others who were more suited to such tasks as watching boats out at sea and tracking down ships' registries.

"I would have," Hiram agreed easily. "But it seems fate had other ideas." His face turned grim, even as his wounds finally stopped bleeding. "Sir, there is something out there in the deep. Something very evil."

Tension filled the room until everyone heard the clanking of bottles near the bottom of the stairs leading to the upper level apartment. Tina.

Zak nodded to John as he headed behind the counter to the door that led to the staircase. He opened it and found Tina standing there, clutching three bottles of red wine to her chest. Her eyes were wide, and she looked adorably startled.

"Is it safe?" she whispered.

Zak considered. "Safe enough, I guess. If you want to come meet our guest, I think it'd be okay. And he can probably still use the wine."

Zak took a couple of the bottles from her and waited while she scooped up a few more, and they headed out into the bakery together. Zak led her over to the table where Hiram was seated again. John had taken a seat at the table next to him, facing Hiram, and they were talking in low, urgent tones. Their conversation ceased as Tina entered the front part of the bakery.

"Honey, this is Hiram Abernathy," Zak introduced them as he placed the first of the bottles on the small table in front of the vampire. Tina was right behind him. "Master Hiram, this is Tina Baker."

She gasped when Zak stepped aside and she saw the rows and rows of bite marks that still showed on Hiram's chest. They weren't bleeding anymore, but they were still there, red and gruesome looking.

"I beg your pardon, lady," Hiram said with old-world politeness. "I am sorry to darken your door in such a way and make such a mess." He looked at the blood smears that made a path to the table and the considerable pool of seawater and blood beneath his chair. "Thank you for helping me. I will gladly reimburse you for your troubles. And, as they say, I owe you one. It is not something trivial to have a master vampire owe you a debt." He winked at her, and Zak bristled.

"What happened to you?" Tina asked in a sympathetic whisper.

"Something in the ocean objected to my presence rather strongly," Hiram replied with wry humor as he looked through the bottles they had brought. "Do you have a glass, a bowl and a small towel?" he asked Tina directly.

She nodded and bustled off to get the supplies he'd requested. Zak stood by the table and watched the vampire. He didn't like the way the bloodletter was flirting with Tina. The bear inside him bristled again at the thought of it, and Zak heard a little growl hit the back of his throat.

Damn.

"Rest easy, young one," Hiram held up a calming hand toward Zak. "She is not for me. I believe the Goddess may have already decided her fate. And yours. No?" Hiram looked up at Zak, a smile in his topaz eyes.

Zak was taken aback. Could he mean…? Could it be?

Tina returned with the items, and a cork screw, which Hiram hadn't requested specifically, but Tina had apparently thought to add. Hiram smiled at her again, and Zak's bear sat up, staring at the man from out of Zak's eyes, sizing him up. The bear wasn't sure what to make of Hiram, and neither was Zak's human side.

Hiram opened two of the bottles, sloshing deep red wine into the glass from one and drinking it all down in one go. Helpful not to have to breathe, Zak thought, when chugalugging. But it didn't do the rather good vintage he'd chosen any justice.

The second bottle, Hiram poured into the bowl, drenching the small towel with wine. Zak watched, surprised, as Hiram placed the wine-soaked towel directly over his wounds, sighing in what sounded like relief as the wine hit his savaged skin.

He drank more glasses of wine while he let the towel sit, emptying the bottle with speed before he opened a second bottle of the better vintage. He started drinking that, too, at a slightly slower pace.

"Normally," Hiram paused in his drinking to speak, "I would share this excellent wine with you, but these are rather trying circumstances. Tonight, you learn one of the secrets of my kind. You are seeing for yourself that we can, indeed, drink wine and that not only can we drink it, but that it also heals us."

Hiram removed the towel, returning it to the bowl to soak up more wine. Tina gasped when Hiram's chest was revealed. Wherever the wine-soaked towel had touched, he was healed. Completely healed. Not even a small mark was left behind.

As Hiram drank down the second bottle, the rest of the marks on his body began to fade right before their eyes, as well.

Zak had seen quick healing. He was a shapeshifter, after all. But he'd never seen anything quite like this. He imagined few people ever did.

CHAPTER THREE

Tina was shocked clear out of her skin. That Hiram guy was getting better by the moment, and all indications were that he was some kind of vampire. An honest-to-goodness vampire, right here in the middle of her bakery. Holy cow!

She'd thought she was going to spend the last few minutes before closing flirting with Deputy Zak, but things had changed drastically in a short time. She was playing hostess to a vampire who was drinking the best bottles of their meager wine collection as if they were filled with water and he had been stuck in the desert for a week. The dude could pack it away, and he didn't seem to get drunk at all.

In fact, if anything, the alcohol made him brighter. More with it. It healed him. The very idea defied logic.

And his eyes had gone from that horror-movie red to a glittering topaz brown that reminded her of a cat. He was really a very dashing fellow. Handsome and built. Just the way she liked 'em.

But next to Zak... Yeah, ol' Hiram paled next to sexy Zak Flambeau. Tina had been hot for the deputy for a week now, ever since he'd been ordered to make sure she was safe in the bakery at closing time. He'd been hanging around, and they'd been talking. She'd learned a bit about his past and his life, his hopes and dreams. And she'd shared the same with him.

She'd thought they'd been making a connection.

Whether that would turn out to be a *love* connection, she wasn't sure, but she had decided she really did want to jump his bones. He was too cute to not want to boink. At least that was Tina's philosophy.

Her sisters might think she was a little wild, but Tina had always done what she liked. She'd done *who* she liked too, though honestly, there hadn't been all that many men in her past. She was particular. And right now, she *particularly* liked Deputy Zak.

She just wasn't sure if he was feeling it too, and she didn't want to be embarrassed if she made a pass and got shut down. That would suck. And it would make her life difficult, since he'd been assigned to see to her safety every damn night. If she bombed out with him, she'd still have to see him. This was a *very* small town, after all. So she'd had to be cautious, which went against her impulsive nature.

"We're going to have to report this through official human channels, unfortunately," Hiram said, drawing her attention. "I had staff on the yacht. Not many, but their families will need to know what happened to them. There will need to be police reports for insurance claims and the like, I imagine."

It struck Tina as odd that a vampire would be talking about something as mundane as insurance. Then again, like the cove's shapeshifters, vampires had to live in the modern world too. They'd have to deal with human laws and procedures from time to time, just to fit in.

"We can help you there," Brody said. "You swam ashore, and Deputy Flambeau found you on the beach, then brought you over to Sven's place. He's the town doctor."

Zak paced a few steps away, dialing his cell phone. Tina heard him talking to Sven, inviting him to join the party at the bakery.

About that time, Tom showed up. He was Tina's newest in-law, mated to her sister, Ashley. He was also the town's lawyer. Brody filled Tom in on the events of the evening while John talked quietly with Hiram. Tina followed Zak over toward the counter as he finished his call.

"You holding up all right?" Zak asked her in a quiet tone, concern clear in his expression.

Tina hugged herself. "I'm okay. This is just a little unexpected, you know? I was just getting used to the idea of shapeshifters. I'd heard there might be vampires too, but I never even dreamed of actually meeting one, much less having one walk into the bakery in such a state."

Zak surprised her by taking her into his arms, but she went willingly. His hug felt so good. Warm and cuddly. Protective and strong. He made her feel secure, which was something she needed, especially after the shock of the evening and her unexpected guest.

"I guess Tom and Brody made my sisters stay away, huh?" she asked in a small voice. Before they'd come to Grizzly Cove, her sisters had been her comforters and protectors. She'd never been left all on her own to deal with it difficult situation like this before.

"No doubt," Zak agreed. "But it's okay. I'm here. Lean on me, honey. I've got you."

She liked the surety and strength in his soft words. And she liked the way he held her, the gentle touches on her back and the slight sway of their bodies as he offered her comfort, asking nothing in return. He was a really sweet guy.

Brody came over with Tom, a few moments later. He cleared his throat to get her attention, and she blushed, realizing she'd been totally sidetracked by Zak's warm embrace. She jumped a little, but he wasn't letting her go so easily. Rather than struggle, she just turned her head to look at her two new brothers-in-law.

"Tom can run you over to his place," Brody said quietly. "Pick up Nell on the way, and you three can shelter with him for a bit while we get this sorted out, okay?" Mutely, she nodded agreement. She couldn't wait to tell her sisters about everything that had happened. She also couldn't wait to be surrounded by their comforting presence...although, Zak was a top notch substitute.

"Zak," Brody went on, "I need you to come down to the office with me. We're going to have to dust off the official forms and get on the computer. This has to be done by the *human* book, unfortunately, and you're way better at that than I am. Plus, you found the guy. It was on your watch." Brody sounded almost gleeful over that little fact, since it probably meant that Zak would have to do the majority of the paperwork.

"Roger that," Zak replied, throwing Brody a casual salute. "Give me five to help Tina pack an overnight bag and lock up."

Brody seemed startled by Zak's words, narrowing his gaze on his deputy, then turning that suspicious look on Tina. She fled. She was in no mood to answer nosy questions—or even questioning looks—from her new brother-in-law.

She hadn't quite gotten used to having brothers-in-law yet, for that matter. The fact that her two sisters were now happily mated to two guys her sisters swore hung the moon and lit the stars still hadn't quite sunken in completely. It was all so new. Only a few weeks old.

Tina ran upstairs, hearing Zak following behind her. She ran up. He took the stairs more sedately, but when she reached the small kitchen, he was only a step or two behind her. Maybe he'd taken them two at a time? And he wasn't even breathing a little faster.

The dude was in shape. But she knew that from the time she'd spent over the past week, ogling his bod. Zak was fit with a capital F, I, and T. And the way he filled out his uniform golf shirt ought to be illegal. He might not be quite as tall as Brody or Tom, but he was a lot taller than she was, and his shoulders were massive, his muscles ripped.

Was it warm up here?

"How long do you think I will have to stay at Tom's?" she asked, looking for something to say.

"Probably just overnight," Zak replied. "Just a precaution, until Big John and the master figure out what's what."

"Are you sure this Master Hiram guy is who he claims to

be?" She frowned, trying to puzzle through their reasoning.

"I think he is, but that's one of the reasons we're taking precautions. John will check out his bona fides—or have me do it while I'm knee deep in computer databases. Vampires don't usually leave a lot of tracks, but I'm pretty good at ferreting out the stuff they can't get around. Plus, we can call the Lords and see what they know, but that'll probably have to wait until morning, just out of courtesy. If Hiram continues to be a good boy, all will be well." Zak moved closer to her, the width of the kitchen table between them as he held her gaze. "If things go south, we can protect you better if you're all together. Don't worry, Tina. You'll be safe at Tom's with your sisters."

"But what about you?" she whispered, unaware until the words were out of her mouth that she was going to speak them.

Zak's expression changed. His head tilted to one side as he smiled slowly, but thankfully, he wasn't laughing at her. Instead, he seemed sort of...touched...by her concern.

"I'll be okay, baby. Trust me." The silence dragged while their gazes stayed locked, unspoken words of concern and reassurance passing between them. Zak finally broke the moment by clearing his throat. "You'd better pack that bag. They're waiting for us."

"How do you know?" she asked, already heading toward her room.

"I can hear them," Zak said, following right behind.

She wasn't sure if she really wanted him to see the state of her bedroom, but it was too late. She grabbed for a lacy red bra she'd accidentally left splayed over her pink bedspread, but she definitely heard Zak chuckle as heat flushed her cheeks.

"That shifter hearing thing is pretty cool," she said, just for something to say while she busied herself finding a small bag and throwing things into it somewhat haphazardly.

She turned abruptly when she heard her bedroom door click softly closed behind him. He had his back to the door and an intense expression on his chiseled features.

"Even shifter hearing has its limits though," he said softly, letting go of the doorknob behind him and walking slowly—predatorily—toward her. He was stalking her, and oddly enough, she wasn't scared. Just...excited.

"Really?" She couldn't think of anything more coherent to say. Not with the way he held her gaze as he prowled steadily closer, coming right for her.

"For example, right now, as long as we keep it low, they won't have a clue what we do up here."

"Is that a fact?" Her mouth was suddenly dry as he stopped right in front of her.

CHAPTER FOUR

Without words, Zak simply held out his arms, and Tina seemed to fall into them, like a magnet clinging to its opposite polarity. His strong arms came around her, and she breathed deep of his masculine scent, burying her face in the hollow of his neck. They were a perfect fit, as far as she was concerned. He was just the right height for her to feel safe and secure without being overwhelmed. As the shortest of her sisters, that was something very important to her.

"I lost about ten years off my life when that vamp walked in," Zak admitted. "I was so afraid he was going to go for you." His arms squeezed her close, and she heard the emotion in his voice.

Wonder filled her at his response. It sounded as if he...cared...for her. Her heart leapt in her chest. She liked that idea. A lot.

"Would he really have bitten me if I hadn't gotten the wine?" she asked, her voice trembling.

"Honey, the wine was dessert. He had me for dinner," he revealed. "Shifter blood is a delicacy to them, and it gave him more energy than your mortal blood would have."

"You let him bite you?" She pulled back, looking up to meet his gaze. Then she checked his neck for bite marks, but he chuckled.

"He took it from my wrist," Zak told her. "And we were damn lucky the guy was a gentleman. He's a master, which means he's an old son of a gun. Powerful. Probably stronger than anyone in this little town. We're lucky he asked politely, because he probably could have just taken whatever he wanted. Including you." He tucked her head into his shoulder and hugged her again. "In the state he was in, he would have killed you. And I would have died too."

That sounded serious. She pulled back to meet his gaze, noting the slight tremble in his hold.

"Why?"

He let some of his emotion show in his gaze and she caught her breath. "I would give my life for you, any day, any way. I would have tried to protect you. Give you a shot at running."

She clutched his shoulders. He was saying something important here, but it still wasn't clear to her. Would he do that for any weak human stuck in that sort of situation? He was the town deputy, after all. He had some kind of duty to protect. Or was it more personal?

Lord, how she hoped it was personal!

"Thank you," she said calmly, her mind racing. "But I wouldn't run. I wouldn't want you to die for me. I'd probably have tried to fight him with you."

"Then we both would have died, and I couldn't do this..."

Zak's head dipped low, his lips catching hers in a gentle kiss that soon turned molten.

Oh, yeah. This is something she'd wanted for a while now. Zak. Kissing her. Making her toes curl in her shoes. Dayum.

She wasn't sure how long the kiss lasted, but eventually, well after her senses were swimming and her equilibrium was shot, he pulled back with a soft curse. She frowned. Why was he stopping?

"I'm sorry, honey. We're about to have company."

He set her back from him, holding her shoulders for a moment until she had regained some of her balance, then let her go. He picked up the bag she'd dropped and stuffed some of the clothing that had spilled out back into it.

"Do you need anything else? Toiletries? Shoes?"

Her mind finally clicked back into the *on* position, and she reached down for a pair of flip flops she kept near her bed. She used them like slippers and sometimes wore them outside, when she didn't have to work in the bakery. Flour-dusted sneakers were the order of the day when she was working, but otherwise, she liked lighter footwear.

She found a stray plastic bag and shoved the flip flops into it. She filled a small cosmetic case with the essentials—moisturizer, face wash, hairbrush and toothbrush. Zak took both of the smaller bags from her and put them into the overnight bag.

Just as he was zipping it up, a knock sounded on her bedroom door.

"You two about ready?" It was Brody's voice, and he sounded perturbed.

Well, that wasn't Tina's problem. Brody was her sister's husband. Let Nell deal with his moods. Tina sailed past Zak, opening the door and heading straight out into the hallway, past a frowning Brody. She didn't look, but she kind of thought the men growled at each other for a moment before following her out of the apartment.

Tina didn't have another chance to be alone with Zak. Brody hustled her out of the bakery and into Tom's truck while he all but ordered Zak to go to the sheriff's office and get the paperwork started. But she saw the way Zak's gaze followed her, just as she kept looking at him until Tom rounded the bend in the road and Zak was lost to view.

She turned around in her seat and regarded Tom as he drove steadily toward Brody and Nell's home in the woods. Tom seemed tense, although it would take someone who knew him as well as she did to realize it. Tina had a talent for noticing things about other people. It was like a sixth sense. She could tell by the set of someone's jaw or the way they held their shoulders what their mood was.

"So this vampire guy showing up…" she said, placing her

opening bid for conversation in the quiet of the pickup truck's cab. "It's a really bad thing, right?"

Tom threw her a glance and seemed to relax a fraction. "Not necessarily. We knew he'd probably come check us out sooner or later. John was aware of his yacht out there at the mouth of the cove for the past couple of days. He figured the master would come visit. We just didn't expect him to show up quite the way he did."

"What happened to him? Did he say anything else about it?"

She should probably have asked the question long before now, but Zak had distracted her. Oh, boy, had he distracted her. And she desperately wanted to be distracted by him again. Real soon.

"Something in the water attacked his boat. Killed the crew. Smashed the yacht. He just barely escaped." Tom sighed, and his shoulders tensed again, ever so slightly. "Whatever's out there, it's not good."

They didn't talk much after that, each lost in their own thoughts. They picked up Nell, and then, Tom drove them all back to his place, where Ashley waited. The sisters reunited with hugs all around while the two older girls made a fuss over Tina, asking for a detailed play-by-play of what had gone down in the bakery that night.

Tom prowled around the house, leaving them alone for a bit, which Tina thought was both considerate, and a little scary. It was pretty clear Tom was keyed up, checking all the windows and doors. He even seemed to be checking the wiring of the elaborate alarm system he'd installed in the house when Ash had moved in with him.

Tina tried not to notice his stealthy movements, but his quiet vigilance was starting to creep her out. She literally jumped when his phone rang, and was glad when he went into his home office to answer questions and rustle papers. No doubt his legal expertise would be needed in dealing with the mess that had been made of the vampire's yacht.

"I can't believe an actual vampire walked right in to our

bakery," Ashley said, leaning against the kitchen counter, sipping the coffee she'd made for all three of them. "Was he sexy?"

"Ash, the guy was so beat up, I couldn't really tell at first. He was scary when he arrived. His eyes were glowing. And red. Blood red." Tina shivered, cupping the hot mug filled with coffee in both hands. "When I came back down later, he was a lot better. And he'd taken off his shirt. He wasn't pasty white, like you see in the movies. He wasn't tan either, mind you, but he was definitely hunky under the healing skin. Muscular. Polite. Handsome. But the freaky part was the way he healed. His torso had these parallel rows of what had to be teeth marks. They were angry and red when I first saw them, then he put a wine-soaked towel over them, drank a few bottles, and when he removed the towel, the marks were gone. Like completely gone. As if they'd never been there."

"Brody heals fast," Nell put in from the other side of the kitchen table. "I think all shifters probably do, but nothing like what you're describing, and the few cuts I've seen heal on my guy didn't involve wine. Brody doesn't drink much. He says alcohol doesn't really affect shifters the way it does humans. They have faster metabolisms, so it takes a lot more to get them buzzed."

"Do you ever feel like Alice, after she fell down the rabbit hole?" Tina asked rhetorically, the conversation having hit a natural lull. All of them laughed at the question.

"I'm glad Zak was there to help you, though I wish it could have been one of the grizzlies. Zak is only a black bear," Nell said absently, finishing her coffee.

"Don't go dissing Zak." Tina was quick to rise to the deputy's defense. "He might not be as massive as your grizzly guys, but he's got it where it counts. I couldn't ask for a better protector. He got me out of harm's way and took care of the problem. He did a great job." Tina was angry her sister would even suggest Zak couldn't handle anything as well as— if not better—than any other bear in town.

"Whoa. Sorry. Peace, little sis." Nell held up her hand,

palm outward. "I wasn't dissing Zak. I think he's a great guy. He's just not as big as Brody or Tom."

"Well, I'm not as tall as either of you, and I can take you both in a fight—at the same time—and you both know it." And she had. When they were younger, they hadn't been above a few cat fights, which Tina had always won, by being quicker, smaller and more devious.

"Methinks the lady doth protest too much," Ashley put in from the side, having held her tongue until now.

Tina spun on her. "What?"

"I think you're getting awfully hot under the collar in defense of a guy you supposedly barely know. Or were you lying all this time when we asked you what you thought about having a babysitter in the bakery at night?" Ashley pressed her case, like the lawyer she was.

"We're just starting to get to know each other," Tina defended herself. "I wasn't lying. But tonight sort of accelerated the process. I know, for example, that I can count on him to protect me, no matter what walks in the door. So don't you dare say anything to the contrary." She gave Nell the stink eye for good measure.

"You know, Ash?" Nell spoke over Tina's head. "I think you're on to something. Sounds like our little sis might just be crushing on Barney Fife." A grin lit Nell's face.

"Don't you call him that!" Tina stood, her chair clattering to the floor behind her with a crashing sound that brought Tom running from the other room.

"What's going on?" he demanded in voice filled with tension.

"Nothing," Ashley said, moving closer to her mate, placing one of her hands over his heart as she snugged herself against his side. "We just think Tina's got the hots for Zak, and she didn't like Nell calling him names."

Tom's shoulders eased as he placed one arm around Ashley. His gaze sharpened as he looked from Nell to Tina, and then he smiled.

"You don't say?" His gaze zeroed in on Tina, making her

want to squirm. "What did you call him, Nell?"

"He's the deputy, so he's Barney Fife, right?" Nell pretended innocence, but Tina still bristled at the insulting words.

Tom tilted his head, considering his words before he replied. "You know," he said at last, "Zak may seem easygoing about how he's the smallest bear in our group, but he's no less deadly than any of us. And in some ways, he's even more dangerous than say, Big John, or even Brody. Zak's a sniper. Did he ever tell you that?" All three women shook their heads before he continued speaking. "The man's an artist with a rifle. Really, with most guns. Doesn't matter the size. And he's pretty good with a blade too. Don't discount him because his bear is a smaller breed than my grizzly. He's the real deal, and me and every man who served with us knew we could depend on him when the shit hit the fan."

Tina nodded. "Like I did tonight. Zak took care of me and kept me safe."

Tom's gaze gentled. "And you have a bit of hero worship because of that, huh?" He smiled, softening his words. "Wouldn't be the first time. Zak's got a way with the ladies. Didn't matter what hellhole of a third world country they sent us to, Zak always drew the female eye."

Tina wanted to argue that what she felt was more than hero worship, but she didn't want to encourage more teasing from her sisters. She kept silent but frowned, just a bit, at Tom. He seemed to understand that she wasn't amused by his words because he backtracked a bit.

"That's not to say that he took them all up on the offers they made. Zak's loyal like a puppy, and when he's with a girl, he's with that girl, only. He's not a player. I didn't mean to make it sound like he was. Sorry." Tom's cheeks reddened a bit, and he extricated himself from Ash's loose embrace. "If everything's okay in here, I have to get back to work."

"Need any help?" Ashley asked. They were setting up their law practice and were going to be partners in work as well as in life.

"Definitely, but it can wait. Catch up with your sisters. Relax a bit. The work will still be there. I'll just get things started."

Ash reached up to kiss him quickly before letting him go. "If you're sure."

"I'm sure." He left them, heading back to his office.

CHAPTER FIVE

Tina and Nell camped out at Tom and Ashley's place that night. The sisters all rode back to the bakery with Tom and Ashley before dawn, which was Ash's usual time to start the bread for the day. She was still working her shift at the bakery, even though she spent her afternoons working with Tom. She was in the process of moving in with him, taking her stuff up to his place a bit at a time, but she spent all her nights at his house now, making the early-morning commute around the cove to the bakery every day.

She wouldn't leave them in the lurch, Tina knew. Ash was solid. And even though she'd spent years earning her law degree, she really did have a gift for the artisanal breads she enjoyed baking. Still, at some point, they'd have to alter the schedule. Tina figured, with the amount of sex both Ash and Nell were currently having, one or both of them would be knocked up before the year was out.

Tina chuckled to herself as she went upstairs to her room, flopping down on the bed. She was still tired. They'd stayed up late talking and then had gotten up before dawn to get Her Ashleyness here to start the bread. It was definitely too early for Tina to be up. She worked nights for a reason. She was *not* a morning person.

Tina woke a few hours later, after the sun had risen and

had a chance to settle into the mid-morning sky. Her first thoughts were of Zak and whether or not she'd be seeing him tonight. She whizzed through her morning routine, showering and shaving, primping and polishing, just in case she managed to get close to the hunky deputy again.

That kiss he'd given her had come out of nowhere, surprising her with its intensity and disappointing her with its brevity. If she got close to Zak again, she wanted to be sure she was ready to take things further…a *lot* further. Like out-of-her-pants-and-into-his further. As soon as humanly possible.

Her mental phrasing made her pause. She had to remind herself that Zak wasn't exactly one hundred percent human. He also had that mysterious bear half that made her curious and a little tingly. Whether the tingles were from fear or anticipation, she wasn't entirely sure. Either way, she couldn't wait to see him in bear form and find out for herself if his fur was soft or wiry, straight or with a slight wave.

She wanted to know everything about him. Including—especially—how he made love. She'd bet his animal made him fierce in the sack, but her sisters certainly hadn't had any complaints about their half-grizzly lovers. In fact, those sappy, satisfied smiles on her sisters' faces made her want to join the sorority and learn, once and for all, for herself, what it was like to be with a shifter.

And not just any shifter would do. No, Tina had set her sights on Zak, and he was the one—the only one—she wanted to take a walk on the wild side with. She just had to get him alone for long enough to give it a whirl.

Tina spent the remainder of her morning primping, then went up to the roof garden to pick a fresh salad for lunch and spend a few moments spying on the cove from her high vantage point. The roof garden she and her sisters had built from scratch was one of her favorite places, and she spent a lot of time up there when the weather was nice.

Today was a bit drizzly, but she persevered, enjoying the fine mist of rain that was so light it might almost have been vapor. The skies were dark, and the cove's waters looked spooky. Or maybe that was just because she knew, after last night's attack on the vampire, that there was something out there in the ocean that could eat yachts.

Nevertheless, she saw one of the few fishing boats returning after a morning out on the ocean. That had to be a very brave man at the helm, to go out there after what had happened last night. Or maybe he didn't know? Tina couldn't imagine Big John letting any of his people go into danger without at least a warning. She decided to ask Zak. It would be something to talk about while they were passing time in the bakery...if he was still on duty tonight.

She didn't think they'd change his routine, but she wasn't privy to everything the sheriff and mayor did. They could easily decide Zak's services were needed somewhere else with this new development.

Happily, Zak arrived at his usual time later that night, just as Nell was going off-shift. Her mate, Brody, picked her up just as Zak walked in, and Tina knew the men timed it that way, to keep the girls covered at all times. It made Tina feel safe after the alarming events of last night, though prior to that, it had seemed kind of silly.

Still, she couldn't fault them for their vigilance. Not after that injured vampire had shown up on her doorstep. The boys knew a lot more about the world—this new paranormal world the sisters had just discovered—and the girls were smart enough to follow their lead.

Zak sat quietly in the corner, as he had done every night since being assigned *bakery duty*, as he called it. There were quite a few customers keeping Tina busy most of the night, but finally, just before closing time, things slowed down and they got a few minutes alone.

"Busy night," Zak commented, coming over to the counter where Tina was cleaning up.

"You can say that again," she agreed. She hadn't even had two minutes to talk to Zak with the near-constant demands of the other guests.

"Brody radioed me a few minutes ago. You're going to have one more visitor before closing," he said cryptically. She wanted to ask who was coming, but he went right on speaking. "While we have a moment alone, I wanted to know if you'd like to go out with me tomorrow afternoon?"

Tina's knees wobbled. This was it! Finally, Zak was asking her out.

"Sure." She tried to sound casual. "I'd love to." That was a little less casual, but his eyes sparkled, and she didn't regret showing her enthusiasm.

"Great." He smiled that smile that made her tummy clench. Damn, the man should come with a warning label. "I'll pick you up around noon. How does a picnic sound?"

"Sounds like fun." She smiled back, unable to resist. He was just so darned handsome. He made her feel good when he looked at her like that. "Can I bring anything?"

"Just yourself. I'll take care of everything else." His gaze held hers and that smile just kept on going...until...

The little bell over the door rang, breaking the spell.

Tina looked up to find the vampire walking in the door again. This time, he was dressed in clothes that didn't have horrendous tears in them, and he wasn't bleeding. And he was also surrounded by bear shifters. Big John, Brody, Tom and a few others were all trooping in behind him, like an honor guard, or maybe a guard detail.

"Good evening, Miss Baker," the vampire said, his voice fluid and strong.

"Hello."

Tina was out of her element. How did one speak to an ancient vampire? Was there some sort of etiquette? If so, it hadn't been covered in her school.

"I wanted to come by before I left town to thank you for your assistance last night. You were very brave."

Whew. If Tina hadn't already decided to jump Zak's bones at the earliest opportunity, her head might just have been turned by Hiram, the hottie vampire. He had a way about him that was exceedingly charming and very old world. Sexy.

But her werebear was even hotter in a more primeval sort of way. Hiram was urbane. Zak was rough around the edges but absolutely honest in everything he did, and that was something Tina truly appreciated. She'd had bad experiences in the past with guys who wanted her to believe the best about them when they really were the worst.

As far as she was concerned, meeting Zak was kind of like hitting the big winner in the lottery. He was the real deal, and her heart—picky thing that it was—had settled on him. It had taken time, but she'd gotten to know him, and now, it would be very difficult for any other man to turn her head.

That's not to say she couldn't appreciate a totally hot man like Hiram, but her heart wasn't going anywhere but in Zak's direction. Interesting. It had taken this little encounter to drive that fact home to her. She looked at Zak and then at Hiram, realization dawning, even as the vampire waited for her to say something. She retreated to common courtesy.

"I'm glad I could help," she replied rather inanely, she thought, but Hiram smiled and stepped forward.

"You were my angel of mercy at a time when I was in desperate need." He took her hand in his and raised it to his lips, kissing her knuckles in that courtly way of his. She was charmed, but she saw the glint of amusement in his eye as Zak visibly bristled nearby. "Thank you, Miss Baker." Hiram released her hand and stepped back. The old vampire turned to look at Zak and bowed his head slightly, just once. "I owe you a debt, deputy. If you are ever in need, call me, and I will come."

The other bear shifters seemed surprised by the vampire's words. Tina got the feeling such a promise from a guy like Hiram was a very big deal. The vampire walked forward so he was standing in the center of the seating area, werebears gathered all around.

"Everything I have seen of your settlement gives me hope that we can be allies from this point forward. You have good people here, John," Hiram nodded toward where John was standing a few feet away. "I extend the hand of friendship to you and yours, Alpha," Hiram went on, walking up to John and holding out his hand for a shake.

John's eyes narrowed, and he paused a moment before taking Hiram's hand. "Our Lords speak highly of you, Master Hiram. I'm glad we can work together and coexist. And I'll go one step further. We've heard reports from the Lords of renewed activity by agents of evil. My men and I are retired now, but we're still warriors at heart. If evil shows its ugly face in this region, we'll be fighting it, and we'll come to your aid if it's in your territory."

"As I will for you, my new friend. I have long stood against the forces of darkness. As long as you and your people serve the Mother of All and fight on the side of Her Light, I will stand with you."

The handshake was as fierce as the men who shared it, and even if Tina didn't understand everything they were talking about, one thing was clear—Hiram and her werebear friends had decided to become allies. Again, she got the feeling this was something momentous.

The men left, John and Hiram in the lead, talking like old friends. Tina closed up the shop, but when she looked for Zak, he was near the door. Tom was waiting to drive her back to his place because Ashley didn't want Tina staying in the apartment alone until the vampire was gone for good. Or so Tom said when she asked.

Zak shrugged and left, letting Tom help Tina lock up. She'd wanted to talk to Zak some more, but it looked like tomorrow would have to be soon enough.

CHAPTER SIX

Zak wanted everything to be perfect for his date with Tina. He spent the morning organizing things and preparing a lunch he hoped she would enjoy. He liked cooking and pulled out all the stops for this special lunch date.

He had a spot picked out near the cove, but not so close to the water that they'd be out in the open. He'd found a secluded area on the property he'd recently purchased that was like a little glade, surrounded by rocks, down near the water. It was open to the beach, but few would see them if they picnicked inside the rocky area, just before the tree line.

Zak picked Tina up at twelve on the dot. She was pretty as a picture, wearing a pair of jeans that hugged her curves and a pretty peasant blouse that was white with colorful embroidery around the neckline and sleeves. It looked Mexican, but Zak wasn't an expert on women's clothing. Still, he liked the outfit. It made her look like the free spirit he knew her to be, unhindered by convention and comfortable in her own skin. He liked that about her. She was a confident woman but easy-going by nature.

"You look beautiful," he told her, wishing he was a little smoother around the edges. He'd spent most of his life in the military, trying to prove his worth to the bigger guys. He hadn't spent a whole lot of time wooing ladies—at least not ones who really mattered.

And Tina really mattered to him. And to his bear.

More and more, he suspected she was the one for him, but time would tell. Zak was younger than most of the other guys in Grizzly Cove and didn't have quite as much experience, though he'd joined them when they decided to quit army life. They'd been his family more than the shitty Clan he'd been born to, and when Big John had wanted to settle down to civilian life, Zak had decided to follow his lead.

"Thanks," Tina said, ducking her head in a shy gesture that charmed him.

She was a woman of contrasts. Confident, yet flustered by his compliment, as if she didn't receive such words often. Zak made a mental note to tell her how gorgeous she was at every reasonable opportunity. Several times a day ought to do it.

"Where are we going?" she asked when the silence dragged on a little too long.

Damn. He'd been staring at her, lost in space. He had to work on his powers of concentration. She had a way of mixing him all up when they were alone.

"Just a little ways down the road. I recently bought some property near town with the idea of building a place for myself, but I haven't started work on the house yet. Still, the property has some gorgeous views, and there's a perfect place for a private picnic between the trees and the beach." He led her toward his patrol SUV while he spoke.

"Sounds perfect," she said as he opened the passenger door of his vehicle for her and helped her hop up into the high seat.

They talked of generalities as he made the short drive from the bakery, which was along the main stretch of roadway at the center of the cove, to a smaller road that led around one side of the horseshoe-shaped inlet. His place was close to the central part of the small town. He'd wanted to be near the action, but also on the water, and this parcel of land accomplished both goals nicely.

"Ready for a little off-roading?" he asked, shooting her a

challenging grin right before he turned the wheel onto his land.

There was no driveway. No road. Just weeds, grass, bushes and trees. The land was wild, as nature had made it, and he had already staked out an area where he would start building. His goal was to have his home make as little impact on the environment as he could manage, while still offering all the creature comforts his human side enjoyed. His bear side wanted the wild places to stay just that way, so he would have territory to roam, mark, and explore.

This place was going to be the perfect compromise between the dual parts of his nature. As soon as he got the place built, that is.

Zak looked over at Tina, to make sure she was okay with the rough terrain.

"How are you holding up over there? Sorry it's a bit bumpy. Nothing's been leveled or graded yet." He raised his voice a bit to be heard over the increased engine noise, accompanied by the scrape of leaves on the outside of the vehicle.

He wasn't worried about the SUV. It was built to handle tougher stuff than this. But he wasn't sure about his passenger. Did human females like off-roading? The males seemed to enjoy it from what Zak had seen, but he'd never really run across a woman on the trail.

"I'm fine," she replied. She'd reached for the handhold that was placed conveniently above the passenger door and was holding on as they bounced along. "This is fun," she added, sending him a grin.

Well, that answered that question. This female—human or not—was adventurous. Just one more thing to like about her.

Before too long, he reached the spot he'd chosen for their picnic. It wasn't too far, as the crow flies—or the bear rambles—from the site he'd staked out for his den, but they hadn't been able to see it from the path he'd taken through the trees. That was partially by design. Zak wanted to show her the floor plan he'd laid out with poles and twine, a little later, and see what she thought of it. He had it all planned.

Picnic first. A glass of wine. The food he'd prepared. Then he'd show her around his new home site.

He parked the SUV at the side of the little glen, surrounded by rocks on three sides. There was a small opening in the rocks on this side, close to where he'd parked, that would give them easy access to the vehicle and the feast he'd packed in back.

Zak got out and rushed around to the passenger side to help Tina down from the high seat. It amused him that she was so petite. She made him feel huge, and that was a feeling he didn't often have since he hung out with massive grizzly shifters most of the time.

Oh, sure, he was larger than most human males, and that had been useful in the service, but the guys he worked with day to day were even more massive. If he'd had a weaker personality or was less sure of himself and his place in the world, it could have given him a complex. As it was, he felt himself grin as he helped Tina slide out of the seat.

He spent a little more time holding her than was strictly necessary, and she didn't seem to mind, so he dipped his head and stole a kiss.

Damn. She was as amazing as he remembered. He'd been wanting to taste her lips again since that very first kiss. She was just as sweet, just as luscious, with a hint of spice that intrigued him. But he counseled himself to leave her be for now. They had a lot of getting-to-know-you stuff to get through before he could jump her bones. At least, that's what he thought human females wanted, and he wasn't going to do anything that might scare her off. She was already too special to frighten away by being too aggressive.

So he let her go, stepping back so she could walk past him, through the rocks and into the little clearing.

"This is amazing," she said, looking out to the water, her hands behind her back as she paced forward. Was it his imagination or were her cheeks pink? He took it as a good sign, though he wasn't entirely sure what that charming little blush meant. "You own this property?"

"Just signed the deed last week." Pride filled him. He'd worked a long time to be able to afford this little slice of heaven right here. "I hope to start construction in the next few weeks."

"It's a gorgeous spot on the cove. Not too far out toward the ocean, and not too far from town." She turned toward him, her expression alight with pleasure. "It's perfect, Zak. I'm very happy for you."

"Thanks." Their gazes met and held for a long moment until her cheeks went a little pink again, and he realized it was probably a bit rude to stare without speaking for so long. "Uh, I've got lunch in the back of the truck. You like spicy food, right?"

"Love it," she confirmed. "Can I help?"

She walked a few paces back toward the SUV while he went around to the back and opened the lift gate. He tossed her the large blanket he'd packed for them to sit on.

"You could spread that out and have a seat. I'll take care of the rest," he assured her as he began lifting parcels out of the back of the truck.

There wasn't all that much. Just a cooler that held their food and the bottle of wine he had on ice. Glasses, napkins, plates and utensils were in a bag he slung over his shoulder. He brought the whole lot over to the blanket she was smoothing over the grass and set it down on one corner.

He felt more than a bit of pride as they shared the meal he'd prepared, especially when she praised his cold Cajun chicken, black-eyed peas and corn bread. The meal was easy and carefree, and they talked about their families a bit. He hadn't expected that, but when she launched into a discussion of her sisters and their new mates, he felt compelled to share a bit of his own background.

He wasn't looking for sympathy, and he especially didn't want pity, but if they were going to get involved, she deserved to know at least the bare bones of his past.

"My father never got over my mother's death," he

admitted, though he'd rarely ever spoken about this topic with anyone. "He blamed me a lot of the time and, sometimes, took it out on my hide."

"He beat you?" She looked appalled, which was what he'd tried to avoid, but he was in it now, and he had to see this through. He figured it was going to be hard to make a human understand how it was for shifters, but he tried his best.

"Some," he acknowledged her question with a shrug. "But when you can both turn into bears, there are other ways—other weapons—besides just fists. And we heal fast. I learned to run fast. And climb really high onto thin branches, where he couldn't reach."

"That's pretty awful," she said, and he dared to look over and meet her gaze.

What he saw there didn't hurt like he'd expected. She didn't pity him. No, she looked angry. Angry on his behalf. That was unexpected. Then again, Tina had more fire than any human woman he'd ever known.

"Well, that's over now. It's been over a long time. I got out of there as soon as I could and never looked back. I joined the Army and met up with Big John and the other guys. Things have been really good since then. They're my family now."

She was silent a moment before answering. "I like that," she said finally. "From everything I've seen of these guys, they're all pretty amazing. Strong. Steadfast. Like brothers who would never leave one of their own in the lurch. I like that you found that and made it your own." She smiled at him, and he felt the impact clear down to his soul.

He leaned over and just had to kiss her.

Finally. She was getting some lip action from Zak. She felt wanton as she encouraged his kiss to grow hotter and deeper. She'd been wanting to kiss him since forever, it seemed, and the little tastes she'd had of him already had only whetted her appetite for more.

She climbed over him, straddling his lap without breaking

their kiss. Feeling bold, she pushed his shoulders back so he was lying beneath her, her hair cascading around them, enclosing them in a private world of hot lips, swirling tongues and pleasure the likes of which she had never felt from just a kiss.

Zak lit her on fire, and she wanted more. So much more. She was through waiting for him to make a move. They were alone, on his land where nobody would trespass, and she had him almost precisely where she wanted him. The time for games was over.

What she wanted most was for there to be no clothing between them. No fabric barriers, nothing to keep her from climbing on his cock and riding him to the stars. Or, at least, that's what she'd been imagining it would be like with him. She wouldn't know for sure until...well...until a few minutes from now, if all went as she planned.

She clutched at his shirt, wanting it gone. Zak seemed to get the message, lifting up to rip it off over his head. Their lips were apart only long enough for the fabric to slip in between their bodies, and then, he was back, kissing her like she'd never been kissed before. There was something special about Zak. Everywhere he touched her, she tingled. His lips brought her to another state of consciousness, it seemed, where all she wanted was more. More of him. More of his lovemaking.

She pulled at her own clothing, helping him remove it until she felt the slight breeze off the water against her bare skin. But he still had his pants on. She reared back, rising up just a bit, knowing he could see everything and reveling a bit in the way his gaze flowed over her body.

His hands followed the path of his gaze, cupping her breasts and then roaming lower. One of his hands toyed with her nipples while the other sought entrance between her legs. She arched into his touch, encouraging his fingers to find what they were looking for.

She had her inner bad girl on speed dial and felt like some sort of sea siren, claiming the man she wanted to fuck.

But this would be more than just a quick fuck. She knew that in her heart. This time with Zak was going to alter the course of her life, and she was okay with that. She wanted that. With him.

Even if he wasn't sure he wanted her permanently yet. She was going to work on him until he gave in, and she was going to grab for happily ever after with her very own cuddly, exciting, badass bear shifter. Zak wouldn't know what hit him.

Speaking of which, she groaned loudly as he found the spot and sank two fingers into her needy core. She couldn't help but move on him, fucking his hand.

"Do you want to come?" he whispered.

And that was all it took. Unbelievably, she felt her pussy contract on his fingers, and she was shaking in pleasure.

Zak laughed, and the vibrations of his rumbly chuckle made her knees go weak. He was holding her up with one arm around her waist, while his other hand remained between them, between her legs, fingers deep inside her.

"You like that, eh kitten?" he mumbled against the side of her face. He'd sat up when she came so she was spread over his muscular thighs, wide open and weak after the quick, hard climax he'd given her.

She took his lower lip between her teeth before moving into a deeper kiss. When she pulled back, she spoke her thoughts against his lips.

"I like everything you do to me, Zak, but I want you inside me. Don't keep me waiting anymore."

"I am inside you," he teased, wiggling his fingers and making her squirm in renewed sensation.

"You know what I mean," she whispered, ready, just like that, for more.

"Say it," he dared her. "Say what you really want."

"I want your cock in me, Zak. I want you to fuck me with that big bear shifter cock until I scream in pleasure." She whispered the daring words against his ear, not sure where the wild child inside her was coming from but glad Zak seemed to like it. Maybe it was his inner bear speaking to some previously unknown primitive part of her nature. Maybe it was that Zak brought out things in her she'd never known before.

And she liked it.

Almost as much as she liked him.

He was going to be hers forever. At least, that was her dearest dream. Now all she had to do was convince him.

Zak surprised her by removing his hand from between her thighs somewhat abruptly. He then picked her up, his muscles bulging in a way that made her mouth water, and placed her on her back on the blanket. She was completely naked, but he still had his pants on. They had to go, but it seemed he wasn't through positioning her just yet.

He lifted both of her legs straight up into the air in front of him, running his hands appreciatively along her thighs and calves. He rested her ankles on his shoulder as he met her gaze.

"Spread your legs wide for me, honey. Show me where you want me," he whispered in that low, compelling tone that made her abdomen quiver.

Channeling that inner bad girl again, she did as he asked, spreading herself in a way she hadn't ever done for another man. She made herself completely vulnerable to him, utterly his slave. She discovered in that moment how much she loved the feel of his gaze on her body.

She watched him watch her from between her thighs. He was on his knees, sitting back on his heels, watching the scene unfold before him. Watching *her* unfold before him. A willing puppet to his mastery.

He licked his lips as he looked at her, and then, his talented hands went to the fly of his pants. One button, then two, then three, and the restrained monster was released. Zak's hardness was revealed, and it was time for her to lick her lips and think about how much she wanted to learn the taste of his body. But judging by his expression, that would come later.

For now, he was stroking his cock, lining himself up for the possession she'd wanted since almost the first moment they'd met. He leaned forward and slid inside.

There was no need for protection. She knew from her sisters that shifters didn't carry disease, and she was on birth control. Nothing would come between them, which was just the way she wanted it.

His gaze swept upward to meet hers

When he was fully seated, he stopped, breathing hard. She realized her own breathing was hitched and ragged. The feeling of fullness was unlike anything she had felt with the few human men she'd been with before. Zak filled her completely, touching areas inside her she hadn't really known existed.

She couldn't wait to find out what it was going to feel like when he moved.

"How are you doing, Tina? All right?" he asked, panting as he held back what she most wanted.

"It's sweet of you to check on me, but if you don't start moving your ass right…now…" She panted between words as she felt her body quiver in need.

Zak chuckled and gave in, starting a slow rhythm that just scratched the surface of meeting her need. She'd never felt like this before. She'd never had this desperate desire, this aching need. Only with Zak, and it felt like only he would ever be able to make her feel whole again.

He pumped within her, changing angles and moving over her so their bodies aligned. He held her gaze, checking on her comfort again, and she felt her heart melt a little at his consideration. But what she really wanted was something a little rougher.

She leaned up and nibbled on his earlobe, biting just once, letting him know her mood. Zak complied, reading her like a dream. He sped up his thrusts and let loose more of the wildness she knew he kept bottled up inside when he was in human form. She needed that passion, that wild abandon. It met and answered the need deep within herself.

A few strokes more and she was calling out his name, coming hard as he joined her in ecstasy.

CHAPTER SEVEN

Zak's impulses said to spend the rest of the afternoon right there, in Tina's arms, making sweet love to her, but he squashed that thought for the moment. He didn't want to overwhelm her. He'd had this whole afternoon planned, and it had already gone way off the rails. Time to bring them back to earth.

He didn't want just a physical relationship with her—though the sex had been amazingly awesome, he had to admit—but he wanted more. A foundation to their relationship that could only be built by being her friend and getting to know her.

He hadn't bothered getting to really know the women he'd bedded before Tina. They hadn't mattered to his bear, except as a way to get some relief. But with Tina, everything was different. His bear *liked* her. Hell, it more than just liked her. It wanted to rub up against her and cuddle.

Never before in his life had his bad-ass, got-something-to-prove-to-the-bigger-bears-he-hung-with bear wanted to cuddle anyone or anything. Not for as long as he could remember. Such soft ideas didn't fly back in the bayou, when he'd been young.

If he'd ever had any softness, his father would have been sure to beat it out of him. And the hard road Zac had traveled since hadn't invited any show of vulnerability. He wanted to be gentle with her and feel her tender touch on him. He wanted to spoon her and just feel her breathe.

Damn. He had it bad.

For a human. His heart sank.

What if she laughed at him? What if she didn't feel the same?

Things were different for humans. They often went from lover to lover from what Zak had observed. So did shifters, for that matter, but not when their beasts started thinking these kinds of thoughts about one particular person.

Shit got serious then. And Zak was very much afraid—and cautiously delighted—that his bear was thinking that way about Tina. At long last, he might have a shot at a mate of his own.

If he could navigate the human rules of dating and figure out if she could truly be his. If she'd been a shifter, he wouldn't be so worried, but she was fully human. She might easily make love to him today and move on tomorrow, leaving him, and his bear, broken hearted.

Uncomfortable with the direction of his thoughts, Zak rose to his feet and stretched, looking out at the water not too far away. He was a man of action, unused to sitting still for so long. Then again, he was seldom in the company of such a delicate—human—lady with nobody else around.

"Want to take a walk down by the water?" he asked, sticking to his plan for the day.

"Sure." Tina sprang to her feet and grabbed her clothes.

Although John had issued warnings about going out on boats or even swimming too far out into the water, Zak figured a walk down by the shore would be safe enough. The thing that had attacked Hiram had been outside the cove, in the deeper ocean, and likely wouldn't venture too close to shore. If it could eat a yacht, it was probably way too big to swim in the shallows near land anyway.

They dressed quietly, but he noticed Tina shooting him teasing glances as she briefly wrestled with him over his T-shirt.

"You look sexy without a shirt," she said playfully.

"So do you," he countered, loving the way she blushed. "When my house is built, you can go topless here any time you like."

She laughed, even as her blush intensified, and she let go of his shirt. "Play your cards right, deputy, and I might just take you up on that." She turned away to finish dressing while he pulled on his shirt.

He'd leave it off except for the chiggers that like to nibble on his human flesh. He knew they hung out closer to the water, and he didn't want to itch for a week. He'd already been there, done that—and wore the T-shirt now to stop it from happening again. There was nothing worse than an itchy bite on your back you couldn't reach to scratch. No, thank you.

He made sure everything was in place—his cell phone, his badge, his weapon—and was charmed when Tina came to his side, surprising him by taking his hand. He liked the way their fingers fit together. It reminded him of the other ways they had fit so nicely together. *Down, boy.*

They walked, hand in hand, the short distance down to the water. There was a bit of a steep incline before the beach started, which would keep his future home safe from tidal changes and storms and would also allow for a magnificent view of the water, once he got his house built. He helped Tina down the dune and then onto the rocky shore.

They walked for a while, moving slowly toward the edge of the water. Little wavelets lapped at the coarse sand, and the occasional seashell, or bit of kelp, littered the path. Gulls cried in the distance, and the peaceful calm of the gentle waves did their magic, bringing their serenity to Zak's spirit.

As did the woman at his side. Tina both excited him beyond all reason and calmed the raging beast inside him. She was a balm to his soul, just by her existence. How he wished he could tell her everything he was feeling, but he didn't want to scare her off. Maybe, in time, he would be able to share more with her. He looked forward to that day with great anticipation.

Tina paused and looked out toward the mouth of the cove, shading her eyes.

"This is a beautiful place, Zak. You have a gorgeous view of almost the entire cove from here."

"Yeah, that's a big part of the reason I chose this spot," he replied, watching her instead of the water. She was so incredible. Her loveliness rivaled that of this beautiful spot he now called his own.

"What the—?" Her words trailed off as she looked down at her feet. Zak saw the dismay on her face before he, too, looked downward.

Something in the water had reached out a... Tentacle was the only word he could come up with for the long appendage currently wrapped around Tina's ankle. She tried to pull free, but the thing wouldn't let go.

"Zak?" A hint of panic laced her tone as she looked up at him.

"Hold on to me," he cautioned, reaching for his concealed weapon. She clutched at his left arm while he sought the gun with his right.

Zak never went anywhere unarmed. It was part of his job, but also something he'd done since leaving home all those years ago. He was a natural with weapons and felt a little naked without at least one on his person.

He pulled the 9mm handgun out of the ankle holster he'd kept hidden beneath the hem of his jeans and took aim at the tentacle that was working its way up Tina's leg. She was holding onto Zak, but he felt the strength of the pull on her body. That thing—whatever it was—was exerting some force to drag her toward the water.

Zak wasn't about to let it have her.

He fired off several rounds, all direct hits on the tentacle, but the slugs just barely slowed the sea monster down. That's when Zak realized he really only had one choice. He had to go bear. He just hoped it would be enough.

Kicking off his shoes and unbuttoning his jeans, he got as close to naked as he could as quickly as possible. Tina was panicking now. He could tell from the way she clutched at his arm.

"I'm going to shift. I'll get between you and it. I won't let it take you," he rasped out quickly. "I promise."

He held her gaze as he let his change come. One moment, he was a man, with Tina clinging to his left arm for dear life. The next, he was a giant black bear. Not as large, maybe, as the grizzly shifters he hung around with, but still far bigger than any regular black bear.

Zak growled as he turned and attacked the tentacle, just clear of Tina's foot. He slashed with his claws and bit with his sharp teeth. The flavor of the creature's blood on his tongue was acidic and like no blood Zak had ever tasted before. It was disgusting. Not fishy, as he would have expected.

Something wasn't right with the creature.

Hell, nothing was right with this situation at all. Sea monsters didn't just appear in the Pacific Northwest and pull unsuspecting women to their depths in the ocean.

Zak applied all his bear strength to tearing the limb off the creature and freeing Tina. All that mattered right now was her safety.

With a final burst of effort, he ripped through the half-foot of flesh that connected the tip of the tentacle with whatever lay just off shore, under the waves. Tina screamed as he broke through, and she was suddenly free. She fell to the ground but was quick to scramble as far away from the shore as she could get, the remainder of the tentacle still twined around her leg.

Zak let out a mighty roar toward the water, a warning of sorts, as well as an auditory victory dance. Round one had definitely gone to the bear. This time.

Zak followed behind Tina, urging her to move farther inland, even as the tentacle stuck stubbornly to her leg.

She made it to the picnic blanket and collapsed onto her side, pulling at the twitching tentacle. Zak came up to her and pushed her hands gently aside, using his bear claws and tough-padded paws to remove the thing and put it aside. He wiped the residual slime off his paws on the grass before shifting back to human form and taking Tina in his arms. She was trembling in reaction.

"It's okay now. You're safe," he crooned to her, holding her as she clung to his bare shoulders.

He knew some of his comrades would be showing up soon. They had to have heard the commotion and the gunshots. That wasn't normal for the cove, so someone would come to investigate and help. His buddies were good like that. Always ready to back each other up when needed.

And, sure enough, he heard the sound of vehicles approaching. He had about five minutes before Brody and John, and possibly a few others, came barreling in.

"We're going to have company real soon," he told Tina in a soothing voice. "The guys will help us figure out what the fuck just happened here." He couldn't keep some of the exasperation out of his voice or censor his words. Had they really just been attacked by a fucking sea monster?

The thing reeked of magic. Even as the severed limb twitched one last time on the grass by their side and finally stilled, it glowed with an unearthly light. That fucker just wasn't normal.

CHAPTER EIGHT

Tina was slowly coming down off the panic high. Zak's arms were around her, and he was so amazingly...amazing. She couldn't believe what had just happened. He'd shot at that...*thing*...that had tried to drag her into the water, and when that didn't work, he'd changed. Right in front of her. He'd turned into his bear, and holy shit! He was massive.

The grizzlies might say he was small, but as far as she was concerned, he was one big, scary-assed bear. Only, she'd known he wasn't going to hurt her. She'd known, deep in her heart, that he only cared about protecting her from that...creature. Whatever it was.

"Octopus?" she wondered aloud, resting her head on his deliciously warm shoulder.

"What?" he asked gently as her wits began to reassemble inside her mind.

"Do you think that was an octopus?" she clarified, though she had a feeling that *thing* hadn't been any regular sort of sea creature. "Or maybe a giant squid?" She held out a vague hope that it could be explained by somewhat conventional means.

"Sorry, babe. I don't think so." Zak looked over at the tentacle, and she followed his gaze. Yeah, that didn't look like any sort of regular sea creature she'd ever seen, or even heard of.

"So what is it?" She was almost afraid to ask.

"Beats the hell out of me," Zak answered almost at once. He moved back, releasing her by slow degrees. "Are you okay now? The guys are on their way in, and I want to scout down by the shore for a minute. Make sure it's gone."

He met her gaze and waited for her answer. Somehow, his calm demeanor, even after what they'd just encountered, reassured her. His actions told her he was a man who had seen worse and survived. He would see her through this. In fact, he already had.

"You saved my life," she whispered.

Zak looked a little uncomfortable, but his gaze remained steadily locked with hers. The moment felt significant.

Tina leaned toward him and touched her lips to his.

The kiss turned molten in no seconds flat. She ran her hands over his shoulders and realized, finally, that he was naked. *Whoa, mama.* How could she have missed something like that?

She wanted to tackle him to the picnic blanket and have her naughty way with him again, but he was already moving away.

Why? Where was he going?

A little bit of sanity returned, and she remembered what he'd said. They were going to have a bunch of guys up here any minute. *Yeah. Okay. Um. Right.*

She could deal.

Sort of. If her breathing would just stop sounding like a choo choo. She had to get a grip and calm down. Especially if—as she suspected—her new brother-in-law, the sheriff, was going to find her, at any minute, tangled up with his deputy. His very *naked* deputy.

Finally, she found the will to let him go.

"Okay. Sorry. To be continued…I hope," she dared to say, even as he got to his feet.

He paused, looking down at her as she sat up. Her mouth watered as she tried *really* hard not to look at what was right in front of her. She met his gaze and did her best to keep her eyes trained there, on his. She was *not* going to ogle his package, though he seemed in no hurry to hide the goods.

"We will most definitely continue this, sweetheart. But not here, and not now. We've got to be safe before we go wild again, okay?" He sent her an audacious wink that heated up her insides before he turned and walked calmly down to the shore.

She couldn't help but stare at his butt. The man was pure muscle. Every solid inch of him was toned, tan and buff. *Sweet Mother of Mercy!*

She hadn't really had much of a chance to look at him before. Their coming together that first time had been like lightning striking—an elemental force of nature that could not be denied. She'd held on and gone with the impulse, riding the lightning bolt all the way to the stars. He'd been that good.

The best she'd ever had, actually. And she wanted more. Much more.

Zak bent over and tugged on his jeans, which he'd shucked down by the water when he shifted. She noticed he kept his eyes on the murky depths even as he dressed. She was sorry to see all that manly flesh covered up, but even she could hear the engines now. The cavalry was about to arrive in force.

Sure enough, Brody was the first to show up. Tina got to her feet and shuddered at the slime trail twined around her leg. The strength of the suckers on the tentacle had even ripped her jeans in places.

"Sitrep," Brody demanded of her, as if she was some kind of commando. She wanted to laugh, but this was no laughing matter.

"That thing..." she pointed to the dead tentacle on the grass, "...tried to drag me into the water. Zak went bear on its ass and ripped that arm, or tentacle, or whatever it is, off the bigger creature, which I guess is still in the cove. Zak's checking now." She pointed to Zak, who was still looking at the beach, bending from time to time as if looking for, or perhaps reading, tracks of some kind.

Brody's face looked grim. "Are you okay?"

"Fine now. Zak took good care of me."

She kept feeling the need to defend Zak to the other men. Why, she had no idea. They respected him. It was clear in the way they treated him. Plus, he'd worked with them far longer than she'd known any of them. But something inside her wanted to jump up and proclaim Zak's capabilities, and the fact that he'd never let her down.

Brody nodded once, then headed straight for the beach. What was it with these guys? They walked *toward* danger, instead of running the heck away. She had to hand it to them, these shifters had brass ones.

"How are you holding up?" John's voice came from behind her, and she turned to find him close, though she hadn't heard him approach. It was spooky, sometimes, how silently these shifters moved.

"I'm okay," she replied, meeting his concerned gaze. "Thanks."

He looked her up and down, then, seemingly satisfied, walked toward the long tentacle stretched out on the grass next to the blanket. He crouched down, looking at it, but not touching.

"What do you reckon it is?" John asked.

Tina wondered why in the world he was asking her, but just then, Brody and Zak stepped into her line of sight, having come up from the beach. Brody crouched at the other end of the long arm, across from John, while Zak came to stand next to Tina.

"Something fey, maybe?" Zak offered. "It stinks of magic."

"Yeah, you're right," Brody replied, sniffing the air above the tentacle. "This is no earthly coloration either."

"And there's a sheen of magic to it. It just about glows, even in daylight," Zak added.

John looked up at Zak sharply. "You can see it?"

Zak nodded slowly. "It's like something I saw, just once, when I was a kid back on the bayou. It was smaller and not shaped exactly like this. It was more gator than sea monster, and it had been brought to this realm by a voodoo lady to guard her lair. She wasn't on our side. She was evil. Served evil." Zak's words slowed as he seemed to remember, and a slight drawl made its way into his speech. Probably the patterns of his youth, Tina realized, that he'd obviously gone to some lengths to lose. "The voodoo woman tried to curse me once, and the gator-thing showed itself to run me off. It glowed a lot like this does to my sight."

John made a grumbling sound deep in his throat as he contemplated the evidence. His frown was one of displeasure mixed with determination.

"We'd better preserve this, somehow," he said, standing from his crouch. "I'll put a call in and see if there are any experts nearby that can help us out."

"I'll take care of the evidence," Brody put in, standing as well. "In the meantime, we'd better warn folks to stay away from the water."

John tilted his head, seeming to consider the sheriff's suggestion. "Humans, maybe," he allowed, but Zak shook his head.

"Everybody, Alpha. Not just the humans. I emptied an entire clip into it, and the thing didn't flinch. Even with my claws, it wasn't easy to break its hold. The beast is quick, silent, and has a hide like boiled leather. Warn everybody," Zak urged.

John nodded slowly. "Okay. Everybody. We've got a council meeting tonight. Let's make it official and turn it into a town meeting. Can you boys get the word out?"

"Consider it done," Zak replied, even as Brody opened his mouth to answer.

"Humans too. Might as well include the Baker sisters, since they know pretty much everything there is to know about our little community now anyway," John added as he turned to walk away. "I'll call off the rest of the cavalry," he added almost as an afterthought. "See you in a few hours."

"Zak," Brody spoke as John left, "maybe you ought to take Tina home." He shot a significant look at her torn jeans as she fidgeted under Brody's inspection.

Since he'd mated her sister, Brody had become a sort of older brother and authority figure all rolled into one. He took the protection of his wife's family very seriously, which made Tina feel a little odd at times. She'd been a free spirit for so long it was weird to have this powerful guy want to be part of her life—all for her sister's sake.

It was endearing, but also a little maddening. Tina knew if she ever wanted to just cut loose, Brody would be there, frowning at her. Come to think of it, Tom would be frowning too. These bears were super protective, and Tina had somehow come under the umbrella of their protection since her two sisters decided to take those boys home and keep them.

Then again, maybe it was about time Tina did the same. She knew which bear-man she wanted. He was standing right in front of her. But she didn't really have the nerve—no matter what her mischievous inner bad girl said—to just jump Zak's bones. Again.

The first time had been spontaneous. Part of a lovely, almost magical, romantic afternoon. It had an ethereal quality to it in her memory already, like a daydream come true—with naughty overtones and pulse-pounding ecstasy as the payoff. Still, it was like something precious, and she didn't really know how to get back to that place—or if Zak felt the same about it.

Maybe to him, it was just a quick bang in the grass. She didn't think so. Everything pointed in the other direction, in fact—the careful planning of the picnic, the way he'd put such care into cooking for her, the romantic setting. But what did she know? Maybe he did that for all the girls. Maybe she wasn't as special to him as he was quickly becoming to her.

She felt insecure, and that tended to negate her wilder nature that wanted to walk right up to him and drag his head down for a kiss. And other things…

"Yeah," Zak replied to Brody, stirring Tina out of her somewhat lascivious thoughts. "I'll drop her off at the bakery and come back with a cooler of ice for that." He gestured toward the tentacle. "Maybe several coolers," he amended.

"Sounds like a plan," Brody agreed. "Nell's at the bakery now. Tell her to shut down for the night. Everybody will be at the meeting anyway. No sense keeping the shop open."

Tina was a little surprised at the idea of closing down the bakery. The sisters had an unwritten rule that they'd do their best to keep regular hours, but she saw the merit in Brody's suggestion. Grizzly Cove wasn't a big city like Portland. Everyone here was part of the small community of bear shifters.

Even though there were a couple of public roads that wound through town now, access was still pretty controlled way out here on the edge of the ocean. Visitors were few and far between. Though in the summer months, that would probably change as the town grew. Yet, the bear shifters here were being very careful about how fast the town grew and who they let in to their community. Which made shutting down the bakery early something they could easily do, since they wouldn't be losing business or offending anyone, with everybody at the meeting.

"I'll start my part of the phone chain," Zak said to Brody, then turned to her. "Come on, honey," he said in a softer tone, holding out one of his hands for her to take. "Let's get you someplace safe."

She took his hand, very conscious of Brody watching their movements. She couldn't tell whether he was frowning at the fact that she was holding Zak's hand, or if he was thinking about the sea monster that had almost dragged her down into Davy Jones' Locker. Either way, she didn't want to chat about it.

She walked briskly to the SUV and let Zak open her door and help her in. He strode around and got in the driver's side, and they were off a moment later.

CHAPTER NINE

The drive back to town didn't take long, and Zak was on the phone for most of it. He gave the details of the change in the night's meeting plans to at least three people, who would probably phone three more, and so on, until everybody had heard the news.

When they arrived at the bakery, he parked in front, turning the engine off. Then he faced her, taking her hand across the center console of the SUV.

"I'm really sorry our picnic got ruined." He seemed so serious, and she was quick to reassure him.

"It wasn't your fault. And up to that ill-fated walk by the water, I thought it was a great afternoon. You treated me like a queen, and then, you did your knight-in-shining-armor act and saved my life." She laughed and was relieved when he smiled too, briefly. "You totally impressed me, Zak, and..." She hesitated a bit, not knowing if what she was about to say was okay, but wanting him to know anyway. "I loved seeing you as a bear."

"Really?" He seemed concerned. "I didn't scare you?"

"Scare me? When you were saving my life?" Her tone was incredulous. "No way. Zak, you're amazing, and I'm so glad you were there. Human or bear, you're still Zak, and you're the bravest man I know." She leaned over and hugged him, pressing kisses to his cheek, his ear, wherever she could reach.

Emotion threatened to overcome her as she thought about the close call this afternoon. Zak was such a great guy. She had deep feelings for him, even though they'd only known each other a short time.

He held her, rubbing her back and stroking her hair as she trembled. The reaction from her brush with danger had never really dissipated. She'd been shaky since the had monster attacked, but she'd kept going. Only now did she realize she was still trembling, emotion clogging her throat.

"It's okay, baby. Let it out, if you need to. I'm here for you," he crooned near her ear, overcoming the last of her resistance.

The tears came then. Tears of anger that she'd been attacked out of the blue, for no discernible reason. Tears for the fear that had gripped her heart and tears of relief. So much relief.

Zak held her throughout, speaking soft words of reassurance.

Zak met Nell's eyes through the windshield of the SUV. She was still inside the bakery, but she'd seen them pull up and could see through the glass separating them that her little sister was upset. Zak nodded to her, glad when Nell took his signal as reassurance and backed away from the window. The last thing he wanted was the family swooping down on his SUV, disrupting this moment.

For one thing, his inner bear demanded he be the one to comfort Tina. The beast had grown very attached to the woman over the past days. In fact, the bear was downright possessive. He wanted to be the center of Tina's universe, even though the human half of him knew her family would always hold a place in her heart.

The other aspect of this situation was even more selfish. Zak just liked holding her in his arms. It broke his heart that she was so upset, but he couldn't help but feel the softness of her body against his, the silkiness of her hair under his hand, and inhale the warm, womanly scent of her wafting to his sensitive nose. She was delicious. Delectable. Delightful in every way. Everything about her satisfied his senses. More than satisfied, actually. With no effort at all, she could light him on fire with the most intense passion he'd ever known.

Oh yeah. This woman was lethal at close range, but what a way to go.

After a few more minutes, she seemed to get herself together. The trembling eased, and her tears died away naturally, leaving her face a little flushed, her eyes a little red, her nose a little runny, but even with all of that, she was still adorable to him.

Zak reached into the door console behind him and came up with a few tissues. Actually, they were paper napkins he'd gotten from somewhere, but they would do in a pinch. She accepted them gratefully, wiping at her eyes and nose as she moved back to her own side of the vehicle.

"I'm sorry for crying all over you," she said softly, hiccupping just once. He had to smile at the way she was trying to put on a brave face for him.

"I don't mind," he answered honestly. "I'm here for you, Tina. Whatever you need."

"Apparently, I needed to fall apart there for a minute. Sorry." She laughed, and he chuckled with her. "You're a very indulgent guy."

"For you? I'll be whatever you want." *Whoa. Too serious?* He watched her reaction to his words carefully. If he had to backpedal, he would, but maybe...just maybe...this afternoon's adventure—and the delicious interlude that had come before—had changed things.

She looked over at him, meeting his gaze. "You're perfect just the way you are, Zak. Anybody else would have freaked out, like I was doing. You took action. You saved me, when all I could do was panic."

"You weren't so bad," Zak told her honestly. "You were a lot calmer than you think. Give yourself some credit. You were actively fighting, buying time for me to figure out how best to attack the situation. You did really good, Tina. Never doubt it. And never doubt yourself. You're an amazing girl, and I'm really sorry our picnic got ruined."

"Hey, that wasn't your fault. There was no way to know that kind of thing was going to happen." She shuddered, but seemed to be holding together a lot better, Zak was happy to note.

"It's my land. I should have inspected the waterfront better before taking you there. I'm really sorry."

He felt terrible that he had brought her to such a dangerous place. All he'd wanted to do was have a nice, romantic picnic by the water. Instead, he brought her onto the set of a horror movie.

"You can't be responsible for the entire ocean, Zak. I know you take your duties as a deputy seriously, but that's going a little too far above and beyond, you know?" She smiled again, and he saw her point...somewhat.

"Well, I can promise you, we're not going to stop until we get to the bottom of this. Nobody is safe until we figure out what's going on in the cove." Zak knew this was going to be a difficult task, but everyone was going to work hard— especially Zak—to nail this down and make the water safe again. "Now, I saw Nell watching us, so you're probably going to be facing some questions when you go inside." He wanted her to be prepared for the sisterly third degree.

"Yeah, I figured as much." She didn't look too thrilled by the idea.

"I'll save you a seat up front at the town meeting. They may want to ask you questions about the creature." He wanted her to be ready, just in case.

"Really?" She didn't look too thrilled with that either. "I suppose... But it all happened so fast."

"If anything, they might ask about the thing's strength. How hard it was pulling you toward the water. Stuff like that. They might ask if there was anything you noticed about the suckers, or the slime. Physical stuff. I'll try to deflect as much as I can from you."

"No, it's okay. They need to know everything they can to fight this thing. It'll be okay."

He loved the way she found her courage. He was so proud of her. Zak reached over and kissed her.

The kiss wanted to turn hotter than it should for the front seat of his town-issued SUV, but he controlled himself. He backed away, letting her go by slow degrees, until he was looking deeply into her eyes. The moment felt significant.

"What was that for?" she whispered.

"For how strong you are, how brave, and how lovely," he replied in the same hushed tone of voice.

She dropped her gaze, smiling shyly. "I'm not brave."

"I beg to differ." He let her move away, each retreating to their own side of the vehicle. "You handled yourself really well today, Tina. Don't ever think differently. I was very proud of you and the way you handled yourself. I'd pick you for my team any day of the week."

He was glad to see her smile at that last bit. He thought she would be okay now. Zak opened his door and got out of the SUV. He jogged around to her side, opening the passenger door with a flourish.

"Thank you," she said demurely as she stepped down out of the vehicle.

He was probably standing too close, but he couldn't help himself, and she didn't seem to mind. In fact, she stepped closer, almost pressing against him as her gaze lifted to meet his.

"You'll be all right with your sister?" He found himself worrying about her. She nodded in response.

He still had a job to do, and for the first time in his life, he found himself conflicted between his duty and his desires. If he followed the latter, he'd stay with Tina all day, just following her around, making sure she was safe. That would probably annoy the hell out of her in short order, but keeping her out of trouble and away from all possible harm was something his bear half demanded of him.

He tried to convince himself Tina would be safe enough with her sister. The bear side wasn't quite buying it, but the minute he caught sight of Tom and Ashley sitting at a table near the front window, he relaxed just the tiniest bit. Tom was there. Tom was a large grizzly. A good bear and a good friend. He wouldn't let anything happen to any of the Baker sisters.

And all three sisters would be gathered in the bakery. Circling the wagons, so to speak. Keeping everyone together for protection. It was a good move. Zak's bear approved.

Only then could Zak step back, giving Tina room to move away from the vehicle.

* * *

Tina hadn't seen Zak since he'd dropped her off at the bakery. Tom and Ashley had stuck around all afternoon. Just before the meeting, Tina turned the sign on the door of the bakery to *closed*, and they all headed over to the half-finished building site that was going to be the new town hall. Just adjacent to the unfinished building, there was an area that had been cleared of brush and most of the trees, that would eventually function as a fully landscaped town square.

At the moment, it was still a bit rough around the edges, but there was plenty of grass for people to sit on, as well as several benches scattered around the area. There was also the beginning of a platform, which would one day become a gazebo-type building where musicians could set up and play during tourist season.

Big John had big plans for the town. This experiment in integrated bear shifter society would eventually include many more humans both living in and passing through their town. The tourists would bring in money to keep the place running while the town council carefully screened who they let in as permanent residents. They could get away with such highhanded tactics because Tom had gone to great lengths with all sorts of legal paperwork, relying on both U.S. federal laws and those governing the local Indian reservation, since part of Grizzly Cove was technically on Native American land.

The local tribe had been very willing to work with Big John, and the shaman had welcomed the *bear spirits*, as he called them, to their land. Native Americans were one of the few groups of humans who actively knew about shifters and, in most cases, welcomed them. Bear shifters, in particular, were considered good omens, as well as good neighbors to have.

Big John had spent a lot of time negotiating with the tribal elders, and Tom had drawn up many agreements between the two parties. Theirs was a symbiotic relationship. The shifters would help bring prosperity to the tribe, as best they could, while also protecting the land and preserving it for the next generation.

Tom had explained a lot about the origins of this crazy little town to pass the time during the afternoon spent huddling together at the bakery. Tina hadn't wanted to talk about her experience on the beach just yet, and thankfully, her sisters understood. Beyond a few hugs of reassurance, they had left her alone for the most part, allowing her to speak or not, as she wished.

Tom had been good company. She'd enjoyed getting to know him better this afternoon. Before he'd taken up with Ashley, he'd never been to the bakery before, so of all the people in town, he was probably the one she'd known least before a few weeks ago. Since then, of course, he'd become part of the family.

Tina liked him more each time they got to spend a little time together. Today was no exception. He'd done a wonderful job of keeping her mind off what had happened earlier in the day.

But there was no escaping those scary thoughts once she caught sight of Exhibit A sitting on ice up near the platform. They'd strung together a series of rectangular foam coolers with U-shaped holes cut out of the sides. Ice filled the containers, and the tentacle was stretched out within them, all twelve-plus feet of it.

"Holy shit," Ashley whispered as she caught sight of it. "That's what attacked you?"

Tina grimaced. "Part of it, anyway. I didn't really realize how long it was. Damn." She couldn't stop looking at it.

And then Zak was there, right in front of her, blocking her view of the tentacle that had tried to drag her under. He smiled at her, bending to kiss her cheek and whisper close to her ear. "How are you holding up?"

"I'm good. How about you?" she answered, so incredibly glad to see him again.

"Been running nonstop since I left you. It took a bit of legwork to find all those foam boxes, but I finally got enough for the display. Brody figured everyone ought to see this thing for themselves, so they know what it looks like and get a whiff of its scent."

"Good idea," Tom said from over Tina's shoulder. He'd come up behind them, sticking close to his mate.

"Thanks for what you did," Ashley said to Zak, blinking back tears as she reached out to give Zak a hug he clearly wasn't expecting.

His expression was somewhat confused as he patted her back and looked from Tom's indulgent face to Tina. She laughed and winked at him as Ashley finally let him go. Then it was Nell's turn to hug him, thanking him for saving Tina's life.

Her sisters were nothing if not demonstrative in their affection, and profuse in their thanks. Zak looked a little uncomfortable with the whole thing, but he soldiered on, accepting Nell's hug with a little less confusion.

"I saved space for you up near the front," he told Tom and the girls, "but Tina should probably sit up on the platform with me."

Tina gulped. She didn't like being the center of attention, but then again, with a twelve-foot tentacle sitting on ice right in front of her, she doubted anybody would really be looking at her. Plus, she'd be next to Zak, and if she had a choice, that's probably what she'd pick any day of the week. He was quickly becoming necessary to her existence, which was more than a little scary.

But the tentacle—and the sea monster it belonged to—was way scarier.

CHAPTER TEN

The meeting didn't turn out to be so bad. Zak sat next to her, and everyone in town took seats all around in small groupings on the grass. It looked like a giant picnic, or maybe how the concerts that would be held in the future on this spot might look, except for the mile-long tentacle sitting up on the stage.

Everybody wore serious expressions and listened attentively when John opened the meeting. He laid out what was going on in a succinct, military-style briefing before turning over the floor to Zak. He stood and told the story from his point of view, again using that military-style format that was brief, while leaving nothing out.

He went on to describe what he had observed of the beast's strength and what it had felt like to both claw it and chew through it. He described the taste and the smell on levels Tina guessed you'd have to be a shifter to appreciate. To her, it just smelled fishy, but Zak's report made her realize that shifters experienced things about the physical world that were way beyond human senses.

The talk turned to magic, and that's when Tina realized she really wasn't in Kansas anymore. They spoke of magic as if it was a real thing. A thing with substance and origins and rules. She'd never thought of it that way, and she was getting a heck of an education just from listening to Zak's brief descriptions of what he saw when he looked at the severed arm of the beast.

Then it was her turn to be asked questions. She tried to be as concise as the men, but she found herself floundering a couple of times. No, she didn't know how to describe the pulling force of the tentacle other than it was really strong. And no, she wasn't really aware if it applied torque while it tried to drag her into the ocean.

Tina didn't even know what *torque* was. But Zak helped answer the questions she had no clue about, and between the two of them, she got through the Q&A session with most of her pride intact. She was glad her sisters were in the audience and Zak was at her side. With her sisters, their new mates, and especially Zak nearby, she felt safe.

She knew most of the other people in town from their visits to the bakery, but this was the first time she'd seen most of them in what she thought of privately as *battle mode*. They were like bloodhounds on a scent, looking for any clue to pick up the trail of the monster that had attacked out of the water.

However, it soon became apparent that the answer wasn't going to be found right there in the half-finished town square. It might not be found at all, for that matter. John took over the meeting again, filling everyone in on his plans for the *evidence*, and the calls he had made earlier that day.

"We're shipping this thing to the Lords for examination by the High Priestess. She's the best equipped to get to the bottom of the magical nature of this beast. I am going to keep a hunk of it to show to the Native shaman on my next visit. I'm also going to pass on the warning post-haste, in case this thing isn't limited to the cove. It's a big ocean out there, and our Native friends fish in it, same as us." John waited for the nods of agreement to run their course before continuing. "I'm also talking to Master Hiram later tonight, after he rises." This time, some of the shifters jerked their heads up in surprise. "He's been around a long time, and his yacht was munched on—possibly by this thing, or one of its larger cousins. I want to compare his experience battling the beast to what we have here. Lou, Granger, I want you both on the intel side of this." John pointed to two men sitting toward the back. They both nodded.

Tina knew them. Lou was an accountant who did taxes for most of the folks in town, and Granger was a bit of a recluse who was a wiz with all kinds of electronics. He'd fixed the bakery's wi-fi several times already and had volunteered his services anytime the sisters needed tech help.

"Drew, Sig, I want you on the lookout from your boats, but I don't want you out there on the water if you sense the least bit of trouble. In fact, I'd say the town can do without fresh fish for a bit, until this mystery is solved. I don't want to lose either of you, even if you are both pains in my ass," John groused good naturedly, drawing chuckles from the crowd and casual little salutes from the men in question.

Both men were commercial fishermen. Drew went out almost every day, catching all sorts of fish that he sold on to Sig, who owned the local fish market, bait and tackle shop. Sig fished closer to shore in the mornings, then opened the shop later in the day, while Drew preferred fishing out farther in the ocean and not dealing with people at all, besides Sig.

The meeting broke up with a few more tasks handed out and a general admonition to stay away from the water unless absolutely necessary. Everyone seemed to accept John's advice with a sense of determination rather than fear. It was clear to her that these people were used to facing adversity and overcoming it. It felt to Tina like they planned to do so again with this obstacle.

Nobody looked afraid, which gave her a bit of added strength. If this community of hella strong bear shifters couldn't deal with this little sea monster problem, she had the feeling nobody could.

* * *

The sisters went back to the bakery to wait for Brody and Zak. Both of the town's lawmen had to deal with the *evidence* before they could knock off for the evening, and they all planned to meet up at the bakery.

A few of the locals decided to follow the sisters, and they spent an hour or two selling bread, sandwiches and sweet treats to their fellow cove residents. Talk was general, and only a few dared ask Tina more about her run in with the creature.

A single stranger drove up, just after dark, in a vehicle that had a Seattle courier firm's logo on the side. Much to Tina's surprise, it was a special delivery from Master Hiram. He'd sent three cases of the finest vintages the famous Maxwell Winery had to offer, and a note of thanks for helping him when he was in need.

Deciding she deserved a little treat after the day she'd had, Tina cracked open a bottle of merlot and shared it with her sisters. Before she knew it, Zak was back, Brody coming in right behind him.

Brody claimed Nell and took her off to their home in the woods. Tom and Ashley left next, only after asking several times if Tina was sure she'd be okay. She assured them she would be fine and sent a few pointed looks at her sister, making Ash finally realize Tina wouldn't be alone if she had her way. She just needed her well-meaning sister to leave.

Ash gave her an exaggerated wink and a double thumbs up on the sly. So at least one of her sisters approved her of hooking up with Zak. That was good. If Ash thought Zak was okay, chances were Nell would too.

Finally, Ash and Tom left, and Tina locked up behind them. She didn't ask Zak to leave, and—heaven be praised— he didn't look like he was going anywhere fast.

Finally. They were alone.

Tina hit the lights as she walked slowly toward Zak, putting a little extra sway in her hips. She picked up the half-finished bottle of wine they'd been working on and let it dangle from one hand as she sauntered right up to Zak and put her free arm around his neck, drawing him down for a kiss.

No words were exchanged, but she told him as eloquently as she could how she wanted this night to end. His kiss was his agreement, and they spent long moments drinking each other in before he finally ended the kiss and turned toward the stairs.

He hit the final light switch before they entered the private staircase, heading up to the apartment together.

When they reached the top of the stairs, Zak was careful to lock the door behind them. He took security very seriously, and she appreciated his attention to detail. In fact, she hoped he'd give that same attention to something a lot more private in the very near future.

She led him toward her bedroom, the wine bottle still dangling from her hand. She had taken over the master bath when her sisters had moved out. It was right next to her room and boasted an extra large jetted tub. Perfect for what she had in mind.

Zak quirked an eyebrow at her when she led him into the bathroom instead of her bedroom, but smiled, letting her lead. At least for now. He was very easygoing that way, and she liked that about him. His slow, almost lazy, smile did things to her insides that probably ought to be illegal.

Man, the guy was lethal.

She shivered, knowing they had the whole apartment to themselves. Blessed privacy. The perfect setting for debauchery of the finest caliber. At least, as much as she could make up in her somewhat limited imagination. The inner bad girl hadn't had all that much experience at letting loose, but she was trying to cultivate the vixen a bit more. Zak had a way of bringing it out in her.

She left the wine bottle on the countertop and turned to Zak. Her fingers got busy on his buttons, so she could shove his shirt out of her way and freeing his lovely tanned skin. She kissed and nibbled as she went along, baring his torso rather quickly with his help.

She spent a little more time on his lower half, drawing out the scene as much as she could. She wanted him to enjoy this as much as she was. She wanted to make him pant, to make him sweat, to make him want her as much as she wanted him.

Judging by the bulge in his trousers, her plan was working. She smiled as she unzipped him, pushing the pants down over his hips.

He kissed her, moving close, his hands grasping her upper arms as he moved her back toward the wall. She was still dressed, and that couldn't be allowed to continue much longer. She wanted to feel his skin against hers. The fabric between them was annoying. She didn't want anything to keep them apart.

She tugged at her clothes, as he did, the tempestuous kiss making them both a little clumsy. Eventually though, she felt the shirt go, and the bra. And then, he was crushing her chest against his, even as he continued to kiss her like there was no tomorrow.

Her nipples hardened and practically begged for his touch. He drew away, moving downward, his hands making short work of the rest of her clothing. Soon, they were both bare, and he was kneeling at her feet, her back against the wall.

He smiled up at her, and she caught her breath. What was he...?

Oh. My. God.

Zak had leaned in and applied his mouth to the apex of her thighs, zeroing right in on the little nub that made her entire body clench in pleasure. Her head went back, rolling against the wall as he brought her to a quick, breathless peak. Sweet heaven above, he was good. He seemed to know exactly what she needed to drive her straight out of her ever lovin' mind.

"Zak!" she cried out when things got a little too intense. She didn't want to move this fast. She'd had big plans for him—what she wanted to do with him and, especially, *to him.*

Zak chuckled, and she felt the rumble of it against her clit. He drew away with a last lingering lick, only to stand and take her into his arms.

"That's what I like to hear," he said, smiling even as he lifted her over the edge of the big tub. "My name never sounded better, honey. You say it that way every time, and you can have anything you want. Guaranteed."

"What if all I want is you?" she challenged, letting her inner vixen out to play.

"You got me, baby. Any way, any time, any place. I'm yours." He held his hands out to his sides almost comically, but his eyes were serious. Something big was happening here. She could feel it.

And she wanted it. She wanted it all. She wanted him...forever.

"Same goes for me," she dared to whisper.

But she chickened out before he could respond, grabbing the bottle of wine off the counter and taking a hearty sip. Dutch courage? Maybe. But she had a few other ideas about what to do with this fine vintage.

He took the bottle gently from her hands and took a long sip of his own. Then he put his thumb over the top, pouring out a little bit on her shoulder, letting it drip down her chest, onto her breasts.

Apparently, their minds had been thinking along the same lines. She giggled, realizing he'd reversed her fantasy. She'd thought she would be doing this to him, not the other way around, but she was willing to go with the flow. It felt too decadent not to see where he was leading with this imaginative foreplay.

"This is one of the finest vintages from one of the finest wineries in the world, you know," Zak said, almost conversationally, as he allowed more of the wine to dribble down her body. "It is spectacular on its own, but on you, my dear, I think it's going to be even better." He licked his lips and grinned at her before leaning down to capture her nipple—and the droplets of wine that had caught there—in his warm, wet, welcoming mouth.

Tina's knees went weak as he licked his way over her chest

211

and eventually down to her belly button. Her knees gave out when his fingers swept into her body, pulsing and rubbing against that secret spot inside that only he had ever found.

Zak caught her, bringing her down beside him in the large tub. He placed the wine bottle on the floor, then reached behind himself to turn on the taps, mixing hot and cold until he found the perfect temperature.

The big tub filled quickly with them both in it, and he flipped the switch to make the bubbles come on. They'd both had a long day, and a quick soak was probably a good thing. Especially considering the bruises she could now see forming along her leg. Zak noticed the direction of her gaze and lifted her abused leg out of the water, placing it over his shoulder as she reclined against the back of the tub.

"My poor baby," he whispered, kissing the booboos that were a harsh reminder of everything they'd been through today. As far as eventful days went, this was one for the books. "Does it hurt a lot?"

"Not really," she answered as he examined each bruise in minute detail. "Just when you press on it. Or when I move the wrong way. Otherwise, I think it's just going to be colorful for a while."

"Yeah, I hate to say it, but these are going to look worse before they get better." He lowered her leg back into the effervescent water. "You're in for a colorful few days." He held her gaze as he moved through the water to take her into his arms. The giant tub was big enough for them to move around a bit. "You'll tell me right away if anything we do hurts your leg, right?"

The request almost sounded like an order, but she understood his concern. Zak was nothing if not thoughtful. She thought it was sweet that he didn't want to cause her any more discomfort than she was already feeling.

"I promise. But honestly, when we're together, I only feel the good stuff," she assured him, patting his chest and smiling up at his handsome face.

"I like that," he said, holding her gaze. "With you, Tina,

there's nothing but good stuff. And I have to tell you, that's new for me."

"For me too," she admitted shyly.

He stopped talking, diverting his attention instead to lathering up her body and his own, cleaning them off, one limb at a time. He paid special attention to her damaged leg and, much to her surprise, seemed to be very serious about getting them both clean. He might've stroked her skin a bit more gently than strictly necessary, but he didn't allow her to touch him, even when she tried to give him a bit of what he'd already given her.

"Patience," he counseled, moving her roving hands away from his cock. "I'll give you everything you want, honey, but I want to do it in a bed this time. You deserve gentle care after everything you went through today. Bathtub sex isn't for wounded girls. There's too much potential for further injury. I'm going to keep you safe tonight, Tina. And that means a soft bed under us."

Her heart melted right then and there. What a great guy.

A few minutes later, after he'd dried every inch of her body with one of her fluffy towels, he carried her into her bedroom and placed her on the bed. He wouldn't let her lift a single finger, convincing her that he would do all the *work* tonight.

"Aren't you going to let me do anything?" she asked.

"Nope."

"Ever?" she wheedled.

"Well, maybe some other time, but not right now, okay? I'm enjoying this too much."

She didn't argue. It was enough to know that at some point, in the future, it would be her turn.

"Okay, but I have plans for you when it's my turn, big guy," she told him with teasing promise.

He agreed that sounded like a whole lot of fun, but for tonight, he would be calling the shots. The first of which seemed to be getting inside her.

She wasn't objecting. She'd had plenty of foreplay in the

bathroom. She was more than ready for him to be inside her, but after he slid in…slowly…inch by inch…he just…stopped.

He stopped and looked deep into her eyes. It was like their hearts were beating in time. Like the whole world had stopped spinning on its axis for this moment out of time.

"This is something special," he said in a voice so low and rumbly she almost came right there on the spot. "Tell me you feel it too."

"I do," she whispered. "I feel it."

Something that looked like triumph entered his gaze. "Say you'll be only with me, Tina. I want this to be exclusive."

Oh, hell yeah! She smiled up at him. "If you promise the same, I'm yours, Zak. I don't want to share you with anyone else."

His grin lit his face. Damn, he was so incredibly handsome. How in the world did she manage to catch a guy like him? What pagan god had smiled on her and given her this amazing man, who wanted to be exclusive with her…whatever that turned out to mean down the line?

She wasn't going to look a gift horse in the mouth. If they were taking this one step at a time, he'd just taken a big one. Exclusivity after only one real date? Yeah, by human standards, they were moving fast. By shifter standards? She wasn't sure. Those boys her sisters had brought home had moved awfully quick from dating to mating. But if Zak wanted to take things a little slower, she wasn't going to argue.

"I'll be true to you, Tina. My bear doesn't know any other way to be. And it likes you a lot. It wants to wrap you in our arms and keep you safe from anything that might ever possibly hurt you. It was so angry at what happened today, and so proud to be able to free you from that thing's clutches."

"I loved seeing your bear, Zak. I loved that you saved me." She almost admitted she loved *him*, but that would never do.

If he wanted to go slow, she was going to abide by his rules. He was calling the shots. At least for tonight. She'd agreed to those terms, and she'd stick with it.

He let out a sound that was like a low rumble through his chest, like the bear was growling, although it wasn't a scary sound. It was more like purring. A happy, satisfied sort of rumble.

"The bear likes what you said. It likes when we make love, and it really enjoys when I lick you." His grin turned devilish, and his eyes glinted with naughty amusement.

"You don't say?" She caught his teasing mood, willing to go with the flow. "I wonder what he'll think when I lick you." She felt his cock jerk inside her, and she chuckled.

"Not tonight," he cautioned, almost as if he was reminding himself as well as her. "Not until your leg is healed."

"Spoilsport."

She stuck her tongue out at him, and he swooped down and caught it in his mouth.

He kissed her as he began a steady, increasing pace that ultimately led them to the oblivion of a pleasure so great she passed out for a few seconds right there at the end.

That had never happened before.

It was scary good.

Zak stayed inside her almost constantly that night, waking her every few hours to make love again. She loved every scandalous, delicious, overwhelming moment of it. And she wanted him like a drug she had just become addicted to.

Zak was lethal in the sexiest way possible, and she wanted more.

She woke him in the morning, dragging him into the shower for a quick wash before she finally convinced him to let her go down on him. She wasn't taking no for an answer, even though her leg had stiffened up a bit overnight. She simply made him stand in front of her while she sat on the bed—after their shower but before they were dressed—and she licked him like a lollipop. A hard, long, devastatingly masculine lollipop.

Naughtiness ensued, and pretty soon, she ended up back on the bed, her legs in the air. He was careful of her stiff leg, but he definitely let her know how much he'd enjoyed her attentions, in the most delicious way possible.

When they were done, they had to hop in the shower again, but neither of them minded. Tina had a permanent smile on her face as she took her time finishing up in the shower, and Zak went on ahead to raid the kitchen, searching for breakfast.

CHAPTER ELEVEN

Zak looked perfectly at home in front of the stove, wielding a spatula like the knights of old probably wielded their swords. In other words, he was the consummate professional, with multiple pans filled with different enticing dishes, all going at once. There were scrambled eggs, laced with finely chopped chives and peppers freshly picked from the rooftop garden, seasoned potatoes that smelled divine, bacon cooking to perfection with a hint of maple in the air, and it looked like chocolate chip pancakes as some sort of dessert.

Dessert with breakfast? She wasn't going to argue. She knew from being around her brothers-in-law that bear shifters ate an awful lot. Zak would probably pack away most of this feast, but she wouldn't mind tasting at least a little bit of each of the dishes he was preparing.

She walked up to him, and he turned with a smile, leaning down to kiss her.

"Mmm. Good morning," she said, still a little sleepy. "Wish we didn't have to get up so early today."

"Sorry. Have to. I'm on duty at nine. I hope you don't mind I took a look around up on the roof then helped myself to some of the produce you grow up there. It's really amazing what you've done with the garden." He seemed so wide awake—bright-eyed and bushy-tailed as the saying went— that she couldn't cultivate her usual morning grumpiness.

Especially not after the night before. He'd shown her things she'd never known existed about pleasure. If their interlude in the grass had been hot—before being disrupted by a sea monster—last night had been explosive. Chernobyl-meltdown explosive, but in a good way.

His lovemaking was powerful, but not harmful in any way, except maybe to her heart. Yeah, after what they'd shared last night, she was well and truly in love with the guy. Bear. Man. Bear guy. She shrugged. *Whatever.*

She was still groggy when Zak stepped away and poured her a cup of coffee. He placed it in her hands with a smile, and she sipped.

Heaven. Somehow, Zak had a talent that even made regular coffee beans taste better. He was some kind of genius in the kitchen, she was quickly discovering.

They sat down to breakfast side by side at the kitchen table, spending the time together just enjoying each other's company. Tina wasn't a morning person as a rule, but just being with Zak improved her disposition. She couldn't seem to stop smiling, and everything he'd cooked tasted out of this world.

"You ever think of opening a restaurant?" she asked between bites of the fluffiest, tastiest eggs she'd ever eaten.

"All the time." He looked almost shy as he answered quietly. "I love to cook. Always have. But my life's path hasn't always been of my own choosing. Being a shifter limits you in some ways."

She contemplated his words as she nibbled at her small serving of spicy potatoes. "But the trade off is pretty awesome." She smiled at him and was glad to see the humor return to his expression. "I think you'd be a great restaurateur. I'd help. And the bakery could supply all the bread you need. Unless… You don't bake, do you?"

He chuckled. "No. I don't have the patience for it."

"Okay then. So what's standing in your way?" She sensed

a problem she could help solve. She'd already been through the creation of two new food businesses—the one here and the original in Portland. She'd learned a thing or two.

"Mostly, it's a matter of money," he revealed. "I don't have enough to build my house and start a business at the same time. I thought maybe after I got the house built, I'd begin saving up for the restaurant, but I don't have the kind of funds some of the guys do, and I don't really want to be indebted to any of them. I've run the numbers, and it'll be years before I could even think of turning a profit in this remote a location, even with the projections Big John has on increasing tourism in the summer months."

"I'm impressed. It sounds like you've really looked at this seriously," she said, meaning every word. She hadn't dreamed there was such depth to her deputy. "But if it's what you really want to do, there's got to be a way to figure out how to make it happen. Like I said, I'll help. In any way that I can."

"I appreciate that, Tina. I really do." He held her gaze for a moment before returning to the project of demolishing the huge portion of eggs and bacon he'd dished up for himself. That, it seemed, was the end of that.

Tina decided to let the topic lie. She'd heard the disappointment in his voice when he'd talked about the realities of the situation. She had learned something important about Zak in this brief exchange.

He had a dream, but he didn't have the resources to make it work just yet. Maybe he never would. But Tina was no slouch when it came to business. She resolved to quietly look into things. Maybe there was something she could do to help.

As it turned out, when the mail arrived just after Zak had left for work, a potential solution presented itself. Master Hiram had sent a thank you letter—along with a very fat check. His note said the money was to cover any clean up or *inconvenience* his recent visit might have caused.

She snorted at the euphemism. It would have been really *inconvenient* if he had killed someone in his blood-starved state. Zak had explained what he knew about vampires and the dire straits Hiram must've been in when he arrived, bleeding, on her doorstep.

Tina couldn't accept such a large check from the Master, but his letter did give her an idea. She just had to call John to run it past him first, since the Alpha bear might object to getting the Master vampire involved any further in the doings of Grizzly Cove.

Later that evening, after speaking with John, and just before Zak usually arrived at the bakery to keep watch over her for the night, Tina had a window of opportunity. She placed the call to Hiram's private number just after dark.

"Master Hiram? This is Tina Baker in Grizzly Cove." She was nervous, but she would do just about anything to help Zak achieve his dream.

"What can I do for you, Miss Baker?" If the vampire was surprised by her call, his urbane manner hid it well.

"I wanted to thank you for the wine and let you know that, while I appreciate the gesture, I cannot accept the check that arrived today." She didn't pause to let him argue but forged right ahead. "However, I do have a proposal I'd like to put forth, with Big John's agreement."

She drew breath while, it seemed, Hiram thought over her words. Finally, he broke the silence.

"I must admit, I am intrigued. What do you propose, Miss Baker?"

"The deputy, Zak Flambeau, is a close…uh…friend of mine." Darn it. She could've phrased that a little better. "It turns out, he has always dreamed of opening a restaurant, but he doesn't have the capital yet to both build his new home on the property he just purchased and build a restaurant. If you're willing, the Alpha has agreed that the money you so generously offered to give me could be put to better use building a new business here in Grizzly Cove, in which you'd be a silent partner. You can work out the political details with John, but when I spoke to him, he liked the idea of a closer alliance between his people and yours and thought this might be a good first step."

She skipped the part about John thinking it was hilariously ironic that a vampire who couldn't eat food would be part owner of a restaurant.

"Does your...*friend*...know about your ideas yet?" Hiram sounded amused.

"Zak? Um, no, not yet. He should be arriving here in a few minutes, and I wanted to talk to you first."

"My dear, I admire your pluck." Hiram was chuckling quietly on the other end of the line. "By all means, lay out your plan for the deputy and let him know that I can easily double the sum, if needed. I will, indeed, call John Marshall to confirm and clarify all points of this arrangement, but I, too, like the sound of an alliance. Everything I've seen of your little community impresses me, and I think it's important for those of us on the side of Light to band together at this time."

She didn't understand everything he was implying, but she shivered, realizing the vampire Master had confirmed some of the exact thoughts John had shared with her. This was more than a business partnership. This was going to be the beginning of an alliance between the Master vampire—and those under his command—and the shifters of Grizzly Cove. Tina hadn't realized it when she'd come up with the idea of how to use Hiram's money, but apparently, she was brokering a diplomatic deal here, even as she tried to help Zak start his business.

"Thank you so much," she said, realizing Zak's dream was well on its way to coming true with Hiram's backing.

"You're very welcome, my dear. Now, I heard you had a run-in with a mini version of what attacked my yacht," Hiram said, surprising her.

She told him what she could about the tentacle that had come out of the cove to grab her leg, comparing notes with him on his own experience. They arrived at the scary conclusion that whatever had attacked Tina had, indeed, been a much smaller version of what had chomped on Hiram's yacht and injured him so grievously.

"I think it's best that we all stay far away from the water for the time being," he concluded. "Until we figure out what, exactly, is down there, lurking in the depths, it seems we are all in danger. I will talk more with John about this, but thank you for sharing your experiences. Now, about the restaurant—I'd be obliged if you told Zak that I can arrange for the best vintages from the Maxwell Winery, if he'd like. Similar to the cases I sent you. Atticus Maxwell is an old friend of mine, and he owes me a favor."

Tina had an inkling of what a coup that would be for Zak's business, since the Maxwell Winery was one of the very best in the world and had limited distribution. To be able to count on serving their wines in Zak's restaurant was a very exciting prospect.

"Oh! I'll tell him. Thank you so much, Master Hiram. I know he was really impressed with the bottles we opened last night. He told me all about the awards Maxwell had won and how hard it was to come by some of his best vintages."

"Please, my dear, call me Hiram. I sense your discomfort with my title, and to be frank, you are one of the first mortals I have spoken to casually in a very long time. I'd like it if you might consider me a friend."

Tina thought about that for a moment, then smiled. "Then please call me Tina, Hiram. I'm glad you found my bakery when you needed help, even if I was a bit confused about the situation at the time."

"Confused is much better than frightened, I assure you," he admitted in a quiet voice. She got the feeling he didn't confide in anyone, and her heart went out to him for what must be a very lonely existence. "Zak is a very brave individual, and I think you will find great happiness together. I'm glad to be part of building your future, even in this small way. Please feel free to call anytime, Tina. I find I have enjoyed talking with you." He seemed almost surprised by his last statement.

"When we open the restaurant, I hope you can come to the party."

"I'll discuss that—and many other points—with the Alpha, but I think this marks a new era of cooperation between our communities. I confess, I am somewhat amazed that this has all come about due to your generous thoughts and actions. I did not know mortals still had hearts so big that they could accept and even want to help those of us who are so different."

"I don't think you're that different, Hiram," she said softly. "You can still be hurt, even with all your power. You still feel. You still have hopes and—like Zak and his restaurant—dreams. What I've seen since I learned shifters were real, and now knowing that your kind exists as well, tells me that we're not all that different inside, where it counts."

"You are very wise for one so young," Hiram said after a moment's pause. "I look forward to seeing what you and Zak build together, and I wish you all the best."

"Thanks, Hiram. I'm sure Zak will want to thank you himself when he learns of my scheming, but I know he's going to be so very grateful. He really is a genius in the kitchen, and I think he's felt as if he hasn't contributed any *art* to the whole artists' colony concept here. If he has a kitchen of his own, there will be artistry, I can assure you. And the whole town will benefit. Thanks to you."

"Mostly to you, my dear," he corrected her. "Without your generous heart, this project would never have been devised."

They hung up after a few more words, and Tina couldn't keep the smile off her face. Zak was going to get his restaurant a lot sooner than he thought.

CHAPTER TWELVE

Zak couldn't really believe how fast things started moving once Tina decided he should open his restaurant. Not only had she figured out a plan to make it happen, she'd cleared it with John and Master Hiram even before telling Zak about it.

Nobody had ever gone so far out of their way for him before. He felt...loved.

They hadn't talked about their feelings since he'd dared to ask her to see him exclusively. He was trying to go slow, to win over her human sensibilities, but then she went and did something like this...

He didn't know what to think. He was touched. Humbled and touched so very deeply. He couldn't voice his feelings. He only knew how to show her. And he did his best to show her each and every time they made love after that amazing night when she'd gone out of her way to help him make his business dreams come true.

Zak spent every night in the apartment above the bakery with Tina and almost every moment off-duty with her. She was helping him plan the restaurant, and Big John had given him the empty lot next to the bakery to build it on. With Hiram's money, they were able to fast-track the project, getting architectural plans prepared sooner than Zak would have believed.

About a week after she'd surprised him with the business proposal for Hiram's money, she was seated beside him as his building plans went up before the town council for consideration and approval.

The process wasn't overly complicated, but even though Brody and John had seen the plans, the rest of the top lieutenants would get a chance to comment and make suggestions before the project could get started. John ran the group that way. Always had. He was a lot more democratic than many shifter leaders. Then again, bears were a lot more independent than most other groups of shifters. And this group was made up of many different kinds of bears.

John was the kind of leader who could hold such a diverse group together. Few others had the kind of charisma and patience it took to deal with this crazy band of shifters and the social experiment they were all engaging in by building this new community.

"Up for consideration next is Zak and Tina's new restaurant," John said, catching Zak by surprise, finally turning the agenda to Zak's big moment.

Copies of the plans were spread out on the big table around which the town council was gathered. A few of the guys leaned in for a closer look at the blueprints, and Zak held his breath until he saw them nodding as they examined the plans.

"Financing for this deal is something special," John went on, regaining the attention of the rest of the group. "The lovely and talented Tina Baker has brokered a deal with Master Hiram of Seattle. He's fronting the money to build the restaurant and will be a silent partner."

"Is that wise?" one of the men asked. "Do we want to be that deeply entwined with the vampire master?"

John sighed deeply before answering. "I think we have no choice but to embrace a closer relationship with anyone who's on the right side of things. Hiram is sworn to the Light. As are we. If that sea monster and its ugly friends are on the other side—which I tend to believe—we might need all the allies we can find. Plus, with what's been going on in the wider world—all the strange and troubling events of the past few months I've been briefed on by the Lords—I like the idea of having an ancient and powerful vamp to call on if we need help out here."

"This arrangement also helps Master Hiram keep up his façade of mortality. We can all swear to seeing him eat, right? And he gets to be a restaurateur in a town that will back him up, no questions asked," Tom added.

"Hiram has good contacts too," Tina put in, doing her best to help. "He's arranging for the Maxwell Winery in Napa to provide some of their rarest and best vintages for the cellar. That might bring in more of Hiram's people who want to spend an evening at the seaside, which means more revenue for the town. From what I understand, most of those vampires are loaded."

Zak had to chuckle at Tina's enthusiasm. He put his hand over hers on the table, and she beamed over at him. With her on his side, he couldn't help but come out on top, right?

"What it boils down to is this…" John said, taking over the meeting once more. "We all know how good Zak is in the kitchen. Food prep is his art. It's what he can contribute to the community, even more than being the deputy sheriff. Frankly, if we keep growing—and I think we're on a good path for growth right now—we're going to need to expand the police force anyway. More than that, we're going to need more businesses for the townsfolk and all those tourists we hope to attract down the road. We have the bakery, but as hard as the sisters try, they can't offer three meals a day for everyone in town, and a lot of us bachelors still don't know how to cook much more than steaks on the grill. Am I right?" Nods all around greeted the Alpha's rhetorical question. "Zak's place will offer an alternative. Something a little heartier than the sandwiches and sweets at the bakery. Something we can enjoy for dinner that we don't have to cook ourselves or hunt in our fur. What do you say?"

A quick vote was taken, and the plan unanimously passed

without much further ado. Tina laced her fingers with Zak's, squeezing hard as her excitement bled through.

They could've left then, but there was only one further item on the agenda, and Zak was interested to see how the vote was going to go. A proposal had been put forward by two human sisters who wanted to open a bookstore. The plan had made it through Tom and Ashley's first look, and up to John's level. Now it was going to be put before the council.

"Last item for tonight," Tom took over, opening his file. "Ursula and Amelia Ricoletti. Human sisters. They want to open a bookstore. We've checked them out, and they look like they would fit in well."

"What do we need a bookstore for?" Sig, the owner of the one and only fish market, asked.

"Some of us like to read, Sig," Tom replied with a chuckle.

"Some of us *know* how to read," Peter, the Russian, quipped, throwing a wadded up paper lightly in Sig's direction.

Sig laughed with them, holding up his hands in mock surrender. "Okay, okay. Keep your hair on."

"They're female, Sig. Who cares what kind of store they open?" Drew, the other fisherman in the group, joked. "Look how well the last three worked out." He sent Tina and Zak a knowing look. "It'd be nice to have more women around here. Maybe give the rest of us a chance to find a mate. Even a human mate is way better than no mate at all."

The vote was taken, and the decision made. The town was growing—slowly but growing. Things were changing in Grizzly Cove.

Talk turned to the sea monster and what they'd been able to find out about it so far. Not much, as it turned out, though experts were still looking into it.

The meeting broke up with the continuing admonition to stay away from the water for now, and to keep sharp eyes out for anything odd. Everyone was on watch.

Tina and Zak walked back to the bakery arm in arm. They'd walked the short distance down Main Street to the meeting and paused on their way back in the lot next door to the bakery, looking at the site where, very shortly, construction would begin on Zak's dream. Now it seemed to be Tina's dream too—for him.

Zak couldn't really get over it. She'd gone behind his back to arrange things for him in an act of sacrifice and care that humbled him. She could have easily pocketed the very generous check Master Hiram had sent her, and Zak never would have thought twice about it. Instead, she'd refused to accept Hiram's generosity on her own behalf and, instead, had talked the vampire into investing in him—in Zak.

How had he gotten so lucky to find a woman like her? Zak felt truly blessed for the first time in his life. As if the Goddess Herself was looking down on him and smiling, giving him a chance to have things go right—really right—for the first time in his private life.

He'd thought he felt the blessing of the Lady of Light a few times in his work. In the field, he'd gotten away with moves that should've seen him eating a bullet one too many times to doubt that the Goddess existed and gave the occasional helping hand to those who had sworn to serve Her.

Zak's faith was powerful but also very private. He knew humans believed differently, but he hoped Tina would agree to be his mate in the shifter way, with the blessing of a priestess. He'd have to figure out the best way to ask her, though. As it was, he hadn't even been able to tell her how much he loved her yet.

He wanted to spend the rest of his life with her, but he wasn't sure she fully understood shifter mating. Bears mated for life, and now that he'd found Tina, he knew there would never be another woman for him. Even if she refused his proposal, he would never be able to commit to another. She was it for him. His one chance at a life full of the love he'd always craved, and had never really believed he would find.

He was truly blessed to have found her. Now he just had to figure out how to convince her to spend the rest of her life with him.

"The kitchen will be about here, right?" she asked, having left his side to walk over the empty lot that would eventually become home to their new restaurant. Zak joined her, putting his arm around her shoulders.

"Yep," he whispered into the early evening darkness, illuminated faintly by the streetlights on Main Street, which were more for decoration and charm than security, and the brilliant moon above. "Kitchen will be back here. Stairs going up to the apartments above and a communicating door with the back of the bakery. We can meet in the hall for a little hanky panky when things are slow," he teased.

Her sister, Nell, was covering for her in the bakery tonight since she'd wanted to be with Zak at the meeting. It was a rare night off for them both, and although they probably should go back and relieve Nell, Zak couldn't help but want to spend more time alone with his mate.

"Or any old time," she whispered back, looking up at him, her eyes glinting in the faint light.

"Will you marry me?"

Zak didn't mean to blurt it out just like that, but the moment had overcome him. Her beautiful face, lit by moonlight. The hope of the place where they stood. He'd just been moved to ask.

And now he was nervous as tears filled her eyes. She looked so startled. Like a deer in headlights that was going to cry, but whether in joy or heartbreak, he wasn't sure. He had to say something to make it better. He'd been an ass to blurt it out like that. *Dammit.*

"I mean..." He searched for words. "You're my mate, Tina. My bear knew it from almost the first time we were together. It just took my human side a bit longer to catch up and gather the courage."

She remained silent, and he didn't know what to do. Finally, he realized there was something missing. Something he'd never admitted to her out loud, though he'd done his best to show her every time they made love. But the time was now. He had to tell her.

Zak drew a deep breath, then bared his soul. "I love you, Tina. I love you with everything I am, and I will love you for eternity. Please say you'll be mine."

The tears fell then, and she lifted up on tiptoe, drawing closer to him.

"I love you too," she whispered into the magical dimness of the moonlit night. "I love you, Zak, and I want to be with you forever. For always."

"You'll be my mate?" He gathered her trembling hands against his chest, not daring to believe she was agreeing.

"Yes, I'll marry you. Mate you. Whatever you want. I want us to be together."

He lifted her in his arms and spun her, his happiness overflowing his heart and lighting up the world. At least it felt that way.

He kissed her, tasting the salty tears of joy mixing in. Hers. His. It didn't matter. They were both feeling too much to contain. Too much joy. Too much happiness. But never too much love.

Long minutes later—how long, he didn't know—he let her down to stand on her own feet again, though he kept his arms around her. They were standing in the empty lot that represented so much hope for their future...together.

Tina cupped his cheek in her hand, drawing his gaze to hers in the moonlight. She looked so serious all of a sudden, he frowned a little.

"Are you disappointed I'm not a shifter?" Tina asked, fearing his answer. But she had to know the truth.

"Never," Zak answered immediately. "Never think that," he whispered more tenderly.

His eyes were shining as she knew hers were. The moment was emotional, and she liked that he didn't hide his reaction from her. He was such a strong man he could never look weak to her. Even overcome with emotion, he only showed his confidence and strength of personality. He was such a great guy. She didn't know what had made him fall in love with her, but she'd do all she could in the future to keep him as happy as they were at this moment.

"The Goddess made you just for me," Zak went on, surprising her. "You are perfect just the way you are." He placed gentle kisses on her face that made her feel cherished in the most amazing way. No man had ever made her feel as special as Zak did.

He surprised her by dropping to one knee, right there in the grass and wildflowers, taking her hand in his. He looked up at her, his face illuminated by the glimmering, romantic moon. He was so handsome it stole her breath.

"Will you marry me in a ceremony the way humans do?" he asked, looking up at her so earnestly she could only nod as tears fell freely once more. "And will you also join with me under the blessings of a priestess of the Lady? The way shifters do? I want it to be official in every way possible, recognized by my people and yours, legally and spiritually, in front of your God and my Lady. What do you think?"

He looked so nervous that she dropped to her knees right there in the empty lot and took both of his hands in hers. The moment was solemn in a way she'd never expected.

"I'd be honored, Zak. And I'm incredibly touched that you'd ask." Tears were rolling down her face, but she didn't care. "I love you so much. I've loved you for a long time, but I never dared dream you'd feel the same. I want what you want, Zak. I want you to be happy and to have all your dreams come true."

"You've already shown me that," he replied, laughing through the tears. "I can't believe what you did with Master Hiram, and giving up all that money so I could build my dream business."

"*Our* dream business," she corrected him. "When I heard how you felt about the restaurant, I decided then and there to figure out a way to make it happen. Hiram only accelerated my plans, which I think is a sign from above that we're on the right track. We're meant to be together."

"That we are," he agreed, resting his forehead against hers. "The Goddess made you just for me, Tina, and She knew what She was doing when She brought us together."

He kissed her then, and it felt like the Goddess's Light was sparkling down around them. When he cracked his eyes open a bit, he thought he saw the magic of Her divine touch, and he knew their future was blessed.

EPILOGUE

With Master Hiram's money, Zak was able to get construction started, not only on the home he was building for his new mate, but also on the restaurant. In the meantime, they were living above the bakery, sharing every night together, making plans and dreaming dreams.

The problem of the sea monster in the cove hadn't been solved yet, and everyone was staying clear of the water as much as they could. In the meantime, experts were being consulted, and plans being made for how to deal with another incursion, should it occur.

There were a few beings in the Spec Ops community who were uniquely skilled in the ocean and with its creatures, and they were being consulted as well, though they were tied up in other parts of the world at the moment. Still, the Morrow brothers and their Navy Admiral father were on the short list of people Big John would call in when and if things came to a head. Two of the brothers were Navy SEALs and not-quite-human. The other—a step-brother—was a badass Army Green Beret who had served with the oldest of the Redstone brothers from Las Vegas, and though he was one hundred percent human, he had earned quite a rep among shifter Spec Ops warriors.

John had already talked to the Admiral. The old man had

promised that as soon as his sons were done in the Middle East, they'd be heading out to the Pacific Northwest—or wherever the sea creatures showed up next. Though he couldn't call his sons off their current assignment fighting terrorists, he'd send them one at a time, if he had to, as they came off their current duties. For now, they had commitments to the human government the Admiral had to allow them to fulfill before he could send them off on an assignment that wasn't necessarily sanctioned officially by the U.S. government.

In the meantime, life beneath the waves was becoming increasingly perilous. Inhabitants of the sea were being hunted and had to be especially careful when they ventured near the shore, where the land peoples dwelled. But those who lived with a foot in both worlds had to be especially wary. The sea sirens and mermaids, the selkies and water sprites—they were all in particular danger.

Especially those who dwelled in the waters off what was now called Grizzly Cove.

# # #

ABOUT THE AUTHOR

Bianca D'Arc has run a laboratory, climbed the corporate ladder in the shark-infested streets of lower Manhattan, studied and taught martial arts, and earned the right to put a whole bunch of letters after her name, but she's always enjoyed writing more than any of her other pursuits. She grew up and still lives on Long Island, where she keeps busy with an extensive garden, several aquariums full of very demanding fish, and writing her favorite genres of paranormal, fantasy and sci-fi romance.

Bianca loves to hear from readers and can be reached through Twitter (@BiancaDArc), Facebook (BiancaDArcAuthor) or through the various links on her website.

WELCOME TO THE D'ARC SIDE…
WWW.BIANCADARC.COM

BOOKS BY BIANCA D'ARC

Brotherhood of Blood
One & Only
Rare Vintage
Phantom Desires
Sweeter Than Wine
Forever Valentine
Wolf Hills
Wolf Quest

Tales of the Were
Lords of the Were
Inferno

Tales of the Were — The Others
Rocky
Slade

Tales of the Were — Redstone Clan
The Purrfect Stranger
Grif
Red
Magnus
Bobcat
Matt

String of Fate
Cat's Cradle
King's Throne
Jacob's Ladder
Her Warriors

Grizzly Cove
All About the Bear
Mating Dance
Night Shift
Alpha Bear
Saving Grace

Dragon Knights
Maiden Flight
The Dragon Healer
Border Lair
Master at Arms
The Ice Dragon
Prince of Spies
Wings of Change
FireDrake
Dragon Storm
Keeper of the Flame
Hidden Dragons

Resonance Mates
Hara's Legacy
Davin's Quest
Jaci's Experiment
Grady's Awakening
Harry's Sacrifice

Jit'Suku Chronicles
Arcana: King of Swords
Arcana: King of Cups
Arcana: King of Clubs
Arcana: King of Stars
End of the Line

StarLords
Hidden Talent
Talent For Trouble
Shy Talent

Gifts of the Ancients
Warrior's Heart

Guardians of the Dark
Half Past Dead
Once Bitten, Twice Dead
A Darker Shade of Dead
The Beast Within
Dead Alert

TALES OF THE WERE ~ THE OTHERS
ROCKY

On the run from her husband's killers, there is only one man who can help her now... her Rock.

Maggie is on the run from those who killed her husband nine months ago. She knows the only one who can help her is Rocco, a grizzly shifter she knew in her youth. She arrives on his doorstep in labor with twins. Magical, shapeshifting, bear cub twins destined to lead the next generation of werecreatures in North America.

Rocky is devastated by the news of his Clan brother's death, but he cannot deny the attraction that has never waned for the small human woman who stole his heart a long time ago. Rocky absented himself from her life when she chose to marry his childhood friend, but the years haven't changed the way he feels for her.

And now there are two young lives to protect. Rocky will do everything in his power to end the threat to the small family and claim them for himself. He knows he is the perfect Alpha to teach the cubs as they grow into their power... if their mother will let him love her as he has always longed to do.

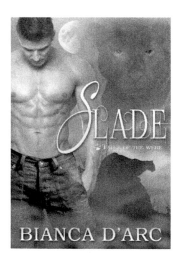

TALES OF THE WERE ~ THE OTHERS
SLADE

The fate of all shifters rests on his broad shoulders, but all he can think of is her.

Slade is a warrior and spy sent to Nevada to track a brutal murderer before the existence of all shifters is revealed to a world not ready to know.

Kate is a priestess serving the large community of shifters that have gathered around the Redstone cougars. When their matriarch is murdered and the scene polluted by dark magic, she knows she must help the enigmatic man sent to track the killer.

Together, Slade and Kate find not one but two evil mages that they alone can neutralize. Slade finds it hard to keep his hands off his sexy new partner, the cougars are out for blood, and the killers have an even more sinister plan in mind.

Can Kate somehow keep her hands to herself when the most attractive man she's ever met makes her want to throw caution to the wind? And can Slade do his job and save the situation when he's finally found a woman who can make him purr?

Warning: Contains a tiny bit of sexy ménage action with two smokin' hot men..

TALES OF THE WERE ~ REDSTONE CLAN 1
GRIF

Griffon Redstone is the eldest of five brothers and the leader of one of the most influential shifter Clans in North America. He seeks solace in the mountains, away from the horrific events of the past months, for both himself and his young sister. The deaths of their older sister and mother have hit them both very hard.

Lindsey Tate is human, but very aware of the werewolf Pack that lives near her grandfather's old cabin. She's come to right a wrong her grandfather committed against the Pack and salvage what's left of her family's honor—if the wolves will let her. Mostly, they seem intent on running her out of town on a rail.

But the golden haired stranger, Grif, comes to her rescue more than once. He stands up for her against the wolf Pack and then helps her fix the old generator at the cabin. When she performs a ceremony she expects will end in her death, the shifter deity has other ideas. Thrown together by fate, neither of them can deny their deep attraction, but will an old enemy tear them apart?

Warning: Frisky cats get up to all sorts of naughtiness, including a frenzy-induced multi-partner situation that might be a little intense for some readers.

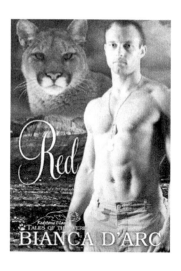

TALES OF THE WERE ~ REDSTONE CLAN 2
RED

A water nymph and a werecougar meet in a bar fight… No joke.

Steve Redstone agrees to keep an eye on his friend's little sister while she's partying in Las Vegas. He's happy to do the favor for an old Army buddy. What he doesn't expect is the wild woman who heats his blood and attracts too much attention from Others in the area.

Steve ends up defending her honor, breaking his cover and seducing the woman all within hours of meeting her, but he's helpless to resist her. She is his mate and that startling fact is going to open up a whole can of worms with her, her brother and the rest of the Redstone Clan.

TALES OF THE WERE ~ REDSTONE CLAN 3
MAGNUS

A tortured vampire, a lonely shifter, and a deadly power struggle of supernatural proportions. Can their forbidden love prevail?

Magnus is the quiet brother. The one who keeps to himself. But he has good reason for his loner status. Two years ago, he met a woman. Not just any woman. This woman made his inner cougar stand up and roar. Even in human form, he purred when she stroked him, a sure sign that she was his mate. And mating is a very serious thing among shifters. Too bad the lady had fangs...

Mag discovers Miranda being held captive. She's been tortured to the point of -madness. Mag frees her and takes her to his home, nursing her back to health and defying all convention to keep her with him. He doesn't ever want to let her go again, but he knows the deck is stacked against them.

When a vampire uprising threatens, Mag and Miranda are in the middle. More than just their necks are on the line when a group of vampires seek to kill them and overthrow the current Master. But they have powerful allies, and their renewed relationship has made both of them stronger than either would ever be alone.

Can they stay together forever? Or will the daylight—and their two very different worlds—tear them apart again?

WWW.BIANCADARC.COM

9 781523 499939